To [M...]

A good friend
of Marla, I
hope you enjoy the
book.

Libby Beasley-Perdue

August 25, 2012

God Wove a Tapestry

Libby Beasley-Perdue

CROSSBOOKS
PUBLISHING

CrossBooks™
A Division of LifeWay
1663 Liberty Drive
Bloomington, IN 47403
www.crossbooks.com
Phone: 1-866-879-0502

First published by CrossBooks 3/26/2012

ISBN: 978-1-4627-1404-9 (sc)
ISBN: 978-1-4627-1403-2 (e)

Printed in the United States of America

This book is printed on acid-free paper.

Any people depicted in stock imagery provided by Thinkstock are models,
and such images are being used for illustrative purposes only.

Certain stock imagery © Thinkstock.

To my husband, Bob, for being so supportive
of me as I wrote this book.

Session 1

While she waited in his office, she noticed that the dark paneled walls smelled freshly polished. Two lush ferns graced either side of the large window looking out over Peachtree Street below. Being on the tenth floor, the traffic noise was thankfully buffered. The built-in bookcase behind the desk was filled to capacity with impressive-looking books. She was sitting too far away to read the titles and she felt too timid to get up and peruse his library. The desk was uncluttered with a small clock facing away from her. The lighting was dim enough to create a sense of serenity, yet bright enough to read the diplomas and certificates on the wall. The upholstered Queen Anne chair in which she sat was extremely comfortable. The whole atmosphere of the office had an air of calm, yet she couldn't have been more nervous.

She frantically dug through her purse for some gum then stopped short when she remembered that she had chewed her last piece in the car. Tears began to well up and she wondered if she'd get through the hour without her chewing gum. She really needed it because it seemed to take the tension out of her jaws. Hearing the door knob turn, she dabbed at her eyes with a tissue she had taken from the box on the desk and smoothed her skirt.

"Hello, Catherine. I'm David Hill," said the attractive middle-aged man, as he closed the door. "I'm so glad you finally decided to come in." As he walked over to her, she jumped up nervously to shake his hand then slowly sank back into the chair with a heavy sigh. His eyes were blue and caring, and his smile was genuine and warm. With a little gray in his hair and the dark suit, he looked distinguished, but not overly formal and stiff.

"Catherine, why don't you tell me what brought you to my office today."

Her voice cracked as she sobbed, "Mr. Hill, my life is falling apart." With lips quivering and tears flowing freely down her cheeks, she sighed a jagged breath. Her throat ached from unsuccessfully trying to hold back the tears.

"Catherine, you can cry as long as you need to." He moved the box of tissues closer to her. Amazingly, when David said it was okay to cry, the desire to fall apart into a wet mess ceased. Just the act of giving her permission to weep seemed to dry up her tears immediately. Maybe she could go through with this session without becoming a blubbering idiot.

Dabbing at her eyes, she was now stricken with the thought that her mascara was probably running and her nose was most likely beet red, probably making her look like some forlorn clown. Her looks were important to her, especially to the opposite sex. She smiled briefly at this kind man and relaxed when she began to realize he wasn't interested in her looks.

"Why don't you start at the beginning."

At the beginning? At the beginning of what? Her life? Her marriage? Her troubles? It would take years of counseling if she started at the beginning, wouldn't it?

David observed Catherine's hesitation. She was a pretty woman, but extremely troubled. Worry lines had begun to form on her forehead. Even the soft blonde bangs couldn't cover the fact that she was in emotional pain. Her intake sheet stated she was 43, but she looked much younger. David knew that would change if she didn't get the help she so desperately needed. Emotional angst could take a terrible toll on one's body, especially the face.

"Why don't you start with what brought you in today."

Her lips quivered as she said, "My husband is thinking of leaving me. I had an affair recently and he doesn't think he can handle my infidelity." Tears began slowly trickling down her cheeks.

"Steve, my husband, is a salesman. He's gone a lot because he covers the whole southeastern territory. When he is home, he's tired and withdrawn. I've been a stay-at-home mom, so life has always been a little lonesome because of Steve's job. We have one daughter, Zoe, who is attending college in Paris. The house is so quiet during the week and I've been so lonely. When I met Austin at the library, it was all so innocent. He liked horses and so did I. I noticed his book on the library table and commented that I'd like to look at it when he was through. We struck up a conversation and, well, you know the rest of the story."

"Do you love Austin?" David said softly.

"No. I know now it was just infatuation. I'm a Christian and this whole situation goes against everything I believe in. I don't think for a minute adultery is acceptable. Austin has horses and I went to his ranch in Cobb County to see them. The whole time the Holy Spirit was warning me not to go, but I thought I could just ride one of the horses then go home. Obviously, it didn't happen that way." She lowered her eyes in obvious shame.

"What did happen that made you go against your beliefs and your conscience?"

"After riding, he suggested we have a cold drink in the house and cool off. It was so hot that day. You know how Georgia summers can be. I was so parched that I readily agreed. Inside it was so cool and I just relaxed on the sofa while he fixed the drinks. When his hand brushed mine, it was like an electric shock between us.

Austin is part Native American and his dark eyes seemed to penetrate my soul. He bent down and kissed me with his warm lips. I instinctively wrapped my arms around his neck. Steve had been so wrapped up in his career that we hardly made love anymore. To have a man so attracted to me was like an aphrodisiac. We made love, but immediately afterwards, I was struck with hideous shame and guilt."

David could hear the anxiety and self-reproach in her soft voice.

"I yanked on my clothes and tore out of the house. Austin

tried to catch me, but I ran like a scolded dog to my car. I was so mortified."

"How did Steve find out?"

"Austin called the house and Steve answered. I don't know what Austin said, but Steve came flying into our bedroom and confronted me. I was so scared. I begged Steve to forgive me. He just looked at me with contempt. I had never seen that look on his face before.

I've never been unfaithful to him, but he won't give me another chance. I know I was wrong, but Steve has been wrong to neglect me. I feel his total disregard for me as his wife made me vulnerable for something like this."

"Are you blaming Steve for the affair?" David was concerned about her subtle way of transferring some of the blame to Steve. He wanted to get deeper into Catherine's feelings and belief system to make sure he didn't misunderstand what she was saying and thinking.

"Yes and no. If he had been the kind of Christian husband he needed to be, I wouldn't have looked twice at Austin. I love my husband, but I need more than a dry peck on the cheek at night. I'm only 43 and I still want romance. But, no, Steve didn't force me into an affair. I willingly made that immoral choice." David could tell Catherine's demeanor had gone from looking shameful to exhibiting a little defiance to shame again.

"You know I'm a Christian counselor, Catherine. So, we will be taking a biblical approach in these counseling sessions. You may discover a lot about yourself that you have buried deep within you. Christ wants to expose any sin to the light."

"I know that adultery is a sin and it ruined my marriage."

"Catherine, we will go beyond your act of adultery into areas of your life that you may never have examined before."

"Mr. Hill, I don't want to sound disrespectful, but I'm here to try to salvage my marriage, not dig into my past." David noticed that Catherine seemed a little annoyed with his counseling plan.

"Catherine, you need to understand a few things. Because your husband is not here, I will not be dealing with his problems.

You and I will work together on you alone. Also, because he is not here, there is no guarantee your marriage can be saved. Even if he was here, there are no guarantees in counseling. It all depends on several factors."

Catherine's lips began to quiver again and David noticed her shoulders droop. He was hoping she wouldn't walk out before they even got started.

Tenderly he said, "Catherine, this whole situation is not hopeless. God can do mighty works with flawed people like us. He wants your marriage to survive and grow. Here's what we're going to do.

I'm going to be praying for you and Steve during this whole process. You need to go home and pray, too. Fully confess your sins to God and receive his grace and forgiveness. Ask God to soften Steve's heart. Also, ask Him to create something good out of this tragically sinful event in your life. Some people might use the word mistake, but we're going to be honest and call it what it is-sin."

"I will, but it may be too late. Steve was discussing moving out in a week or so. Once he's moved, he'll be too stubborn to come back. I've ruined everything and I feel so hopeless."

"It's not hopeless. I'll see you next week and we'll pick up where we've left off today."

After David prayed, she rose from her chair. Her slim body seemed to be carrying the weight of the world. Giving him a melancholy smile, she opened the door and was gone. David made a few notes in his book, closed his eyes and began to pray in earnest.

Session 2

Catherine came in the same way she left the week before-somber and defeated-looking. She flopped into the chair and let out a weary breath.

"How are things going, Catherine?" David responded in a genuinely interested tone.

"Ok, I guess." He could tell she had been crying. Her nose was red and her eyes were glassy.

"What's happened since we saw each other last week?"

"Well, Steve moved out, like I said he would. Nothing I said would change his mind. I cried, begged, but nothing seemed to penetrate that cold look in his eyes. He took his suitcase and left. He's staying at a motel across town, near his office. I thought the house was quiet before, with Steve being gone all the time, but knowing he won't return has made living there sheer torture. The silence is so loud, if you know what I mean. Since I don't work and Steve's not there to cook and clean for, I've found myself either sleeping too much or watching television a good part of the day. This isn't like me. I'm so depressed I just want to crawl into bed and die there."

He saw that her hair didn't seem as beautifully coifed as before and sadness permeated her whole being. She was definitely depressed.

"Catherine, do you feel suicidal?"

"Not really. It's like I don't want to live, but I don't want to kill myself. I just want to cease existing."

6

"You need to think of your daughter. When will she come home from college?"

"Not until Christmas. I haven't called her with the news yet. I'm just too tired and she'll want to know why Steve left. She's got her studies to concentrate on, so my life-tragedy can wait." A little cynicism was creeping into her voice.

"Your daughter is an adult now. She'll have to be told the truth eventually. You and Steve should discuss how you will tell her the news."

"Right. Just like we discussed his moving. Steve doesn't seem to want to even talk to me right now. He's not returning my calls to his cell phone."

"You'll have to talk sometime, so be prepared to talk to him in a calm manner about your daughter. Hysterics will make him clam up. He needs to see that you're ready to dialogue with him in a mature, serene manner. I think you'll see he'll be more open. Men tend to be repulsed by hysteria.

On another note, since you don't work, is Steve going to continue to support you?"

"Well, all I know is the bills are paid for this month. He's always given me discretionary money and I saved some of it. I'm OK for now."

"I'm glad to hear that. We can now concentrate on getting you to the spiritual place you need to be, without you worrying about money."

"Mr. Hill, I'm here about my marriage. My spiritual health is not in question right now. I know I've sinned and I've repented and asked God for forgiveness."

"That's wonderful, but part of repairing your marriage will be repairing parts of you that need to be fixed. After all, a truly happily-married, spiritually-grounded woman would not have fallen for Austin's seduction."

"I know what you're saying. I guess we'll do it your way," she stated unenthusiastically.

"Catherine, I want you to tell me your earliest memory or some significant event from your early childhood."

"We're going back that far? Why?" she almost shouted.

"Your parents or the significant adults in your early childhood, along with the environment in which you were raised, are extremely important to your childhood development."

"Well, this seems silly, but I'll think of an early memory." With her eyes raised toward the ceiling, she sat quietly until a little scowl crossed her face. "I remember my fifth birthday party. This would be a significant event in my life. Mother had gone to a lot of trouble making me a special birthday cake. Father was on the phone, as usual. It was just a party of three, but there were balloons, party plates, and two gifts on the table.

Mother asked Father to please get off the phone so we could light the candles. Five pretty, pink candles waited patiently in a sea of white frosting. I couldn't take my eyes off the cake or the gifts. I was ready for the party to begin. I glanced at Mother's face as she looked anxiously at Father to end his phone call. Again, she motioned with her hands to put the phone down.

Father got an angry look on his face like he wanted to say something very mean to her. He did that sometimes. His voice got louder on the phone and he began to wave around his free hand to punctuate what he was saying. I started clapping my hands together in excitement. Mother turned again to Father. He slammed down the receiver and turned to us. I'll never forget what he said, although he didn't say it, he screamed it.

'Kathy, I'm talking to one of my most important clients and all you can think about is this stupid birthday party.' His face was red and full of fury. Mother seemed to cower a little. She got that broken little smile on her face that she always had when Father's anger was starting to escalate.

Sarcasm dripping from his voice, he said, 'Well, I wish all I had to do was bake a cake and sing happy birthday. Instead I've got to make a living for you two, so you can have this life of ease. Don't you know it's hard to make a living these days!'

'Ron, that's not fair. You know I work hard around the house. Please calm down and let's enjoy some cake and ice cream.'

Mother's voice got more and more suppressed as she pleaded with Father.

'Woman, after you interrupted my important phone call, do you really think I want to eat cake and ice cream? I'm going to the office for some peace and quiet.' A moment later the front door slammed shut and the house was suddenly very quiet.

I looked at Mother's face. She was beginning to cry softly, all the while my happiness started oozing out like a slow leak in one of my pretty, pink balloons."

David could see the anger and pain on Catherine's face as she spoke. From the way she described it, he could picture that little girl's broken heart.

"We had our little party, if you want to call it that. Mother and I picked at our pieces of cake and the ice cream slowly melted in our bowls. I slowly opened my presents. I was happy with the baby doll she gave me. Father's gift was a necklace that said, 'Daddy's little girl.' I don't think I ever wore it."

"Catherine, it sounds like your father was the dominant one in the house. Was your father always so critical and frustrated?"

"You know, I never thought about him being frustrated. I always thought he was mean and distant. And, yes, he was the dominant one. Whatever he demanded, it was done, by me or my mother. Mother was from the old school that believed the home was the man's castle and he was the king. She waited on him hand and foot, never raised her voice, or demanded anything of Father."

"Tell me about your relationship with him. Did you spend any daddy/daughter time together?" Catherine shook her head slowly.

"Father was all about work. If he wasn't out on sales calls, he was working in the yard, or tinkering in the garage. He never had time for either of us.

Mother didn't drive. She had had an accident when she first learned to drive and she never drove again. Father took us every Saturday to a strip shopping mall. He'd drop us off and come back exactly three hours later. Mother and I would have lunch at the drugstore, which I enjoyed so much. We shopped at the 'five and dime,' then do our grocery shopping. We'd be outside the store at exactly 3:00 so Father would not have to wait. He hated to wait for anything. All my fond memories are of Mother. I always tried to avoid my father and, no, we never played together, ever."

After being lost in thought for a moment, she looked at David and said, "Isn't it interesting that I married a man very similar to Father? I just thought about that. Steve and I hardly talk because he's just as devoted to work as Father was."

"It's not unusual for a woman to marry a man like her father. Even if her father was abusive, she may marry a man just like him. Subconsciously, she may be trying to rewrite history, thinking things will be different with her husband and she can get from him what her father neglected to give her. Of course, as you can expect, that hardly ever happens."

"I feel just as lonely with Steve as I did with my father."

"Let's discuss Steve later. How was your relationship with your mother?"

"Mother, she was so sweet and kind. Everyone in the neighborhood and at church loved her. I just adored her. I always felt she was the only person who really cared for me. She always wanted to make me smile. I miss her so much. She and Father were killed in a car wreck about six years ago. Father didn't want to wait for the train to pass. He went around the crossing guard and miscalculated how fast the train was going. It was so awful. I often think about mother's last moments of life. She had such a fear of driving and car accidents."

"You were an only child, right? What were some of your interests back in your childhood?"

"I loved playing house and being the mother. I had a lot of dolls and they would be my babies. I would talk to them like they were real. I'd try to imitate my mother. I'd occasionally ride my bike down the street, but I mostly played indoors."

"Did you have a lot of friends?"

"No. I had a girl two doors down come over and play house

with me once a week, but that was about it. I was shy, plus Father didn't like noise."

"Tell me what kind of student you were."

"I made very good grades. I would strive to always make all A's.

My teachers always liked me because I was studious and well-behaved. The only time my father would give me any affirmation was when I made all A's. Mother would show him my report card, he'd study it, look me in the eye, and say, 'Good job!' That was the only time I got any recognition from him. I wanted him to love me and I thought good grades would win his love."

"Tell me about how you met Steve." David saw a little smile trying to emerge on Catherine's pretty face.

"It was at college. I was in my freshmen year. Steve was a senior. I was looking for a girlfriend in a classroom. Entering the classroom, I saw a few students had their chairs in a circle and Steve was doing most of the talking. I kept trying to get my girlfriend's attention by waving, but she was engrossed in filing her nails. She obviously was only in the room because her boyfriend was there.

I accidentally caught Steve's eye and he motioned for me to come over. I was a little embarrassed to have the attention of the group focused on me, so I quietly entered the room and sat near my friend.

Steve was talking about finances. He sounded so confident and knowledgeable that I found myself intently listening and watching his every move. He was handsome, with light brown hair and blue eyes. He wore navy slacks and a pale-blue dress shirt. After awhile, I forgot why I had come to the class in the first place. My errand of finding my girlfriend was long forgotten as I began to daydream about Steve. In the dream we were sitting on a park bench close together and he was leaning over to kiss me.

Right about the time he was going to kiss my lips, chairs scraped on the floor and I was abruptly jarred back into reality. I ducked my head to hide whatever look I might have had on my face. Before I could turn to speak to my girlfriend, Steve touched my sleeve.

'You seem very interested in finances. That's unusual for a college girl as pretty as you.' His sweet smile made my heart pound and I started stuttering to say something, anything.

'Actually, I came to talk to Laurie.' I could feel a blush rise up in my face.

'I see.' He didn't look disappointed. 'Well, how about some lunch and I can find out what you really think about money.' He hesitated then said, 'Maybe you and your friend have other plans. Or, you may have a boyfriend.' Curiosity filled his eyes and I could tell he was teasing me.

'Not really. I don't even remember why I needed to see her.' I couldn't believe I said that, since it made me sound like an airhead.

'Great! Let's meet out front in five and we'll go to a burger joint,' he said.

'I'd loved to,' I said a little too loudly. I couldn't seem to contain my excitement. Mother always said boys want a girl who's not too available, but I couldn't help it. I hadn't had a lot of dates with boys and to have such a good-looking one wanting to take me to lunch, it was so thrilling.

And as they say, the rest is history. Steve and I got married as soon as he graduated. He had an entry level job at a bank. I quit school as soon as I found out I was pregnant six months later."

David asked, "When do you think trouble started in your marriage?"

"Steve worked hard at the bank, but he had normal business hours. I stayed home and raised Zoe. We had the typical suburban life and I loved it. It was so different from my childhood."

"Different in what ways?"

"First of all, Steve didn't act like a tyrant, like my father. I wasn't afraid of him like my mother was of Father. Also, Steve was a good father. He played games with Zoe, rode bikes with her, and had real conversations with her. As long as Steve worked at the bank, we had what I call a real marriage."

"What is your definition of a real marriage?"

"Well, the husband is home for dinner at night. He really connects with his family. The wife is happy and thinks of her husband as her lover and partner, not a boss."

David leaned forward in his chair and asked, "When did things change in your marriage?"

"Steve was always so good with money. We never did without and we had a large savings account. Steve began to feel like he was never going to succeed in life financially as long as he worked for a bank. He wanted more potential to make what he called 'real money.' That's when he began to interview for sales positions with large corporations.

Because he's so smart and goal-motivated, it didn't take long for him to land a job working for a pharmaceutical company. He's was out late some nights with customers, but it was OK. He was home more than he was away at night. I was happy to see Steve so happy.

Steve did so well that after a year he was promoted to regional sales manager for the southeastern district. That's when things really changed.

He would be gone from Monday until Friday every week. When he was home, he wasn't really home. He'd either be resting or working on his computer. Zoe and I would have been home all week by ourselves and we wanted to spend time with Steve. We looked so forward to him coming home.

As it turned out, Friday nights became a bust for Zoe and me. Steve would come home tired and irritable late Friday night. He'd sleep-in Saturday, eat breakfast, maybe cut the grass, then be on the computer all afternoon. Saturday night we'd go out for dinner, but I could tell his mind was on his work. He'd be quiet while Zoe and I would talk about our week. After awhile, it was apparent that Zoe and I were really only talking at Steve, not with him, because he wasn't really listening.

It wasn't long before he didn't want to go out to eat on Saturday night. He'd complain that he ate out on the road and didn't want to stomach another salty, fatty meal when he was in town. I would tell him I'd cook for him, but he'd encourage Zoe and me to go out so he could get some work done. So, even Saturday night became a bust for us. I don't think I had ever felt so lonely in my adult life.

Money was plentiful, but I couldn't make Steve understand I didn't want all this money, I wanted him. He would come back with the argument that this was for Zoe's college and our future. He loved to talk about how wonderful it would be in the future. Then we'd travel and have romantic walks.

Sure, I wanted Zoe to have a college fund, but I began to wonder if he and I would ever have a future together. How can you put your marriage on hold then reconnect years and years later? His words began to ring hollow for me.

Life with Steve became an exercise in futility. The more I begged Steve to spend time with me and Zoe, the more withdrawn he became. I finally stopped begging him and retreated to my television. After getting sick of that, I decided to expand my mind and go to the library. I had to get some comfort somewhere, so I decided to lose myself in books. I've always loved to read.

I never would have known a simple trip to the library would destroy my marriage. That's where I met Austin. And I've told you that story already." She almost whispered her last statement as tears began to slide down her cheeks.

David sensed that Catherine was tired. Although they had a few minutes left in the session, he decided this was a good stopping point.

"I'll think we'll wrap things up for today. I'd like to close this session with prayer. From time to time I'll be giving you homework to expand what we've discussed. I won't do that today because these two sessions have just been an opportunity for you to give me your basic life story. Next session we'll start getting into the Bible and begin to help you become the woman Christ would have you to be."

Catherine got a puzzle look on her face. "Christ? What about what I want?"

"You're going to find out that what you want is not the answer. If you surrender to God, He will take you on a journey you could never imagine. You'll be amazed what He can do when He's the Potter and you're the clay." David's warm smile made her drop her defenses.

"Right now I feel like the journey I'm on is a dead-end," she laughed half-heartedly.

"Yes, in a way, you are, but that will change. Have patience and hope."

He bowed his head and began to pray for her. As she bowed, too, she began to feel a little peace. It wasn't much, but she'd cling to it all the same and hope that it would last her until next session.

Session 3

"Come in, Catherine. I've been waiting for you. How's your week been?" David gave her an encouraging smile.

Catherine always felt he was truly concerned for her and she really needed that in her life right now. Except for her daughter, she felt alone, unwanted, and unloved. She gave him as warm a smile as she could muster, considering her discouragement.

"You'll be doing a little writing today. Across the top of this page I want you to write down four messages you received from your childhood. I'll give you an example. My mother always said I needed to lose weight."

"Mr. Hill, you don't look like you need to lose a pound!"

"I don't and I didn't. My mother always wanted me to be slender like her father, but my body type was more like my father's. So go ahead and write the four messages and they don't have to be all negative."

Catherine sat for a moment before her pen moved. Once she started though, she wrote faster and faster.

"Done."

"Tell me what you've written."

"Well, the message from my father was only good grades would warrant his attention. Remember, I told you he'd say 'good job' after I earned all A's on my report card. That was the only time he gave me attention and acted like he was proud of me. I guess you might say I had to earn his love.

The second message was from my mother. She always told me

how much she loved me and I knew she meant it. So, the message was mothers give unconditional love.

The third message was from her, also. Husbands are to be obeyed, no matter what. Father was strict, unbending, and many times unreasonable, so Mother never stood up for herself or got her way. The message was men are selfish.

The fourth message was from my teachers. Their message was you're a good girl because you make good grades. My teachers liked me, but I wonder if they would have felt the same about me if I had flunked a class or showed little interest in what they were teaching. Again, the message is caring and attention must be earned."

"Now, under each message I want you to tell me how each message made you feel."

Without hesitation Catherine wrote down her feelings. It was like they were right there on the surface of her mind to be quickly retrieved.

"Done."

"Why don't you share what you've written."

"My father's message made me feel anxious and needy. My mother's first message made me feel secure and loved. Her second message made me feel anger and fear. My teachers' message made me feel anxious and proud.

I guess I shouldn't have felt that way. Most of those feelings I had about all those messages were bad, especially those that related to my parents. But, I couldn't help it!" Catherine got a remorseful look on her face.

"Catherine, feelings are neither good nor bad. They just are. God made us to have emotions. You can't help how you feel. It's what you do with those feelings that matters."

"You mean even anger is alright?"

"Yes. Even Jesus got angry, but He never lost control of Himself. For example, John 2:12-17 tells how Jesus was angry with money changers.

Think of feelings like spices. Spices make a dish tasty and enjoyable, yet too much of certain spices, like pepper, can ruin the dish. If anger is pepper, you don't want too much of it in your life or your life will be unpalatable.

Remember, feelings aren't wrong, but what you do with those feelings can be wrong. For example, if you're feeling anger towards a person, you have several options of what you'll do with that emotion. You can stuff those feelings down, you can reciprocate and retaliate against that person, or you can remember you're a child of God and act appropriately."

"What exactly do you mean by that last option?"

"We're going to go more in depth about this later in our counseling process, but basically, because you're a Christian, Christ lives in you. Plus, you're a daughter of the King. You can choose to behave like one."

"I never thought of it like that. I've been beating myself up about some of the negative feelings I've had lately. I need to stop that."

"When we experience those feelings we call negative, we need to ask ourselves, why am I feeling this way? Going back to the emotion of anger, we need to consider why this person or what this person is saying or doing is making us angry.

Let's say a person says you're lazy. If you immediately feel very angry, you need to ask yourself why that statement bothers you so much. It may be that your father unfairly called you lazy as a child, even though you weren't. You obviously would have deep-seated feelings about being called lazy.

This brings us to our next exercise. You've told me the messages you were given as a child and the feelings that resulted from those messages. Now I want you to write down what beliefs resulted from those messages and feelings.

"I don't think I understand what you mean. Can you give me an example?"

"Sure. My mother always told me I needed to lose weight. This made me feel insecure about my body. I began to believe that only slender people were happy and loved, and if anyone had a little weight on them, they were a failure. Do you see how the message leads to a feeling which leads to a belief?"

"I think I do."

"Let's start with your father's message about earning his love. He only gave you attention when you received all A's on your report card. You said this resulted in you feeling anxious and needy. Explain to me in more detail about these feelings

"Well, I felt anxious about my grades all the time. I worried that if I didn't score well on tests and papers that I'd get a bad grade on my report card. I was driven to make all A's. I felt emotionally needy because I wanted my father's love so much that I was willing to give up everything to make good grades."

"What do you mean you were willing to give up everything to make good grades?"

"I'll give you an example. My sophomore year in high school I was invited by my Spanish teacher to join a group of students to go to Mexico during spring break. This was going to be a fun trip, even though it was going to be educational, too. I didn't go because I had a major writing project for English class due two weeks after spring break. I stayed home just so I could work on that project and make it as perfect as possible."

"Do you regret that you made that decision?"

"Oh, yes. The kids had a great time. I got my A and my father's 'Good job,' but I missed out on a once in a lifetime opportunity. That's what I mean about being so emotionally needy when it came to my father."

"I want you to write down what were your beliefs due to your father's message and the subsequent feelings."

Catherine had to think for a minute then she filled in the blank space on the paper. "I believed you had to earn a man's love. I believed that the woman had to do most of the giving to get approval and acceptance from a man. Love wasn't free with a man; it took hard work."

"Catherine, we're going to talk about this in real detail later in our counseling process, but I want to tell you that how we feel about our fathers has a lot to do with how we feel about God."

"Really? I don't understand because I think God is loving."

"Like I said, we will discuss this later, but while you think

God is loving, we will explore whether you think you have to earn God's love like you did with your father."

"I'm going to have to really think about that one."

"Let's continue with the beliefs you had because of your mother's messages and the feelings that followed. Explain what you mean when you say you have to earn a man's love, it's not free."

"Mother was always doing the giving in her relationship with Father. Father never made her life easy. Everything had to be his way, on his time. That's what I took into my relationship with Steve. I thought I had to do all the sacrificing, although Steve was not quite as demanding as my father was. That is, not until Steve started putting his business before everything. Even his family took a backseat to his work. I began to feel that I was giving too much and not receiving enough. That's why I fell into that trap with Austin so quickly."

"Let's discuss the beliefs you received from your teachers."

Letting out a sigh, Catherine said, "I'm beginning to see a pattern with my Father and my teachers. I had to earn their love and respect. You know, Mr. Hill, I think that's another reason I feel so tired. I'm tired of earning people's love. Love shouldn't be that way. My mother's love was pure and free, but she's the only one who showed me that type of love."

"What about Zoe? Is her love not free?"

"Yes, it is, but she's my child. I'm talking about adults in my life. I always felt with Mother that she'd love me no matter what I did." Tears began to blur Catherine's vision, so she had to wipe them to focus on David.

"Catherine, we will talk more about this in later sessions, but God loves you even more than your mother did and His love is unconditional."

"My head knows that, but it hasn't gotten to my heart. Not really. I have a hard time believing I don't have to earn God's love."

"There's nothing you could ever do that would be good enough to earn His love. That's why it's a gift." Catherine observed that

David's face reflected the joy he felt knowing God's love was unconditional. Catherine nodded her head, but sadness remained in her eyes.

"We're going to talk about the coping mechanisms you created to protect yourself from more rejection and hurt. This is what the Bible calls flesh. These mechanisms are ways you have dealt with life in your own strength. God had no part of it because you were trying to cope on your own.

Let's go back to my own personal example. The message I received from my mother was that a trim body was the key to happiness and people would like me if I was slender. My flesh was trying to either diet myself to death or avoid social situations as much as possible when I failed to lose the weight. Can you see how I was struggling on my own? I had not prayed about my weight situation with God. I had not asked Him what was best for me. No, I was coping in a most unhealthy way to protect myself from the fear of people not liking me because I wasn't skinny."

"I think I understand what you mean. To protect myself from the rejection of my father and teachers, I worked myself silly to get good grades.

I didn't want their disapproval. I only wanted their love and I had to work to get it. I even felt that if I sacrificed my happiness for Steve he would never stop loving me. Man, was that sick or what?"

"Catherine, we all have what the Bible calls flesh. The secret to the abundant life is to submit yourself to God and allow Him to help you to not only cope with life, but thrive in it."

"But, isn't that like working to earn God's love?" Catherine looked confused.

"No. Again we will talk about this more in detail later, but God has our best interest at heart, even more than your mother did."

"You know, Mr. Hill. I'm beginning to understand what you're talking about."

"Good. From what you've told me thus far, I think one of your coping mechanisms was being self-disciplined about school work. You put unrealistic expectations on yourself. You feared making any mistakes, so you became a perfectionist. How does it make you feel to be a perfectionist?"

"Tired, emotionally and physically. I live in fear of failing. I feel anxious about it. Sometimes, it has made me want to just quit because of all the pressure I've put upon myself."

"Quit in what way?"

"Sometimes I've wanted to just lie down and die. I wanted to just go to heaven and rest."

"Do you think it's God's plan for you to feel all those negative feelings and do all you've killed yourself to do, all in the effort to earn people's love?"

"No, but I don't know what to do!" Catherine lowered her head and began to weep. David gave her time to compose herself. After she wiped her eyes, he began again.

"Have you been living the abundant life Jesus talked about giving his followers?" She shook her head.

"I've got good news for you. In the near future, if you follow through with our sessions and do all I teach you, you will know you're living the way Christ wanted you to live all along."

"I sure would like that." A small, sad smile graced her lips.

"The second coping mechanism I think you have is being a people pleaser." Before he could finish, she put her hand to signal him to stop and shook her head.

"Now, what a minute. I thought the Lord wanted us to love and help people. That's in the Bible, so how is that flesh?"

"Remember, flesh is what you do to protect yourself. It's more of a defensive action than a proactive one. What the Lord wants is for us to love and help others the way He did. He had no agenda for Himself. He was a Servant and He sacrificed for others. Your flesh is all about you. It's that way for all of us when it comes to the flesh."

"I see what you mean."

"You were always trying to make others happy. You may have not been aware that you were really being controlled by others, because all your hard work was for them to respond to you. You didn't make good grades for your betterment or for the sense of accomplishment you would get. You did it to protect yourself from the disappointment that might occur if you let your father or teachers down. You let them control your life. Your whole life was and has been to please others so they would love you.

You could never be truly happy living that way. After you made a certain good grade, you would become anxious again because there is always another test or another paper around the corner. You always had to strive for the next A. Am I correct?"

A subtle frown formed on her face. "You are so right and I'm just this minute realizing how my whole life has been a sham. I've done things just to get love so I haven't really lived. And the sad thing is, I don't know how to live any other way."

"You will, I promise. Don't be so hard on yourself. I will show you how we all have suffered from the flesh. I'll begin next week by explaining this diagram to you. It's a biblical picture of man."

"You mean our time is up for the day?" She gave David a quizzical look. "I feel like we just got started."

"You know, Catherine, it felt that way for me, too. As God begins to open your eyes to His truth and Satan's lies, you will become more and more eager to learn all you can. I can see it already in you."

"I can, too," she said softly.

David noticed that Catherine's shoulders didn't seem as slumped when she exited his office. He couldn't help but inwardly smile.

Session 4

Her blonde hair gently bounced as she cheerfully came into his office. Her smile seemed genuine and David could tell Catherine had taken a little extra effort with her make-up and outfit.

"Wow, who's this bright person walking into my office?"

"Mr. Hill, I went home last week and thought long and hard about all we talked about. My motivation for all I've done has been wrong. I haven't thought enough about myself. I went and got a new outfit and a new hair style. From now on, it's going to be all about me!" She pointed boldly to herself. She was expecting David to say, "Right on!" or something to that effect. Instead his countenance darkened somewhat.

"Catherine, if that's what you heard me say last week, then I have completely missed the mark. All of us already think too much about ourselves. Our focus should be on Christ and others. That's not to say we should ignore or abuse ourselves. Everything should be in balance."

She began to look anxious and downcast. "I thought you'd be thrilled to see me more upbeat."

"Catherine, I am. It's your statement, 'It's going to be all about me,' that concerns me. Also, Catherine, you're too concerned about what others think about you. You always worked hard to get praise from others and it looks like you're trying to get it from me, too."

Looking embarrassed, she averted her eyes. "You know, that's just what I did. I want you to like me, of course in a professional way, and I thought you'd be cheered to see me happier."

"I do like you, Catherine, and I am cheered to see you happier, but you need to remember that you're not here to earn points with me. I'm here to help you become the Christian woman God wants you to be. There are no grades or points to earn in this ministry."

She felt a little chastised, but decided to not let it interfere with their counseling relationship. Had this happened before her sessions, she would have doubled her efforts to get him to compliment her, or broken down in tears. She had now come to realize that those efforts were backed by the wrong motivation. She also realized that when she did those types of things, it really was all about her and feeding her neediness. David was right about her.

"Well, let's get started with the biblical picture of man."

He gave her a picture of three concentric circles. The circle in the middle was labeled spirit. The next circle surrounding the first was labeled soul. The last largest circle, surrounding the other two, was labeled body.

"Catherine, man, meaning woman, too, is made up of three parts. There's the body, soul, and spirit. First Thessalonians 5:23 makes this very clear. The body is the physical part of man-your actions, senses, speech, brain and other organs. The soul is made up of your emotions, mind, will, and personality. When people say, 'I know that person,' besides the physical body that they see, they're referring to one's soul. It's the part that interacts with people and with oneself.

The spirit is our true identity. I would say this is how God sees you. Yes, He knows all of you, but this is the part that concerns Him the most."

"I never thought of man this way. I thought we were just material and immaterial." David noticed that Catherine seemed genuinely interested in this topic and it pleased him immensely.

"Unfortunately, we are all born with a spiritual problem. Some say we have a dead spirit. Whatever you call it, it means there is a wall between us and God. Isaiah 59:2 makes that perfectly clear.

What separates us from God is our sins. Since we don't have a connection with God, in other words, we're lost spiritually, we live out of our own resources. Remember last week when we talked about your coping mechanisms or flesh. The flesh is also called the self-life. Remember in the Bible when Jesus said He was the vine and we were the branches. When we live in the flesh, we're cut off from our life source, which is Jesus, and we're trying our best to survive anyway we can.

Jesus died on the cross for our sins. John 3:16 says if we believe in Him we are saved and have eternal life, His life. Romans 5:10 adds even more to this topic. I'll write all these Scriptures down for you and you can read them at home."

"You know, I think I'm familiar with all these verses, but I've never put all the parts together like this. This is truly amazing. You can go to church all your life and never know the whole truth." She just shook her head.

"Catherine, it's not that Bible-believing churches are trying to confuse you. Many times the Bible is presented in bits and pieces through sermons and Sunday School lessons and the big picture is not presented, not like I'm presenting it to you.

Let's continue. Jesus didn't just die on the cross to save you from your sins. He gave His life to us so He could live through us. You've heard the expression, I'm sure, that we're Jesus' hands and feet on earth today.

This brings us back to the picture of the circles. After salvation, instead of having a dead spirit, God gives us life in our spirit. We are reconciled to God and have a relationship with Him at that point. There is no separation anymore. We're a new creature. I encourage you to read Second Corinthians 5:17-21 to solidify this in your mind. This is all good news, but unfortunately, we can still have our flesh. One reason may be because we may have a distorted view about God. Another reason can be because we haven't surrendered completely to Christ. Do you recall what your description of your father was?"

"I think I said he was mean, distant, and dominant." Catherine got a little smirk on her face.

"Remember I told you we would discuss how our feelings about our father can be transferred to God?"

"Yeah, but I said God was loving."

"Why do you think God is loving?"

"Because the Bible says so."

"That is an absolute fact, but I wonder if your mind believes it to be so, but it's never sunk down into your heart." David made this sound more like a question than a statement. When Catherine didn't reply he continued.

"I want you to draw a picture of God."

She snorted. "I can't draw and I sure can't draw God!"

"You can use stick figures if you have to," he said as he handed her a tablet of paper.

She gave David a look, then began in earnest to draw. She really was more artistic than she gave herself credit. A picture of God began to form. She drew a man in a long robe. His arms were crossed as someone does when they're angry or upset. He had a stick in his hand that pointed to a clock. His eyes looked unforgiving and his mouth was turned down.

"I want you to include yourself in the picture, too."

Catherine sketched a small girl on her knees, with palms together and arms upraised, as if she was begging for love or mercy. She was crying and her mouth was shaped in a most pitiful fashion. Her eyes showed fear.

David took the picture from her and studied it. "Let's discuss what you've drawn here."

Catherine instantly regretted being so honest with her drawing. David could see a concerned look cross over her face, so he smiled warmly to let her know her drawing was no cause for concern.

"Catherine, I didn't want a Sunday School picture of God. I wanted your real opinion of God and I'm glad you chose to be candid. I can tell you have a similar impression of God that you have of your father. Would you say that's correct?"

"Unfortunately, I would. But until I started drawing, I had no idea that I really regarded God as regimented, unfeeling, and unforgiving. It's like you said, I kept a Sunday School picture of

God in my mind because I felt it was blasphemous to think of God in any other way."

"Do you think God can't handle your honesty?" Catherine didn't answer, but shrugged her shoulders like a child would.

"Well, He can. But He doesn't want you to live a lie. It's a lie when you have a distorted view of God. It's not truth and God is all about truth. He wants you to understand Him as much as a human being can. Good relationships are built on trust and honesty. I can tell from your picture that you've got God all wrong." He said this with a smile so she wouldn't feel reprimanded.

"I guess I do," she said with uncertainty. "But look at my life. My father was an unlovable ogre to me and my mother. My husband began to ignore me for his career. My life hasn't been a love fest, especially when it comes to men, if you know what I mean."

"Many people would say the same thing. Life is hard and cold a lot of the time because we live in a fallen world. When you go home today, read Genesis 2 and 3 to get a full understanding of why our life can be difficult. Sin not only affected man, his relationship with God and others, it even marred nature. You can also read Romans 8:22.

Just because life can be tedious, that has nothing to do with God's goodness. Let's do this for a few minutes. I want you to write down every good thing in your life on your tablet."

Slowly her list began to grow. After about two minutes, she stopped and handed the tablet back to David. "Well, I think I'm done."

After perusing her list, he smiled. "This is a good start."

"Good start? That's all there is. That's it!"

"I noticed you didn't put down good health. Has your health ever been bad?"

"Beside just the normal childhood diseases, no."

"Have you ever been lacking in food, clothes, or shelter?"

"No."

"Have you ever been sexually or physically abused?"

"No."

28

"Have you and your husband been able to provide a stable home for Zoe?"

"Yes."

"Catherine, I think you get the point. God is good."

"Then why do bad things happen to people? For example, my mother. She was sweet and loving and look at the life she had."

"You can't blame God for that. Maybe your mother didn't pray earnestly about her decision to marry your father to see if he was God's choice for her. Maybe your father willfully sinned by letting his emotions rule his life, which in turn, caused your mother and you so much pain. God gave us a free will. We're not puppets on a string that God manipulates. Are we?"

"No."

"Then, as free-will agents we choose to sin and sin causes damage to ourselves and others. Your father is a prime example of what sin does."

"I see now what you're talking about."

"Another important person was not on your list."

She looked curious. She had put down her mother, Steve, Zoe, and a few good friends. "I'm not putting my father on that list," she growled.

"No, I wouldn't expect you to. The person I'm talking about is Jesus Christ. He's the greatest example of God's goodness because He died on the cross for our sins, desires to save us and give us abundant life."

"How could I have left Him off the list? I guess I've been so self-absorbed with all my problems that I haven't given Him much thought."

"Even though you haven't thought of Him, He's thought of you," David said warmly.

She glanced at her watch and realized it was time to go. The sessions seemed to go by so quickly. "I guess our time is up," she said disappointedly.

"It is. We'll pick up on our circle diagram next week. There's so much more to share with you."

"Mr. Hill, even though my situation is still awful, I really believe you're helping me. I want to thank you for that."

"Catherine, I know I'm in God's will and doing what He would have me to do when I hear comments like that. I appreciate it."

"Steve wants to meet with me this week and talk about our situation. He spoke to me in his serious, business tone of voice. It made me feel like I'm really losing him for good." David could see she was wanting to talk some more, even though their time was up.

"That's another subject we can discuss next week. We'll do that first thing when you come in. OK?" He closed up the folder and walked to the door.

Catherine hesitated as she rose from her chair. She wanted to talk about Steve and release her fears, but she knew another client was waiting to be with Mr. Hill. Her timing had definitely been off today. She had begun their session together boasting about herself. Now she realized she should have brought up Steve instead. She'd have to wait a whole week to unload.

Session 5

The following week, when she was scheduled to see Mr. Hill again, Catherine woke up slowly. She seemed to be walking through the morning in a daze. The conversation with Steve the night before seemed like a bad song that kept running through her mind over and over. It was as if she was on autopilot as she made her bed and went through her morning beauty routine. Nothing registered with her except the unnerving sound of Steve's voice, playing over and over in her head. She had to hurry or be late for her appointment.

Stepping outside, she turned and stared a long time at her home. This stately Tudor house had been theirs for ten years. She had always loved this place. For her it meant family, security, and beauty. Now looking at it on this dull gray day, she realized it might be taken from her. She wiped the tears away and got into her luxury sedan. Feeling the comfortable leather seat against her back, she wondered if this, too, would be lost to her. Pulling out of her driveway, she headed for the only bright spot in her life right now, Mr. Hill.

Not seeing his early model sports car in his designated parking space made her heart jump. She just had to see him today. Her broken heart needed to release some of the pain she was feeling. Walking into his waiting room, she was relieved when his receptionist told her Mr. Hill would see her shortly.

He appeared at his door and motioned her in. "Catherine, how are you doing?" She never felt he asked this question just to be polite. He seemed genuinely interested.

"Terrible," she said as her voice began cracking from attempting to hold back the tears. "I got really scared when I didn't see your car out front. I thought our appointment had been cancelled."

"You never need to worry about that. If there had been an emergency, my secretary would have called you." Pushing the box of tissues her way, he said, "Why don't you tell me why things are terrible."

"Well, I didn't get to meet with Steve until last night. Business had backed up his schedule." This last statement had a hint of sarcasm in it. "He came to the house, which I mistook for a good sign. I thought once he came into the house he would realize we need to patch things up and be a family again. But he wasn't having any of that. He came in with a legal pad and said we needed to talk about distribution of our property. I was shocked and told him so. We hadn't even talked about divorce in any serious way and here he's talking about distribution of property." She stopped as she realized her voice was getting too loud. After calming down, she continued.

"My first impulse was to scream and cry and beg him to reconsider, but I remembered what you said about talking with him in a mature manner. I told him I thought this was a little premature since we hadn't discussed divorce. I did tell him I didn't want a divorce, that I still loved him. Sarcasm was dripping from his voice when he said, 'Yeah, you really were loving me when you had sex with that creep, didn't you?' I couldn't hold back the tears, but I stayed composed. I asked him not to make such a big decision until we had given it time to heal. He just stared at me like I was insane. The he said harshly, 'Catherine, some wounds never heal. You've hurt me too badly. It can't be reversed. I want a divorce, period.'

His face showed little emotion when he spoke. At that point a little ember began to burn within me. I started thinking of all the sacrifices I had made for him and how he had done me wrong all these years and the venom began to spew from me like a volcano.

I told him he had been a terrible husband and father and it was because of his neglect I had ended up in the arms of another man. I wanted to hurt him right that moment just as he was hurting me. I rashly said something that wasn't true and I regret saying it now. I said five minutes in Austin's arms was better than the last five years in his.

"I could see the hurt in his eyes, but I didn't care. I felt like a wounded animal that wanted to strike out at anybody and everybody. But that feeling didn't last long. As he gathered his note pad and began to leave, I felt the rage in me fizzle. At the door he told me I should contact an attorney soon. After he closed the door, I literally fell apart."

"Catherine, I think before we go any further, you need to get right with God about this. Otherwise, we won't make any progress in our session, because God will not bless a person with unconfessed sin."

She agreed and bowed her head. With a heart full of sorrow, she verbally confessed her sin and asked God to forgive her. David saw she was sincere and felt she was ready to resume their session.

"Catherine, most of the time God will allow us to experience the consequences of our sins. He does this so we won't be so eager to jump back into them. One of the consequences of your adultery may be divorce. It may not seem fair that the whole family structure will be destroyed over one sin, but adultery is extremely damaging to a marriage and a family.

In Genesis 2:24 God says in marriage the man and woman become one. This oneness goes beyond sex. It's like the couple become one unit. In a Christian marriage, the unit is the man, the woman, and Christ. First Corinthians 6:18-20 talks about how sexual sins are against your body and your body is the temple of the Holy Spirit. Adultery invites a stranger into the holy unity of the married couple and God. Do you see why it's so despicable to God? In the Old Testament, adulterers were actually stoned to death. It was that serious."

"I knew adultery was wrong, but I never thought about it violating the union between a man, woman, and Christ. That makes adultery sound even more disgusting. Why did I ever do it?" Catherine looked contrite and humble. "I wish I had never even met Austin. What a disastrous mistake! What a fool I was. I never even stopped to consider the fallout from my sin."

"Catherine, sometimes one sin can ruin a person's life. The prisons are full of such people." David paused as she wiped some tears away from her downcast eyes. "I would say at this point, you need to bathe this situation with Steve in prayer. I'll be praying for both of you. God can work on Steve's heart, but, remember, Steve's got a free will. He'll ultimately do what he wants to do about the divorce. Let's discuss more about this after you see what Steve's next move will be."

"I'm not getting an attorney yet. I'm going to fight for my marriage. It may not do any good, but I'm not ready to throw in the towel."

"I'm glad to hear that. Couples nowadays are too quick to jump into divorce. They don't take their wedding vows very seriously. Of course, Steve has a biblical reason to divorce you. That doesn't mean he should though. Sometimes we need to surrender our rights for the greater good."

Getting out the diagram with circles, David said, "Why don't we pick up where we left off on the circle diagram we discussed last week." Catherine didn't seem too interested, but David knew this material was too important not to discuss. "Ok, we left off with Christ making our spirits alive as we accept Him as our Savior. But, just because we're saved, that doesn't mean our flesh is done away with. Remember, the rejection we experience in life, especially in childhood, has an effect on our emotions and our mind. We begin to depend on our flesh, which results in coping mechanisms. Unfortunately, as we try to cope with our present problems and our past rejections, we will experience conflict and frustration. This is because we were never meant to depend on ourselves. We are to depend on God. Just like Adam and Eve did in the beginning.

Our ineffective coping mechanisms lead to stress, which we all know leads to all kinds of health problems, physical and mental.

We may resort to self-pity or withdrawal. It may make you a controlling person, an obsessive person, or a self-righteous person. The manifestations of the flesh are numerous. Ranging from being passive to being hostile, being a people pleaser to being self-absorbed, being prideful to being self-depreciating."

"It sounds like flesh is our way of trying to just keep our head above water. Sometimes that's the best we can do, isn't it?"

"Catherine, it's the best we can do ourselves, but that's not what God wants for us. He wants the best He can do for us, which is far superior to anything we can do on our own.

We have negatively programmed flesh when we have experienced many traumas and rejections in our life. I believe that would fit you.

Positively programmed flesh results from few traumas and rejections. The manifestations are usually pride, self-righteousness, being judgmental, and being controlling, because we think we've got it all together.

While positively programmed flesh may look better, it's still flesh. I believe you deal with your world from performance-based acceptance."

"What does that mean?"

"It means you have been indirectly taught that when you are good and you do good works, people will accept you. You may not have been conscious of it, but you've always looked for love and acceptance by performing or working for it. Would you agree?"

"I hadn't thought about it, but now that you've pointed it out, I can see all my life I've bent over backwards to make people approve of me and like me. That's all I've ever known. I just wanted people to love me and I didn't think they could love just me for myself. I had to give them something to earn their love. I've been so stupid all these years, haven't I?" David felt a wave of sympathy for Catherine. She looked like a forlorn little girl who just discovered Santa is not real.

"Catherine, don't be so hard on yourself. We all have some manifestation of flesh. The good news is, unlike so many people who go through life blind to what is wrong with them, you are

35

discovering what your flesh looks like and with the help of God you will break free from it.

God uses circumstances in our lives to teach us His truths. Whether it's positively or negatively programmed flesh, He wants to root it out."

"But how is this going to help with my problem with Steve?"

"God wants you to live in truth, dependent on Him, not yourself. Whether you and Steve reconcile or break-up, you need to be free from the bankruptcy of your flesh. No matter which way this situation plays itself out, you will be more of the person God would have you to be than you have ever been. You will live your life in a completely different way."

His encouraging words didn't seem to penetrate her melancholy. Her body language was saying, "So what? My life may be completely ruined soon anyway."

"I know you feel like your life is crashing down all around you. But remember, the very fact that you were led to my office means God is guiding you to a better life. This trauma you are experiencing is being used by God to mold you closer to Christ's image."

"I wished He had picked a different way than a possible divorce."

"Catherine, we only grow during times of trouble. When everything's going well, we seem to not depend on God as much. We become a little too self-sufficient and self-absorbed. It takes adversity sometimes for God to get our attention." The look on his face let Catherine know he was talking from experience.

"I know you're right. I've prayed more in the last weeks than I've prayed in the last few years. I know it grieves God that we ignore Him when things are running smoothly. I'm so guilty of that."

"So what is your plan for the coming week as far as your relationship with Steve?"

"I plan to pray that God can soften his heart so Steve will forgive me. I'm not going to contact an attorney yet. I want to see what Steve's first move is. Other than that, I don't know what else to do."

"Catherine, have you ever given any thought to expanding your horizons, so to speak?"

"What do you mean, travel?" She looked confused.

"No, I mean get involved at your church more, volunteer at some worthy charity, or get a job? Now that Zoe is reaching adulthood, this may be the time to be thinking about being more than a stay-at-home mother."

"You mean, think about what I'd like to do with my life? I thought I was to concentrate on others, not myself."

"This would be about helping others, but at the same time, the added benefit would be that you'd be helping yourself. Let me ask you something. Now that Zoe is away at school, do you think you have too much time on your hands? Many times when we have nothing to occupy us, we tend to start looking inward, which can lead to concentrating on our problems too much. What do you think?"

"I guess. When I was alone at home and Steve was gone so much, I really started feeling sorry for myself. I guess that's why I almost jumped into Austin's arms. I'll give your suggestion some thought this week."

"Great. I'll see you next week and we'll discuss some more diagrams, OK?" Catherine nodded then departed quietly.

After straightening up his papers, David walked over to the office's tall windows. The sun was shining in that way that made you glad you were indoors. He happened to look down at the street and noticed Catherine buying a newspaper at a stand. Maybe she would start looking for an opportunity to get her mind off herself and her problems. If Steve went through with his threat to divorce her, she would most likely need a job. The days of a wife getting alimony for the rest of her life were long gone.

He was concerned for Catherine because her life was possibly getting ready to turn very turbulent. While his prayer for her and Steve was reconciliation, Steve would most likely divorce Catherine. From what she has told him, Steve didn't seem very flexible or forgiving. He hated to see a marriage of twenty-odd years evaporate. They had a daughter and a divorce would rock her youthful world, even though she was almost an adult. Divorce was so messy. Like the ripples in a pond, a divorce eventually touches everyone in the family.

Before the next client arrived, David felt the Holy Spirit's prompting. He was being urged to pray right there for Steve, Catherine, and Zoe. After rising from his knees, he ended his petitions with, "Lord, may Your will be done."

The next day Catherine cancelled her next appointment for the following week. Normally David would take that in stride, but he decided to do something he hardly ever did with a client-he called her to ask why. He was worried about Catherine's fragile state of mind and wondered if something with Steve had sent her into a tail spin.

The phone rang several times before she picked up. She sounded a little groggy. It was the late afternoon and the sound of her voice sent a shock wave of fear into David. Had she been drinking or worse yet, taking drugs?

"Catherine, this is David Hill. Are you alright?"

"I'm OK. What's wrong?"

"When you cancelled your appointment for next week, I got a little concerned. Normally I wouldn't call, but . . ." His voice trailed off and he wondered if he had made a mistake about calling.

"The reason I cancelled for next week is because I have a job interview on our usual day. That's all." She didn't sound as upbeat about the job prospect as he thought she might, but that was discussion for another day. Maybe she was frightened about interviewing for a job.

"That's great, but I have other slots open on other days. Do you want to reschedule?" Now he really felt awkward and maybe a little pushy. He should have trusted Catherine to have a good excuse for canceling.

"You know, I think that would be a good idea. I'll call your secretary tomorrow. By the way, thanks for being concerned."

He could hear the smile in her voice. She didn't sound as groggy either. Maybe she had just woken from a nap.

Catherine did call the next day to reschedule her appointment. David was relieved. He didn't feel as though he was getting too involved with this client, but he'd have to be careful. One of the greatest dangers for a counselor was to get too vested in a relationship with a client. It can only lead to problems later on, for counselor and client alike. Either the counselor gets taken advantage of by a manipulative client or the counselor becomes in the eyes of the client a savior, or worse, a lover. Neither of these scenarios is healthy and can be downright dangerous. Clients can destroy a counselor's reputation and practice. Counselors in turn can destroy the trust a client may have for any authority figure or advisor.

David only felt concern for Catherine, but it had to stay on a purely professional level. Catherine was too emotionally needy right now. It would be easy for her to transfer her feelings for her husband to David. He was a happily-married man who didn't need that kind of difficulty in his life. He had known of counselors who had clients fall in love with them. The consequences ranged from disappointing to dangerous.

One client he knew of terminated the counseling relationship when she saw the counselor had only professional regard for her. While a counselor may be relieved that the relationship has ended, he would still be concerned for the client's emotional and spiritual problems, wondering if she would seek help elsewhere.

Another client had started stalking a counselor because she fully believed he was equally as in love with her as she was with him. She began calling at all hours when she discovered his home phone number and even showed up at his house one night. The client was arrested and put in jail. Needless to say, his family had been terrorized by this emotionally-disturbed individual. Upon release from jail she spread vicious lies throughout his hometown about him. Had it not been for his impeccable reputation, he would have been destroyed by her maliciousness.

He didn't feel Catherine was like that, but still he would not call her home again. There was no sense cracking open a door for the Devil. Their relationship was just where it needed to be and he was pleased with the progress, albeit slow, she was making.

Across town, Steve was opening the motel door. He tossed his briefcase on the couch in exhaustion. After stripping off his coat and tie, he looked in the small refrigerator for a cool drink. Half a bottle of water was all that was left. Unscrewing the top, he downed the cold liquid in one large gulp. A grimace crossed his face when he thought of the prospect of another fast-food meal tonight.

It's funny, but before he moved into the motel, he had been accustomed to traveling for business. Motels and quick food were part of the sacrifice one made to work one's way up the ladder. But knowing this was his home for now made him chafe. He wasn't doing this for business; it was all because of his wife's unfaithfulness.

Every time he thought of Catherine in another man's arms he wanted to pound his fists into something until his knuckles bled. How could she do this to him? Here, he had been toiling for her and Zoe and what did he get in return-his wife sleeping with another man. He understood she had been lonely, but what about him? Many a night in a motel room he ached to go home, but he didn't fall in bed with someone else to ease the pain.

The fact that she only did it once didn't seem to help. In fact, it made it feel like she went out on a one-night stand. Disgusting! Catherine had behaved like a common tramp. It might have been different if she had fallen in love with him. But she just fell hook, line, and sinker for this creep's offer of riding horses. What a joke!

She had cried and cried for him not to leave her, but he was afraid if he didn't go, he'd do something rash, like slap her. He had never touched Catherine except in a loving way. Now he wasn't sure he'd want to ever touch her again.

And what about Zoe? So far they had kept everything low key with her. That would change and when it did, it would be ugly. Steve thought of his sweet daughter and knew she'd be so hurt when she found out her parents would be divorcing. He didn't plan to smear Catherine's reputation just for revenge, not even to Zoe. That would hurt Zoe deeply. While he hadn't spent as much time with her as he would have liked, he still loved her dearly. Why did Catherine have to go and screw everything up? Wasn't everything just fine as it was?

Changing into jeans and a t-shirt, Steve dialed the delivery pizza place. While waiting for the pizza, he grabbed the remote. After scanning countless channels on the tube, he settled for the news. Maybe they would report something so tragic he would feel better about his situation. After that annoying weather-girl finished her dubious predictions, he shut it off in disgust. He didn't care if it snowed, rained, or whatever. What did it matter? He'd be stuck living in this cookie-cutter room until who knows when.

A little voice was telling Steve he wasn't being entirely honest about the situation, but he didn't care. He was outraged and he had a right to be mad. He had kept his end of the bargain by providing well for his family. He deserved a lot better than what Catherine had done. When he thought of all those late business dinners and tacky motel rooms in some of those dreary, little towns, it made him fume. Did she think he enjoyed all that greasy food, surly waitresses, and smelly rooms? It wasn't like he was living high on the hog when he was on the road. Except when he took a client out, he always cut traveling costs as much as possible. He felt that would be another contribution to the company's bottom line. His boss had never told him to do that, but he wanted to look like a team player.

Catherine didn't have a clue how much everything costs. The mortgage alone was astronomical. He wanted his family living in a safe neighborhood with good schools. You had to live in expensive subdivisions to get those kinds of perks. He was proud of all he had done for his family. He always felt that all his hard work was paying off, but now he began to wonder. He wasn't even living anymore in that luxury home he labored so hard to purchase and maintain.

The knock on the door startled him. He had drifted into a one-man gripe session in his head and had forgotten about the pizza. He over-tipped the scraggly teen with the nose-ring to get rid of him quickly. As he was closing the door the teen held it open and peered into the room.

"Hey, I know this motel. When my uncle got out of jail, he moved here. Boy, this place is really nice. We had some good times before he got kicked out for fighting in the parking lot." He got this dreamy look on his acne-scarred face like he hated that those fun-filled times came to an end.

Steve smiled politely then slammed the door tight. He now felt more depressed than before after hearing that story. Looking around at the cheap motel furniture with the artwork on the wall that would make Picasso vomit, he just shook his head. Yeah, this is some place.

After eating one slice, he put the remainder of the small pizza in the equally small refrigerator. Leaning back on the couch, which had a faint musty smell, he looked up at the ceiling. He could tell people had smoked in here, even though it was supposed to be smoke-free. The ceiling tiles had a tinge of yellow that every smoker's house eventually developed. While this was one of the better motels near his office, it was a long way, figuratively and geographically, from his home. How depressing and humiliating!

Cutting the tube back on, he muttered to himself, "Catherine, why? Why did you do this to me?" Leaning back again, it wasn't long before his internal tirade ended and snoring began.

Session 6

David was stretching his back, when the receptionist beeped and said Catherine had arrived. Upon opening the door, she flashed him a small smile and sat down.

"Well, how has your week been?" David had a way of making Catherine feel so comfortable from the very beginning of their sessions.

"I'm doing quite well. I took your advice and started looking for a job. I think I may have found one." Excitement gleamed in her eyes.

"What kind of job is it?"

"It's working for a museum, a Western art museum. It's just an entry-level job, but that doesn't bother me. I would be giving tours to school-age student groups. I love kids and being around all that artwork of horses and the West would really be fun. They're going to call me back next week and if I get the job I'll be trained for two weeks. So, what do you think?"

"Catherine, I think that's great. I'm very proud of you. It would have been so easy for you to slip into depression and stay there, but you're really moving forward. Have you told Steve?"

"No. I don't want to say anything to anyone until I get the job."

"I understand. Well, let's get back to where we left off last week. Today I'd like for us to get back to our diagrams. I'd like for us to first look at Galatians 2:20." He already had the place marked in his Bible and he handed it to Catherine.

After reading it to herself, she looked up at David. "What does that exactly mean?'

"Catherine, to live the victorious life Christ promised us, we must stop living out of our flesh and surrender to Him. As we surrender, we allow Christ to live through us. Christ is eternal. For us to have eternal life, He must be in us and we in Him.

I want you to write down a few verses to read later today. These verses will explain how our soul, remember it being our mind, emotions, and will, will be transformed. Romans 12:2 says our mind will be renewed, Psalm 23:3 says our emotions will heal, and Romans 13:14 states our will can choose to depend on Christ.

Basically four changes will occur. We will have freedom from sin's control, we will have our needs met in Christ, we can relinquish our rights, and we will have the mind of Christ. Do you need for me to go into more depth on any of these topics?"

"I think I need for you to explain more, a lot more, about this idea of surrender," Catherine's voice had a worried tone to it.

"Psalm 51:17 says the only sacrifice God really wants from us is a broken and contrite heart. This is the very opposite of a proud heart. For example, a proud heart is a critical heart. A contrite heart is full of compassion. A proud heart says, 'What's in it for me?' A contrite heart says, 'What can I do for you?' Do you see the difference?" She firmly nodded.

"God wants you to be broken so He can recreate you into His masterpiece. As long as you're depending on your flesh and not Him, he can't really use you to your full potential in Christ. You must surrender or be broken by Him. He will use people or circumstances to break you. I think God is going to use your affair to break you of your dependence on flesh and on Steve."

"It would seem God would want us whole, not broken. Broken people are weak people in my mind. I don't want to be weak. I've felt weak for too long in my life. I want to be a strong woman." Catherine sat up in chair a little more and lifted her chin slightly when she said this.

"Was Jesus strong or weak?"

"Strong, I guess. He went through a lot on the cross."

"Jesus didn't classify Himself as weak or strong. He said in Matthew 11:29 that He was meek. Meek means humble, submissive. It's strength under control. Jesus allowed people to mistreat Him, but He never fought back or retaliated. He had all the power in the universe, but He submitted to the Father's will and plan.

Meekness is patience, too. He was patient with people and all their sins and problems. This is what God wants for us, to be meek. You become meek when you are broken. You can fight God about surrendering or you can voluntarily submit. Which do you want to do?"

David waited patiently while Catherine lowered her eyes and silently sat there. "Catherine, there are four barriers to brokenness. They are pride, fear of suffering, lack of trust in God, and fear of losing control. Which one do you think fits you?"

"There was a time I would have said there is no way it's pride, but I guess my comment about not wanting to be weak was prideful. I guess I would say the first three barriers. I'm not afraid of losing control because I have lost control. My life is like a leaf on a raging river, floating madly in the river's current. I have no idea what I'll be doing or where I'll be living next month or next year. My life is all in God's hands now." David couldn't decide from Catherine's expression if she considered that good or bad.

"Let's talk about suffering? Are you really afraid of suffering? It appears you've suffered a lot in your childhood? Would you agree?"

"Yes, I did and I didn't like it one bit. I guess you can't be alive and not suffer."

"Suffering can be good and useful in God's eyes. Second Corinthians 12:9 tells us that Christ's power is made perfect in weakness. God can use suffering to show us how much of a complete failure we are without Him.

Think of all the suffering Joseph in Genesis experienced. But Joseph came to realize that God meant it for good. You can look up Genesis 50:20 later to see that it's right there in Scripture. The outcome of Joseph's suffering was that he was able to provide for his family. From Joseph and his eleven brothers came the whole Hebrew nation. God used Joseph to save His people from starvation and subsequent extinction."

"Do you think what I'm going through will have a good outcome, like Joseph?" Catherine looked pleadingly at David.

"If you surrender your life to Christ, yes, I do."

"Well, I never thought of suffering in this way. But I can see suffering is a universal human experience and it really shouldn't be feared, *if* it is put it in God's hands."

"For you, the barrier to brokenness, I feel, is a lack of trust in God. Because of your feelings toward your father, this has led to a distorted view of God. You see God as being like your father. We've got to work on that. Remember the list of good things in your life you made? I've got it in your file. Let me get it out."

Handing it to Catherine, he asked her to reread it. Once she was finished, she laid it back on his desk and looked at him like, "I see your point."

"This is just the tip of the iceberg of God's love for you. If all He ever did was allow Jesus to die on the cross for your sins *that* would be enough. Imagine a life with no hope, no eternal life. What a wretched existence that would be.

Praise God, we don't have to live like that. God came to earth, wrapped Himself in flesh, and suffered and died for us. If that's not love, I don't know what is?"

Catherine nodded and said, "I know. I know it's love."

"I want you to try something. I want you to trust God in some part of your life. Can you think of something that concerns you, that you should be placing in His hands?"

"Yes. I guess I would say off the top of my head, finances. I don't know how things are going to play out with Steve and me. He's always been a good provider, but I broke his trust, so who knows what will happen."

"Can you step out on faith and trust Him to provide for you?"

"I'll try, but I'm scared. What if I don't get any money from Steve? How will I make the household expenses?"

"That's why it's called faith. You're going to believe God knows best and will provide."

"Boy, this is scary. I've always either had my father or my husband to take care of me."

"Has it ever crossed your mind that God was providing for you through those two men?"

"No, not really, but I'm starting to see it now."

"You need to really be in prayer so God will know you're serious about this. Why don't you make a list of all your household expenses. Then when you're praying, pray over these things one by one. Let's see what God is going to do. Are you willing to do this?"

"Yes. Yes, I am." She sat up in her chair like she was serious.

"I'm going to give you a list of promises from God in the Bible and I want you to meditate on these. You're going to feel better and better about putting your trust in Him." He handed her a sheet with Bible passages, that included Psalm 37:23-25, Psalm 23:1, Deuteronomy 28:11-13, Matthew 6:31-33, Luke 6:38, Malachi 3:10-12, and Philippians 4:19.

"Catherine, let your attitude be one of adventure. See where God is going to take you. Feel the freedom in surrendering to Him. It will transform your life. I promise." She was looking a little skeptical to David. "I can hardly wait until next week to hear what God is doing in your life." David warmly smiled at Catherine and she couldn't help but feel a little excitement stirring within her, although it was very little.

"I've never been the adventurous kind, but I'd like to start, but I'm still scared," she said emphatically.

"Ok, I hear you. I think we will cut things short today, but I'll make it up to you next week. This is a good stopping point and I've got to go to the dentist. The traffic will be murder going to his side of town. I heard today they're doing road construction and I'd like to get a good head start. Is that OK with you?"

"Sure, I've got some errand to run myself. I may just need that extra time next week if I'm stepping out on this new adventure. Good or bad, I'll have plenty to talk about I'm sure."

"Remember, don't think *bad*. If God allows suffering in your life and you're yielded to Him, He'll turn it around for good. Look at suffering as a vehicle to the good things."

"OK, but I'd love to have the good without going through the suffering. Wouldn't you?"

"Flowers don't grow if it's sunshine all the time. You have to have a little rain."

Catherine just shook her head and got up to leave. "I know in my head you're right, but it's got to sink down into my heart, 'cause I'm not feeling it."

Upon arriving home, she noticed her answering machine blinking. "I wonder if it's the museum?" She couldn't help but feel a little excited before pushing the play button. Her exhilaration turned to shock as she listened to Steve's formal voice. There was no warmth at all. Sinking onto her knees, after hearing the whole message through, she cried, "Why, God? Why?" Tears flowed down her cheeks onto her new blouse, the one she had worn for her museum interview.

It was at least an hour before she felt composed enough to walk into the kitchen. Although she hadn't eaten since breakfast, the thought of eating sickened her, but she was quite thirsty from crying. She fixed a tall glass of water and went to her bedroom.

Looking at the beautiful king-size bed and its sheer size, the bed seemed to mock her. What good was a bed that big with only one person to sleep in it! It was looking like she and Steve would never share this bed again. If she could have lifted it up, she'd have heaved it out the window, into the yard. Instead, she fell across it and squalled until sleep finally took over her weary mind and body.

Because she had fallen asleep so early in the evening, she woke up around 3:00 a.m. Looking at the clock, she moaned. "I don't want to toss and turn until the alarm goes off." But, she didn't get up. Instead, she played Steve's message over and over in her mind. He wanted a divorce and he was ready to discuss the distribution of property. He wanted to know if she had an attorney yet.

Normally a quiet person, she yelled at the ceiling, "God, is this your way of making me suffer so good things will come my way? I don't want your blessings! God, leave me alone!" Her throat ached from yelling because it was already sore from all her crying. She pulled her pillow over her ears to block out God. Part of her wished He'd be so angry with her that He would command a solitary storm cloud to appear over her house and have lightening strike her dead, right then.

Later, while she laid in perfect silence, a Voice spoke to her spirit and said, "I will not leave you alone. I love you." But, she would not be mollified. She was angry and she liked the strength of her rage as it coursed through her body. She remembered what Mr. Hill said about this being an adventure and part of her wanted to laugh in his face when she saw him again.

"Yeah, this is some adventure, Mr. Hill. Don't you mean a nightmare?" Catherine imagined herself spitting those words at him. Negative thoughts keep bubbling up, like a boiling cauldron, full of toxic chemicals. She couldn't believe the vicious thoughts that raced madly around her brain. She was furious with God ("Why do I have to suffer? You could fix this!), Steve ("Why can't you be more forgiving?), Austin (Why did you have to even talk to me and seduce me?), and Mr. Hill (Why did I ever come to be counseled by you?), yet deep inside she knew she was being unfair. As her temper cooled, she realized she was really just angry with herself. What a fool she had been! Why is being irate with yourself such a bitter pill to swallow?

Some time in the wee hours of the night, she fell back to sleep. The alarm startled her out of her turbulent dream and she rose to get ready for the day. She would have to find a good attorney. Part of her wanted to call Steve and say, "Just take it all. I deserve to be a homeless, bag lady." But, she knew she was being overly dramatic. Steve would be fair to her, the mother of his child.

Catherine remembered her neighbor worked for an attorney and called her cell-phone. After making an appointment, she took a deep breath and called Steve. He didn't answer and she didn't leave a message. He'd call back soon, especially if he was so anxious to proceed with the divorce. Before taking a shower, she called Mr. Hill's office and scheduled her next week's appointment for that afternoon. She couldn't wait a whole week.

"I'll either come blazing into his office, looking for a fight or wither under the pressure of my dilemma and sob my eyes out. Either way, it won't be pretty," she thought as jerked off her pajamas.

"The phone always rings when you take a shower; it never fails," she thought. But Catherine didn't rush out of bathroom to answer it. While the shower was refreshing, she felt bone-tired and didn't feel up to talking right that minute. It was probably either Steve or Zoe. Either way, it would require too much effort to converse with either one of them.

She switched off her phone and, without drying her hair, she slipped back into the bed. "I wish I could just fall into a coma and wake up when the nightmare is over." Her eyes slowly shut and she murmured to no one in particular, "Please, help me. Please, help me. Please, help me." Then a wave of fatigue washed over her and she was out like a light.

In her dream she was drowning and there was no one to save her. A wave crashed upon her head and drove her deep into the sea. She saw herself sinking slowly into the dark water until it swallowed her into its inky depths. When she finally awoke, she was as tired as before. She cut the phone back on and sat on the edge of her bed, just staring into space.

Across town Steve fretted that he hadn't heard from Catherine right away. "Was she looking for an attorney or what? I can't live in this motel forever. I've got to get out of here and start over!" Picking up his phone he dialed her number. The woman who answered the phone didn't even sound like Catherine.

"Catherine, are you OK?"

After coughing a few times, she muttered, "Yeah, I'm OK." She ran her fingers through her hair. It felt like a rat's nest after sleeping on it wet.

"Did you get my message yesterday?"

"Yeah, I got it." Her voice sounded so despondent.

"Well, have you got an attorney yet?" Steve was getting a little agitated with her short answers.

"No." She had only an appointment with one, so she reasoned that her answer wasn't really a lie.

"Catherine, what's the hold up?" Catherine knew that tone of voice and it began to irritate her.

"Steve, you're the one who wants to get the divorce. Not me. Why can't we just talk this through?" In desperation she whispered, "I still love you!" All she could hear was his breathing into the phone.

"Catherine, I think I still love you, but I'll never trust you again. I can't live like that. I have too many other hassles in my life to be stressed all the time wondering if my wife is sleeping around while I'm working."

"Steve, you act like this was a long affair and I've done it before. It was one mistake. Can't you forgive me?" Tears began to well up in her eyes.

"It's not a matter of forgiveness. I'm just tired. Tired of living in this motel, tired of my work situation, and just tired of trying."

"But, you haven't tried to work things out with us at all. You just left. Come home to your own bed and your own bathroom. It's so lonely here."

"Catherine, I've got a call coming in that I need to take. Let me know who your attorney is when you get one. I want this divorce to be as smooth as possible. I want to be fair, even if you weren't fair to me."

Before he could hang up, she slammed the receiver down. "A smooth divorce. What an oxymoron!"

Dragging herself out of bed, she showered again and got ready for her appointment with Mr. Hill. "I'll probably lay my head on his desk and pass out from exhaustion. Then when I wake up, I'll probably cry myself to sleep again." She could even envision it, with Mr. Hill trying to arouse her with his kind words. Unfortunately, sleep would have to wait until tonight.

Session 7

David was a little startled when Catherine raced into his office and plopped into her chair. Her eyes were swollen and it look liked she hadn't slept in days. Her hair was sticking out in all directions and she didn't even have on any make-up. He decided not to comment on her disheveled look.

"I was surprised when you made an appointment this soon after your last."

"Well, remember the first time I came into your office and said my life was falling apart. I didn't know then how unraveled my life could get in just a few weeks. I thought by coming to counseling things would get better, not worse!" Her mouth twisted into a snarl.

David took no offense at her comment and looked at her with compassion. "Catherine, we talked about suffering and its purpose last session. Things may get worse before they get better. God is still working in your life and will continue to do so."

Getting an aggravated look, she almost hissed, "I wish He would stop working in my life. I can't take all this *assistance.*" Her fingers made exaggerated quotation marks in the air when she used the word assistance.

"Why don't you tell me what's happened since I saw you last."

"Well, first, I haven't heard from the museum yet. Second, Steve wants me to get an attorney and get this show on the road. I don't know why he has to be in such a rush. He said he was tired of living in the motel. There's part of me that wants to laugh in his face about that. He's lived on the road most of his adult life and *now* he doesn't like it? What a joke!

I told him to come home and let's patch things up, but he's not budging. He's made his mind up and that's it. I guess we're really going to get a divorce." Rubbing her forehead, she tried to stop the tears, but she had no control over them either.

"Catherine, the museum may still call, so let's not worry about that right now. This couldn't have been a surprise for you concerning Steve. He's been unbending from the start. Some people are slow to forgive, while others refuse to at all."

"I know, but I thought I could change his mind. I figured the more he stayed away from home, the more he would miss it. And me." Two big tears slipped down her cheek.

"From what you've told me about Steve and your relationship, I didn't get the impression that you were able to influence him much. You said he spent too much time at work and neglected his family. You've tried to get him to change, but he never did. Did you honestly think he'd waver?"

"I had a glimmer of hope, thinking he'd consider Zoe?"

"Has he before?"

"Not really, but I know he really loves her."

"Let's talk about surrender again." Before he completed his sentence, Catherine jerked her hand up to motion *stop*. Before she could utter a word, David gently bowed his head and began to pray aloud. She was so surprised she quickly closed her eyes and bowed her head, concentrating on his words and not the thoughts whirling through her head. David prayed that God would use him as His vessel to minister to Catherine, especially when it came to the topic of surrender. He pleaded with God to give him the right words and for Catherine's heart to be open. Then he raised his head.

"Are we ready to discuss surrender?"

She looked at him sharply and said, "Are you going to just start praying any time I don't want to discuss a topic?"

"No, I just felt the Holy Spirit wooing me to stop and hand this session over to Him." David seemed to have tears in eyes and that really touched Catherine's heart.

"I'm ready to listen to what you, I mean the Holy Spirit, has to say."

"Surrender is not a demand, it's an invitation. There's three parts of surrender: allowing God to work in and through you, being God's living sacrifice as Romans 12:1 discusses, and relinquishing rights.

Let's discuss rights first. You have a right to want to continue being married to Steve. After all, you are bound by the vows you made before God. Is that correct?"

"Yes. I do have that right."

"But, didn't you break your vows by having an affair?"

She lowered her head and mumbled, "Yes."

"Steve has a biblical right to divorce you. Jesus said adultery was a legitimate reason to get divorce in Matthew, chapter 19. Now does Steve have the right to divorce you?"

"Yes, I guess he does, but he doesn't have to." Her voice cracked.

"That's right. He has the right, but he doesn't have to exercise that right. He could surrender it. I wish he would. Unfortunately, it looks like he's not going to do that. But, do you see what I mean? You may have to surrender the right to live happily ever after with Steve. God wants you and Steve to reconcile, but He's not going to force Steve to do anything. You need to put it into God's hands and say, 'God, whatever you want to do with me and my marriage, I'll submit to your will.' If you know how much God truly, truly loves you and wants what's best for you, you'll be more willing to surrender."

"But isn't that just giving up? It's like throwing your hands up in the air in defeat."

"In a war context, if a soldier surrenders, then he's giving up. He's at the enemy's mercy and he knows the outlook is grim. In your relationship with Christ, you're giving up your rights as part of surrendering, but you are surrendering to your loving, merciful Lord and Savior. The outlook is far from grim because

He loves you and wants only what is best for you. Do you see the difference?" After she nodded, David continued.

"When you surrender your rights to having a husband who provides well for you and your child, what do you think will be the outcome?"

"Pain and struggle." Catherine's face looked so forlorn.

"If that is true, you know it will be for a higher purpose. God will weave your suffering into the tapestry of your life and make something beautiful out of it. You've just got to have faith and trust Him." When she didn't comment, he decided to share a personal story.

"Catherine, I had an aunt who lived the American dream. She had two lovely daughters, a gorgeous mansion, and a loving husband. Life was so good for her. One night her husband was returning from a business trip, fell asleep at the wheel, and struck a tractor-trailer head-on. That accident was bad enough, but it got worse.

He had made some really bad investments and when his estate was settled, my aunt was virtually penniless. She lost everything but her faith in God. She surrendered her rights and told God to do what He felt best for her and her daughters. They had to move in with a relative while she searched for a job. For a couple of months, things were really looking bleak. Finally, she found a low paying job at a women's shelter.

You may think at this point that God had forgotten her, but there's more. After working at the shelter for six months, she and her girls were offered a little apartment connected to the shelter, rent-free. Because she thoroughly engrossed herself in learning all she could about helping these women, she eventually wrote a handbook to guide battered women through all the consequences of their situation. The book was promoted by her shelter and thousands of copies have been sold across the nation. She's made enough to buy a small house and is doing quite well today.

I asked her one day if she ever looked back on her old life. She said, 'David, I don't look back. That life is gone. Only heartache would result if I reminisced about the 'good ol' days.' God has brought me through a crisis that I wouldn't want to ever repeat. But, you know, I wouldn't ever want to be the woman I was before. I've got a real life now based on truth.'

I said, 'But you had a real life before. Didn't you?' She smiled and said, 'It was a life based on self and pleasure. I was living a Babylonian life.'

'What do you mean?' I knew she was a Christian.

She pulled a small Bible out of her purse and read Isaiah 47:8 and 10. These verses speak about Babylon and her arrogance, pride, and overindulgence. The verses basically say, 'It's all about me.' At that moment I knew exactly what she meant and why she didn't look back.

David noticed that Catherine was hanging on his every word. That was important because he had another story for her.

"I knew a woman who worked with an agency that sent medical supplies to the refugees of Sudan. The agency spent most of its resources on the cost of the supplies and shipping expenses. Salaries were meager at best. This woman lived most of the year in the States, while going overseas twice a year for a month to distribute the medical supplies.

She was meeting with her mentor more than usual because certain feelings she had been experiencing were bothering her. She was living in a large, urban city and the cost of living was taking most of her salary, leaving little money for a few extras. Her Christian friends were living in large, expensive apartments, going on trips, and shopping at expensive boutiques. She found herself feeling jealous and a little sorry for herself.

She went to her mentor and poured out her heart about this. She was ashamed of her feelings, but at the same time she felt she had a right to have a little more material comforts in life. After all, she was sacrificing everything for the Lord and this ministry. Was it too much to ask for just a few creature comforts?

Her mentor was a wise, older woman who had lived as a missionary in Kenya most of her adult life. She patiently listened to all the younger woman had to say. After exhausting all her tears, the younger woman said, 'I feel like I'm trying to live an impoverished Sudanese lifestyle in an opulent city.' The older woman lovingly reached for her hands and held them.

'Beloved, that's exactly what you are doing. Don't you see? This is the life Christ has fashioned for you. It's not the life He's picked for your Christian friends. You have surrendered the right to have a lovely home, beautiful clothes, and fancy trips. Now you must let the surrender settle in your heart and become comfortable with it. You have already made the choice to surrender, now bask in the warmth of God's approval and the abundant life He has for you.'

The young woman was stunned. This wasn't exactly what she had expected to hear. She sat motionless while the harsh tone of her thoughts began to soften and the melting of her heart, like the winter ice slowly thawing in the spring sun, caused the Father's love to be felt like never before throughout her whole being. She dropped to her knees and hugged her mentor around the waist. Lifting her head, she looked into those wise, ancient eyes and smiled for the first time in a while. She now understood the beauty of surrendering one's rights to Christ."

David finished his story and then waited for Catherine's response. He could tell it had had an impact on her.

"I'll be honest. All this talk about surrender that you have discussed has made me feel uncomfortable. But, after hearing about those two women, I see it in a better light. Relinquishing one's rights is not a negative thing if Christ is the One you are surrendering to.

I have been clinging so hard to the right to be married to Steve and remain in our home. When I think of all the energy I've spent trying to hang on for dear life, it makes me tired just thinking about it. No wonder I was so exhausted all the time.

Mr. Hill, I'm going to change my thinking about this. I'm going to place my rights squarely into Jesus' hands. I guess we will see what will happen, won't we?"

David saw that Catherine's demeanor had totally changed from when she first entered his office today. She was less agitated, more receptive to God's plan, and even exhibited a glimmer of joy in her eyes.

"I want to continue our discussion on surrender, but I don't want to start a new topic when it's so close to our time being up. Did you have anything else you wanted to talk about before you go?"

"No. I've got a lot to meditate upon when I leave here. I've got an idea of what I want to do when I get home, but I don't want to talk about it right now. Let's wait until next week when I may have more to discuss."

"That's fine with me." David rose to walk Catherine to the door. When she reached the door, she turned around and looked solemnly at him.

"You really helped me today. I appreciate all you're doing, even though I may not show it." Catherine could see the gratitude in his smile.

She walked up to the receptionist and made an appointment for the following week. Hoping for better news by then she felt a stir of expectation in her heart as she stepped outside. Even the air seemed a little lighter as she inhaled deeply. Looking into the sky, she breathed a small prayer of thanksgiving to God.

Driving home she considered all she and David had discussed. She wanted to test her new decision to bestow her rights to God. Once inside, she dropped her purse on the sofa and began dialing Steve's number. She was surprised he answered on the first ring.

"Catherine, I was hoping you'd call soon." He hesitated to say more until he could decipher her mood. After all, she had slammed the phone down in his ear last time.

"Steve, I'm ready for you to come over and discuss the distribution of property." She didn't sound cheerful, but she wasn't angry or melancholy either. It was funny. Her tone of voice was unlike any he had ever heard before.

"OK. Will tonight be good for you?"

"Sure. Let's say 7:00."

"I'll see you then."

Steve just stared at the wall when he hung up. He really couldn't decide if this was a set-up or she was moving on. A vicious little thought entered his mind and he could feel his heartbeat quicken. He began to wonder if she was seeing that bum, Austin, again? The more he pondered that possibility, the madder he got. Boy, she didn't let any grass grow under her feet. The last time he talked to her she begged him to come home. Now this. She sounded too calm and collected. If he got over to their house and Austin was there, he would. . . .

What would he do? He had asked for the divorce. He wanted it to move forward as quickly as possible. Why should he care? But, he did care, whether he liked it or not. The thought of Catherine with another man sent him over the edge with fury and jealousy. Except for that one time with Austin, she had always been Steve's. Her body and soul had always been exclusively for him.

He put his head in his hands and endured what seemed like a thousand thoughts and emotions racing through his mind, like a swarm of angry bees. He felt torn, he felt angry, he felt hopeless, but most of all, he felt a deep sadness come over him. The realization that once they divided the property and got a divorce, the only thing that would cause them to have any contact was Zoe.

He had tried to push Zoe out of his mind for now. He called her every Sunday evening to check on her. Wasn't it ironic that the very thing that had split the family apart now caused him to reach out to his daughter like he never had in the past. *God, forgive me for my neglect.* I realize now that all that talk about needing to provide for the family, staying gone days and weeks at a time, all that was really just that-boastful talk. The promotions, the business dinners, the bonuses, that was all for himself really. Those things stroked his ego and boosted his pride. Yes, he provided well for his family, but that wasn't what drove him to overachieve. No. He realized at this late date that he had been a self-serving, egocentric jerk, and it had cost him his family. In a small way, he was no better than Austin, indulging in his own desires without a thought of how it was affecting other people, especially the people he was suppose to love the most.

While he had earlier felt so self-righteous about the divorce, now he understood that he deserved to be divorced, on his own, lonely. The vision of all the years to come, living without Catherine, made him cringe. The chiming of the clock shattered his reverie, and he looked at the time. If he didn't hurry up, he'd be late to see Catherine.

Not too much time later, standing in front of his own front door, he felt unsure about just walking in without ringing the bell, so he pushed the button twice. On the way over he had played different scenarios in mind about how Catherine would answer the door. Would she be crying? Maybe cold and unwelcoming? Could she possibly be hysterical and begging for him to move back? He dreaded any of those possibilities, so Steve was quite taken aback when she answered with a smile on her face and a calm disposition.

"Come in, Steve. I've cleared the dining room table so we can work there. We'll have more room to spread out." He followed her to the table and sat down. He began to pull papers out of an attaché case while she brought glasses of tea and set them into the crystal coasters.

"Before we begin, I just have to comment on your attitude. I was expecting drama and tears, yet you're so calm." He wasn't sure if this was a good thing or not. For some reason, it didn't exactly feel good. He felt unsure about his next move.

"I've been working with my counselor and he's opened my eyes about many things. I'm mentally and spiritually preparing to get on with my life without you, since that seems to be the way things are shaping up." There was no whining in her voice.

"Catherine, are you seeing Austin again?"

She laughed, "Heavens, no. That whole thing was a huge mistake. I hope I never lay eyes on him again."

"Someone else?" His curiosity was getting the best of him, or was it jealousy?

"No. Nothing like that." Catherine didn't look happy, but she didn't look unhappy either. Steve just saw a peaceful expression on her face, one he had never seen before.

Turning to his papers, he said, "I think the first order of business is to sell the house. I can't continue to pay the mortgage and rent a motel room." He sat back and waited for the fireworks. They didn't materialize.

"Our neighbor is a good real estate agent, unless you've got someone else in mind. I would be fine with whoever you chose."

"I don't know any residential agents. Why don't you give our neighbor a call?" This was going too well. It made Steve a little anxious.

"Of course, you will keep your car and Zoe will keep hers. I've already talked to my financial advisor about paying for all your expenses until you get a place of your own. Zoe may want to visit and I want things as normal as possible for her as long as possible."

"That sounds very reasonable."

Who is this woman? I've never seen Catherine so calm about something so traumatic.

"I want us both to split the equity in the house, so let's not rush into accepting the first offer that's made. I want you to be able to have enough money to get a comfortable, little house in a safe neighborhood." Catherine softly smiled.

"Steve, this all seems very reasonable and I'm glad I won't be rushed. We can split the furniture when we both find our own houses." Having said that, she suddenly had to exert all her strength into holding back her tears.

"Is there anything else you can think of that we need to discuss tonight?" *I'm really not anxious to go back to the motel. It's nice having a congenial conversation with Catherine, just like old times.* He wanted to reach for her hand, but that would only be confusing for both of them.

"No, I guess that's it. I'll call the agent this week." She lowered her head and pretended to be brushing invisible lint from her pants.

"Well, I'll go then. Call me when you have some details from the agent." Steve throat was beginning to feel tight. It was time to get out of there before he embarrassed himself and begged to move back.

Getting settled into his car, he allowed himself a few tears as he drove slowly toward the motel. *Catherine seemed a little upset toward the end, but she never revealed her feelings. Why is she being so agreeable? Doesn't she still love me? She didn't even put up a little fight when we talked about dismantling all we have accumulated all these years. That was our home for ten years. Doesn't she still love me?*

Once inside, he fought it no more and wept like a man given a month to live. For the first time, he knew what those love songs meant when they talked about a broken heart. His was breaking and it would have been hard for him to verbalize all the pain he was feeling. He trudged to bed and fell across it. *Oh, Catherine. Why did it have to come to this?*

It wasn't until dawn that he woke up, drained of energy and spirit. His eyes were puffy and his throat hurt. Abruptly, his phone rang. After calming down one of his irate customers, he slowly got out of bed. *Come on, Steve. Get ready for work. It's all you've got left.*

Catherine waited until she heard Steve's car drive away, then she broke down in tears. Yes, she was surrendering the right to be married and have this home, but that didn't mean it wasn't painful. All the pleasant memories created in this house seemed to materialize before her eyes as she stared out into the dining room where they had just been seated.

Her gaze fell on an oversized, beautiful porcelain bowl she had displayed as a centerpiece on her dining room table. Steve had proudly commissioned a local artist to make it for their anniversary last year. Horses were grazing in a pasture as a woman in a long, cotton dress leaned against a fence to observe them. Inside the bowl the words of Proverbs 31:10-31 were written in exquisite calligraphy. The words *a wife of noble character* caused the tears to flow again, this time with greater intensity. If Steve had felt that way about her last year, he hardly did now. She had betrayed him and now she was paying the exorbitant price for that one sin. But, oh, what a sin it was! She had violated the marriage bed with a stranger.

After wiping her tears with a tissue, she picked up the phone and dialed her neighbor. Yes, tomorrow morning would be fine for her to come over. Her bedroom and bathroom were all that needed freshening up since those seemed to be the only two rooms she used. The refrigerator held just diet shakes and yogurt. No cooking took place anymore, unless you considered popping popcorn in the microwave a culinary skill. She always avoided looking at the shiny brass pots and pans hanging over her kitchen island. They held too many memories of relaxed family meals and jovial dinner parties. What would she do with all that cookware when she moved to a small house?

Before she retired for the evening, she knelt beside her bed and asked for forgiveness for all she had done to bring about this calamity in her family's life. Asking God to give her strength to face each day with courage that only He could give, she closed her prayer with words of gratitude of all she still had. Her daughter was excelling in school and she did have her health. Plus, Steve would be helping her financially for awhile. Things could be so much worse and she knew it.

Climbing into bed, she closed her eyes and started thinking of all she'd have to do to get ready to move. The task seemed insurmountable, but she had just asked for strength and she'd trust God to be faithful. Even when she had not been, He had. She had not really trusted Him, but He had been trustworthy. *Oh, Steve, I'm so sorry for what I've done. Please forgive me, too.*

The next day she checked around the house for any obvious dust or dirt. She had always kept a clean house and she wanted the real estate agent to see what a gem of a house this was. She had just wiped out the sink when the doorbell rang.

"Hello, Catherine. I'm so glad you picked me to sell your home. I didn't know you and Steve were planning to move." Kitty had that bubbly personality that was perfect for her line of work. As Catherine led her into the living room, she was thinking she really could do without all that effervesce, especially this morning.

After all the pleasantries were dispensed with, Kitty got right down to business. She explained that Catherine and Steve might be surprised how low the values of houses had dropped in the neighborhood just since last year. Steve had refinanced the house last year so there had been an appraisal done then. Unfortunately the economy was killing the real estate market and it might be awhile before the house would actually sell.

Kitty seemed curious why they were selling, but Catherine remained vague. Although Kitty was her neighbor, they had never really been close. She didn't feel like divulging her problems to just an acquaintance.

"Steve and I feel like it's time to downsize. We don't need this much room anymore." Kitty nodded while she looked through some papers in her satchel.

"You know, I may have just the house for you two when this house sells. It would be perfect." Catherine could almost see dollar signs flashing in Kitty's eyes.

"Slow down, Kitty. Let's worry about one house at a time." Catherine was already dreading months of contact with Kitty. She liked that she was a go-getter, but the pushiness would probably get on her nerves.

"That's fine. We can discuss that later on. Give me a tour of your home. I want you to know it has so much curb appeal. This house may sell faster than the others have in the neighborhood."

Great! That's just what I need-a speedy sale.

Kitty made little comments as they surveyed each room. All in all, there were few things she suggested that needed to be changed. The first order of business was to take down all personal photos, though. Prospective buyers needed to imagine what it would be like if this was their home.

Having already compared the selling prices of other homes in the neighborhood, Kitty discussed a good price to list the house. Catherine was shocked. She couldn't even imagine how Steve would take this. An uneasy thought began to form. *Will Steve change his mind about the money for her?*

Kitty's voice was beginning to grate on her nerves as she raved on and on about the house. She had to get her out of the house and have some time to think, maybe even cry.

"Kitty, I've got a really bad headache. Can we finish this another day?"

"We've done all we need to do for right now. I'll draw up the contract for you and Steve to sign. If it's OK with you, I can have a sign in the yard this afternoon. Won't that be exciting!" Kitty's was one of those people who couldn't read social cues. Obviously, she hadn't noticed the sadness in Catherine's face as they had traveled from room to room in this lovely, lonely house.

Catherine smiled weakly as she showed her to the door. She could already envision her life being invaded by strangers tromping through her home, making critical comments and questioning the agents about getting a better deal. Kitty turned around on the sidewalk and waved brightly, like they were best friends who had just spent the morning together doing something fun.

Before Catherine closed the door, Kitty's cell-phone was already up to her ear. No doubt she was calling her agency to arrange a "for sale" sign to be planted in her front yard. Catherine dropped her forced smile and closed the door a little too loudly.

She immediately called Steve and gave him the bad news. Rather, she gave his voicemail the bad news. Going into the garage, she found some empty storage containers and started taking down the family pictures. Wrapping them in tissue paper as fast as she could kept the tears from welling up. In the future when she unpacked them, that's when she'd have the luxury of crying her eyes out.

After working hard all afternoon, she had just finished wrapping the last picture, when the phone rang. Looking at caller-ID, she moaned. She had expected it to be Steve, but it was Kitty.

"Catherine, I'll have the contract ready in the morning. Do you want to call Steve and let's meet at your house tomorrow evening?"

Catherine wanted to slam down the receiver on that perky little voice. *Boy, she didn't waste a minute, did she?* To be fair, Kitty didn't have a clue that putting up the house for sale was breaking her heart.

"I left a message on his voicemail after you left. He should be calling soon. If it's OK with Steve, why don't we meet at eight tomorrow night?" Catherine knew her voice sounded dejected, but Kitty didn't pick up on it.

"I can't wait. I'm so happy you called me instead of another agent. Catherine, you really are a good friend!"

Catherine smirked. *Where were you "good friend" when I had all the sod to put out in the yard when Steve was out-of-town? Good friend, my foot.*

"I'll see you tomorrow night, Kitty," she said flatly as she hung up.

Steve arrived at the house at 7:30. He hoped to spend a little time with Catherine before the agent arrived. When Catherine opened the door, he presented her with a large bouquet of flowers. Seeing the perplexed look on her face, he stammered as to why he brought them.

"I thought this might help pretty up the house a little." He looked a little embarrassed, just standing on the front step, so she motioned for him to come in quickly.

"They're beautiful, Steve, and I'm sure they'll brighten up the living room. Let me go put them in a vase right away so they don't start drooping."

Steve could hear her opening and closing cabinet doors, looking for a vase. That gave him a few minutes to look around the house. Something seemed different, then it struck him-all the family photos were gone. He began to walk slowly from room to room and it was the same-no pictures of the family anywhere. He could feel his face getting hot.

I can't believe she's already taken down our pictures. I've only been gone a short while and she's erased all memory of us living here. I thought I knew Catherine, but I can see she's moved on, big time!

He was frowning at the wall in their bedroom that once held a large, professional picture of the family. In its place was a watercolor of a seaside scene. *Where'd that picture come from? And, where are our pictures?*

Hearing her footsteps, he pretended he was looking for some

socks. He buried his head in his closet so she wouldn't see how upset he was.

"Steve, can I help you find anything? All your clothes are just where you left them." She walked over to him like she was going to help, but he held up his hand.

"I've got them. I was looking for this particular pair of socks to take home." *Home? When did I start referring to the motel as home? That is the last place I would consider home.*

If Catherine heard his blunder, she didn't let it register on her face. Steve stuffed the socks in his jacket pocket and headed downstairs. Just as he got near the foyer, the doorbell rang. He had never really known many of the neighbors because he traveled so much, so when he opened the door, he had no idea who this woman with the bleach-blonde hair and twinkling smile was; he assumed it was the real estate agent. Before he could even speak, she was already through the door.

"Steve, I'm so glad to finally meet you. This is so exciting for me to list your house. Catherine told me you two were downsizing and I think that's so smart. Instead of a big house to care for, you two can concentrate on a more relaxed lifestyle together!"

So that's what Catherine told her- we're downsizing. Are we downsizing so much we don't need family pictures anymore?

He couldn't decide who was irritating him more right now- the wife he didn't seem to know anymore or this high-pressure saleswoman with the blinding smile. Boy, was she a piece of work! Maybe not knowing the neighbors wasn't so bad after all.

"I'm really quite busy. If you have the documents ready, I need to sign them and leave." He didn't even try to hide his annoyance. He could see Catherine out of the corner of his eye. She was standing there with a coffee carafe in her hand, her mouth ajar, but Kitty never missed a beat.

"That's just fine. Everything's completed. Catherine, I'm sure, explained about the low selling price. It just can't be helped. Let me get the papers out of my satchel and we'll get you going. I bet you've got some big customer to woo tonight, don't you?" Her teeth just sparkled.

He ignored her question and pulled a pen out of his shirt pocket. Catherine had taken the coffee back into the kitchen and slowly sank in a chair at the dining room table. She couldn't figure out why, but she felt like someone had just slapped her hard across the face.

Steve furiously scribbled his name on the appropriate lines, unlike Catherine who moved slowly like she was underwater. In her lovely handwriting, she wrote her name then handed all the documents to Kitty. Kitty, in turn, passed out everyone's copy.

"Well, I guess that's it for now. Did you notice I already have the sign up?" Both Steve and Catherine ignored her. Steve looked at his watch, snatched up his copy, and started walking to the door. Kitty was placing papers in individual folders, while Catherine got up quickly to follow Steve.

"Don't you want to have some coffee? I fixed your favorite blend." Steve gave her that familiar look that told her to drop it.

"Gotta go." He opened the door and didn't look back.

What just happened tonight? Steve brought the flowers and I can't believe it was just for the house. I was looking forward to talking to him after Kitty left. What went wrong?

She watched his car disappear around the corner. When she turned around, Kitty was seated comfortably, like she was there for a long visit.

"That coffee smelled delicious! I wouldn't mind a cup."

"Kitty, I don't know what's wrong with me. I still have that headache. Can I give you a rain-check on the coffee?"

Kitty's mouth drooped momentarily, but then the charm and brightness was back on as she picked her satchel and purse.

"Sure thing, honey. I'm sure we're going to spend lots of time together. Isn't it a shame that your moving away brought us together?"

Yes, what a shame.

Session 8

Catherine ~~was~~ for her appointment with Mr. Hill. When she e~~ntered~~ ~~s~~he was obviously out of breath.

"Whoa, s~~low down~~ you hurried to see me, but now you can relax," he ~~said~~

"I'm sorry ~~I wa~~s cleaning up a little for the agent to show the ho~~use"~~ ~~Catheri~~ne looked forlorn and closed her lips tightly, the ~~way she di~~d when she wanted to hold back the tears.

"Before we g~~et into what I thi~~nk we ought to discuss today, why don't you tel~~l me what's going~~ on."

Taking a deep ~~breath, sh~~e said, "The house is on the market now. Steve came over last night to sign the papers. He came with flowers, so I thought he was having second thoughts. But the funny thing was, after he came inside, his mood instantly changed and he couldn't wait to sign the contract with the agent and leave. It was all so confusing."

"What do you think happened to change his attitude?"

"I really don't know."

"How are you personally handling this situation with the house being sold?"

"I've surrendered my right to having my home. Isn't that what I'm supposed to do?" Tears started to flow slowly down her cheeks, refusing to be held back any longer.

"I'm sorry you're hurting. Suffering always comes before surrender."

"That's just great," she said sarcastically. "Let's get started."

Choosing to ignore her last statement, David said, "Today I wanted to talk about another part of surrender. It's giving God permission to do whatever He wants to do with you. Romans 12:1 says we should present ourselves to God as a living sacrifice. He's more interested in you sacrificing your whole being to Him than in offering material things. Your thoughts, actions, and decisions should be honed to His good pleasure. How do you think that would play out in your life?"

Deciding to focus on what David had to teach instead of her sorrow, she said, "For starters, I should look at this move as a stepping stone to whatever else God has planned for me. I shouldn't fight what is occurring, but make the best of the situation, knowing it will all turn out in the end."

"That's excellent, Catherine." *I hope she's not just saying that, but means it.* "What about your interview at the museum? Have you heard anything?"

"No, not yet. The good news is Steve says he'll pay my expenses until all this is settled. The bad news is the house has lost a lot of equity since last year. I'm worried there won't be enough money to buy me a little house after ours sells."

"Are you going to surrender that worry to God? Can you trust Him to get your affairs in order in a way that will do you good in the long run?"

"I know I must in order to not go crazy over all the changes in my life." She sent a quick, silent prayer heavenward for her trust in God to grow.

"The third part of surrender is being open for God to do His will in and through you. In the Garden of Gethsemane, Jesus didn't want to be crucified, but He told His Father He would submit to His will, and He did. The human part of Jesus probably shrank from the idea of being mutilated and killed on the cross. Yet, even though it was going to be horrific, He went through with it.

What does that mean to you? It means that you will submit to some unpleasant things in your life. Why? To be miserable? No, it is to glorify God with your obedience. That obedience will be rewarded in some fashion."

"I'm already miserable, you know, but I'll submit to His will. What I don't understand is, God ordained marriage, so why doesn't He fix ours?"

"Catherine, that is a good question. He doesn't just immediately fix it for three reasons. First, God gave us a free will. We are not puppets on a string. He wants us to love and obey Him out of our own volition. If He manipulated our every move, we would be like robots. Have you ever wanted to cozy up to a robot?" Catherine giggled at the thought.

"Second, you sinned against your marriage. While we can be forgiven if we ask for it, we still have to bear the consequences of our actions. God rarely allows problems to just disappear. He does this so we will learn. It's the same when we punish our children. We do it so they will not repeat the offense. If we just let them off the hook, they'll be right back at it.

Third, I don't know what God has planned for you and Steve, but He may bring you to back together. With God, nothing is impossible."

She looked unconvinced. "Fat chance. The house is on the market and Steve acts like he hates me. I really can't see any hope for us."

"If God sees that Steve will not forgive and reconcile with you, then He has another plan for you. The hardest thing to do is wait on the Lord, but the Bible frequently advises us to do so. Just be patient."

"Patience is something I'm real familiar with. I have been patient with Steve for many years, but he has no patience for me or God it looks like."

Catherine's sadness touched David's heart. He had been praying for her and Steve, yet he had not seen any improvement in their relationship. If anything, it was getting worse. He knew the divorce could create animosity between them that would prevent any hope of reconciliation in the future.

"I want to talk to you more in detail about the third part of surrender. It is being willing for God's will to be done in and through you. Just as Jesus submitted to being crucified for the salvation of all mankind, so we must let Him work through you. This will not only bring you closer to Him, it should be a testimony of what God is doing, and make you a link between a lost soul and God. When we look at surrendering and suffering in the light of eternity, it gives them value beyond anything this world has to offer.

I know you have surrendered having your home, but what else do you need to surrender to God? What are you afraid of letting go?"

Catherine looked at David and said, "Not being loved. I knew my mother really loved me and I think Steve did, too. Of course, I guess we all take the love of our children for granted, that they'll always love us. I am afraid of being alone and unloved."

"Sometimes God will remove things from our lives if we have an unhealthy attachment to them. This can range from material possessions, to a dream, spouses, children, the list is endless. We may get them back if we can possess them in a way that is pleasing to God, which means they don't come before God in importance to us.

Let me give you an example. There was this woman I knew who loved her husband so much that she put him before God without realizing it. God is a jealous God, you know. It's not the same kind of negative jealousy we see on earth, but a holy jealousy. He created us and we are His alone. He only wants the best for all people. After all, we are made in His image.

She lived for her husband. If he wanted the money she saved for the church, she gave it to him gladly. If he told her to participate in some unholy activity, she would do it, even though she knew it was wrong. This man did not force her to do these things; all he had to do was ask.

She never noticed how far she had drifted from God until her husband left her for another woman. She had sacrificed everything for him and she was left with nothing but material possessions. The love of her life was gone.

When she finally mustered the courage to speak to her pastor, she told him everything that had happened. The wise pastor just listened as the tears and words spilled out of her. When she was finally spent, he asked her what she thought God was saying to her. Mentioning that she had had some time to ponder this, she said God was telling her she had sacrificed her relationship with the Lord for the wrong thing. Unlike her husband, God would never leave her or stop loving her. Only God can make a promise like that.

God took her husband away for a season. The affair with the other woman dissipated and he begged to come back. She told him he could with the understanding that God would come first in her life from now on. He gladly conceded. There was never a more dedicated Christian woman that I knew of after they reconciled. What's interesting is they both now seem happier with each other than they had ever been."

Catherine didn't respond. "Catherine, do you see yourself in this story?"

"Well, I was not as fanatical about my husband as she, but I have left God on the backburner until now. My marriage, my child, and my home were number one in my life. Zoe naturally will be finishing college and having her own life, so I expect her to move on. But the three things that were most important to me are either gone or will be gone. I put all my eggs in the wrong basket."

"It wasn't that your marriage and child and home are wrong in any way. It's that God didn't have the place of honor He deserves in your life. Your marriage and your child should come second in your life, not first."

"You're right. I've had to go through a lot of suffering to learn that lesson." David noticed that there was no self-pity in her voice or facial expression. She was just stating the truth.

"Let's go back to your statement that the thing you have a fear of surrendering is being loved. Would you say you'd do anything to get love?"

"No, not anything, but I can't stand the idea of becoming an unloved, old woman."

"Catherine, God loves you very much, even when you're mad at Him, even when you think He doesn't care, even when He seems to be doing things in your life that are hurtful."

"I know He does, but I'm talking about another adult human being loving me."

"Would I be safe in saying you mean a man loving you?" She nodded, but her blush gave her away first.

"In Matthew 6:33, Jesus said that we are to seek God's kingdom and His righteousness first then our basic needs will be met. Wanting to be loved is a basic human need. Infants have been known to die just from not getting love. You need to devote yourself to loving God first and then see how He will meet your need to be loved. I have no idea what God has in store for you, but He has something planned.

I'd like for you to start memorizing Matthew 6:33. If possible, review it every morning and every evening. This verse will help you through the ups and downs of life, when you think your needs are not being met. Will you do that?"

"Yes, I will. I promise I will." *I hope I can remember to do it.*

She started telling him about Kitty and her irritating ways, her sadness and weariness surrounding the move, and Steve's confusing behavior. She noticed David glance at his clock and knew their time was up. It was just as well. She wanted to go and find some more boxes to start packing, so she was ready to leave anyway. After their session was closed with a prayer, she left David's office with a long to-do list already pressing on her mind.

After stopping by several stores, she had enough empty boxes to make a good start with the packing. Upon entering her home, she could tell someone had been there. The rug in the foyer was a little askew and there were two agent's cards on the round table next to the stairs. She glanced at them briefly then went to check her messages. She had two new messages. She grimaced when she imagined one being from Kitty.

The first message was from the museum and the second from

Zoe. She would want to chat a while with Zoe, so she called the museum first. Her heart pounded as she waited for Mrs. Talbot to pick up the phone.

"Mrs. Talbot, this is Catherine Russell, returning your call." *Why do I sound so timid and scared?*

"Yes, Catherine, I have good news for you. You have been selected for the job we spoke of a few weeks back."

Catherine's sudden elation was tempered by the realization that she would be moving and she didn't have a clue what her future would bring.

"Mrs. Talbot, I have a problem." *I'm sure she won't want me now.*

"Oh, what is that?"

"I'm getting a divorce and I'm not sure what's going to happen to me. I really want the job, but I don't know where I'll be living, what I can afford, and things like that." *Go ahead, retract the offer.*

There was silence on the line for a minute before she said, "Catherine, I was once divorced. I do know what you're going through. I may have a solution to your problem. Let me make a phone call first. Why don't you come tomorrow around 2:00 and we'll discuss the job."

Because Mrs. Talbot's voice was so amiable, Catherine wanted to break down in tears of relief. *Thank you, God. Thank you!*

"I'll be there. Thank you for being so understanding. Good-by."

Catherine couldn't help but sing throughout the rest of the day. Packing was hard work, yet the afternoon seemed to fly. After a quick bite to eat, she returned to the task, not stopping until she realized it was time for a shower then off to bed. For the first time in some time, Catherine had something to look forward to.

The door bell vibrated through the silence of the early morning. Catherine looked at the clock beside her bed. *Who in the world is ringing my bell at 8:00 in the morning!* She threw on her robe and went to answer the door.

Upon opening the door she saw Kitty standing on her door mat in a bright pink suit with matching pumps. She had silver jewelry that glistened in the bright, morning sun. Catherine had to squint to protect her eyes from all this glare.

Ignoring Catherine's scowl, Kitty, in her loud, cheerleader voice, said, "Catherine, do I have good news for you!" She brushed past her into the living room and sat down. Spreading the papers on the coffee table, she made herself right at home.

"I was expecting to smell that good coffee you make." Kitty's bright eyes turned toward the kitchen.

"No, I was actually sleeping when you rang my bell." *It may be rude, but I'm not going to fix any coffee right now. Sorry, Kitty, that might encourage you to stay.* She felt a little prick of guilt for being so uncivil, but she ignored it.

"Well, anyway, I have a contract. Can you believe it? And, it's a good one. When can we get together with Steve and sign the papers?"

"I can call him right now, but let me look at the contract first."

Catherine briefly scanned it and had to agree with Kitty; it was a good one. In this economy, to get close to your asking price was a miracle.

She picked up her phone and called Steve. Even he must have slept in because he sounded a little groggy. After telling him the news, they decided to meet that night at 7:00. Knowing she'd have a signed contract today, Kitty's smile grew even bigger, if that was possible. Catherine stood up to stretch and yawn, then handed the contract back to Kitty. She hadn't made a move to depart, so Catherine picked up Kitty's attaché case and walked to the door.

"Well, I'll see you tonight. We can have some of that coffee then."

Catherine smiled and closed the door before Kitty was off the porch good. A contract this soon was an unexpected blow. She really thought it would take a year to get one. The only bright spot was she wouldn't have a whole year to put up with Kitty. But, that was the only bright spot.

After closing the door, she looked around the living room and sat slowly on the sofa. This life will be over forever when they close on the house. What should she keep, what should she throw away or donate to a charity? She didn't even know how much room she would have in her new house. The uncertainty of the situation swallowed her up into an anxiety-filled abyss. Maybe when she called Zoe back she would feel better. But she doubted it.

Steve was uncharacteristically late that night. Catherine was stuck entertaining Kitty, although Kitty was a show all unto herself, between the radiant smile, sparking jewelry, and nonstop chatter. Catherine could feel Kitty's intensity sucking out her last ounce of energy. *Steve, hurry up, so I can send this woman home and go to bed!*

Kitty had been on the prowl for another home for Steve and Catherine to live in. Catherine didn't tell Kitty they would actually be needing two homes. She wasn't even sure if she'd let Kitty be her agent anyway for her future home. Kitty was like hot sauce; a little of her went a long way.

While they were waiting for Steve, Kitty was showing her picture after picture of homes of all kinds, although she was paying little attention. Her concentration was on the driveway. Just as a watched pot never seems to boil, her impatience grew as the minutes ticked by. As she rose to make coffee, headlights swerved into the driveway and were quickly extinguished. Steve walked in quickly while Kitty jumped up and went forward with her hand extended. Steve ignored it and sat down on the sofa.

"I'm sorry I'm late. Where's the contract?" Funny, he didn't look sorry. He looked like it was an annoyance to be there at all.

"Steve, I've got all the papers laid out in the dining room. I think Catherine has gone to make us some coffee, so we can relax and sign the papers." Kitty was undeterred by Steve's look of irritation.

"I don't have time for coffee." Catherine noticed Steve's tone of voice as she came out of the kitchen. She also noted he didn't even look in her direction.

Walking to the dining room, Catherine gazed at Steve and wondered what happened to the man she had loved for so many years. After signing the papers he finally looked at Catherine and said, "We'll talk later." Then he was gone. Catherine's fury at his behavior was heightened by Kitty's mere presence. Once again she would have to be rude and ask Kitty to leave or else explode into a million pieces right into her face.

After escorting Kitty out the door, she cut all the lights off and climbed the stairs wearily to her bedroom. Kneeling by her bed, Catherine alternately cried and prayed. The moving experience was one thing, but Steve's lack of concern for her situation was so painful. She had seen him neglectful before, but never so cold. Crawling into bed, she drifted off into a fitful night's sleep.

The alarm clock's shrill buzzer rudely woke Catherine from her slumber. The chore of packing was the first thought that came to mind. She pondered how she could possibly know what to pack since she had no idea what Steve wanted, what she would be able to use in her future house, and what Zoe would want. *Oh, Zoe, my heart just aches when I think of telling you the news.*

Catherine decided to put off the packing until after her interview. She didn't want to wear herself out with all that manual labor and the emotional toll of separating her family's belongings. Wanting to be fresh and invigorated for the interview, she went to her bathroom for a short shower and long beauty treatment.

Checking her look in her reflection in a big picture-glass window at the museum, she entered the front door and looked for Mrs. Talbot's office. Knocking on the door, she heard an authoritative voice say, "Come in, Catherine."

Mrs. Talbot was nothing like Catherine had imagined. From her voice on the phone, she pictured Mrs. Talbot as short, plump, and stern looking. She had been dead-wrong. Mrs. Talbot was tall, slender, and had a kind face. While she wasn't drop-dead gorgeous, she was attractive. Her jet-black hair was swept up in a French twist and her suit most likely had a designer label. She looked about her own age with hardly a gray hair or wrinkle.

"Do come in and have a seat." Mrs. Talbot motioned to a loveseat that looked new. Looking around, all the furniture looked like it had just been purchased. It was ultra-modern and it seemed to complement the oversized room.

Reading Catherine's mind, she said, "I just had this office redecorated. While the museum has a western theme, I didn't feel that would be appropriate for my work area."

"I was very excited to get your call. Of course, I explained my situation and I'm a little apprehensive about taking the job." Catherine could feel her face turning a little red.

"Catherine, I'm about to offer you something I have never offered to another employee." She wasn't smiling, so Catherine was confused. She couldn't conceive of what Mrs. Talbot had in mind. *Did I hear her right? Did she say employee? I didn't think she'd give me the job after what I told her about getting divorced.*

Seeing her perplexity, Mrs. Talbot smiled. "Yes, you have the job if you'll accept it. I've already checked your references and done a criminal background check on you. I liked what I read in your resume. I think you'd be an asset to the museum, that's why I'm offering you something that will help you with your move. Walk with me. I want to show you something."

Catherine followed her to the back of the museum. Walking down a narrow hallway, they came to a steel door. Mrs. Talbot was still smiling, but said nothing. Opening the door, she led Catherine into a room with a tall ceiling and banked with large windows overlooking a courtyard. The weeds and small bushes had taken over, but she could just see a pathway circling a Japanese maple. Turning to Mrs. Talbot, she said, "What's all this? It looks like an apartment."

"This is an apartment the museum use to offer artists who were exhibiting large art collections. They would reside here while their art was on display. It made it convenient for the artists to be here, especially when their work was for sale. We discontinued this service when artists began to make too many demands for upgraded amenities. The museum didn't have the funds for such nonsense, so the apartment was closed last year. You can see all the cob webs and dust. But everything works and it has a living room, bedroom, kitchen, and bathroom. I talked it over with the board and we'd like to offer it to you."

Catherine's jaw dropped at the prospect. She wanted to grab Mrs. Talbot and squeeze her neck. Instead she calmly asked, "What is this going to cost me?"

"Catherine, you will be working part-time. This will allow you to have another part-time job. Instead of a paycheck, you'll get the apartment and the utilities free. What do you think?" Now Mrs. Talbot looked concerned that Catherine would balk at the proposition.

"Mrs. Talbot, I can't thank you enough for this opportunity. I'm so glad to have it settled about where I'll live. You're truly a gift from God." Catherine couldn't hold back the urge any longer, so she gently hugged Mrs. Talbot. She seemed surprised, but didn't pull away from Catherine's embrace.

"Why don't you look around the apartment while I go finish the paperwork for you to sign. No rush. Just come back to my office when you're finished."

After the door closed, Catherine surveyed all the rooms. They were all small, except the living room with the tall windows, but this place had so much potential. The wall opposite the tall windows was large enough to put up all her pictures. Her deck furniture would fit in the courtyard. She'd have to downsize from a king to a queen-size bed, but that was no problem. After all, she'd be sleeping alone. Tears began to well up at that thought, but she quickly wiped them away. She would have to suspend a rack for her pots and pans from the ceiling of the kitchen. There were very limited cabinets.

She envisioned how some of her furniture would fit. Not having a tape measure, she walked off the length and width of each room and wrote it on a slip a paper she found in her purse. Then, she bowed her head. *Yes, Lord, You have provided for me. Thank you for your mercy and love. Amen.*

Upon entering the office, Mrs. Talbot looked up from her desk.

"Well, what do you think? Will it suffice?"

"It's just right. I can't wait to get started on cleaning it and moving my furniture in. The courtyard can wait a little while, but I'm anxious to make it a pretty flower garden. It's got so many possibilities."

"Good. Let's get these papers signed so you can get started."

Once home, Catherine felt energized enough to start packing. She decided to pick out all the items that would fit in her apartment. After labeling each box with the word *Catherine's*, she started stacking them in the garage. After a couple of hours, she realized she was going to have to be more discerning about what to move to the apartment, what to donate, and what to store. There was just so much she could cram into that little apartment.

By nightfall, she was dirty and dusty. Her back ached and felt quite stiff. Looking at the clock she decided to stop and go soak in the tub until she loosened up. While washing her hands in the kitchen sink, she heard a car door slam. *Kitty! At this hour! I'm not answering the door if it's her.*

Peeking through the plantation shutters in the living room, she saw it was Steve. *I wasn't expecting him. What a nice surprise!* Opening the door with a wide grin, she was met with a less than receptive face.

"I know I should have called, but we need to talk." His demeanor right away dispelled any thought of reconciliation. Passing a mirror, she saw how dirty her face was, but now she didn't care. Obviously he wasn't there to have a romantic evening. He walked directly by her and sat in the living room.

"Well, I see you've already started packing. I really appreciate you doing this for us. It's going to make our move so much easier than having strangers paw through our things." A very small smile graced his lips.

Anger welled up in her breast. *He thinks I'm doing all this for him. Does he ever stop thinking about himself?*

"Actually, I'm doing it for me. I have an apartment and I'm sorting through things that will fit a one-bedroom." His smile instantly disappeared.

"You sure didn't let any grass grow under your feet, did you?

But, I guess everything is happening the way it should." She would have loved to slap the smirk right off his face.

"Exactly what do you mean, Steve?"

"Well, I came here to discuss finances with you. The sale of the house is not going to allow both of us to get a house in a decent neighborhood. I was going to see if you had any ideas, but I see you've already made your plans. I hope the apartment is not too expensive. I'm not made of money."

She wanted to say what she thought he was made of, but stopped. *I will surrender my desire to retaliate, no matter how tempting it is.*

"It's not going to cost you a thing, if that's what you're worried about. It's all taken care of." She relished that surprised look on his face.

"How is that possible? Have you got another lover?" Narrowing his eyes, he reminded her of Father, when he had verbally abused her poor mother with sarcastic comments that were baseless.

Catherine had never seen Steve act so hateful. He had hit way below the belt this time and she wasn't going to put up with it. *Surrender, my foot.* Before she knew it, her fury possessed her like a demon. Picking up an antique cut-glass vase, she threw it in his direction. She had no intentions of hitting him; she just wanted him to know how deep that disgusting question cut into her heart.

It sounded like an explosion as it hit the Bombay chest they had purchased on their honeymoon. Immediately, the shock of Catherine's action left them both speechless. The silence after the crash was deafening. Getting up from the sofa, he walked to the door and quietly exited. Catherine slumped across the cream-colored sofa, facedown. Clutching a pillow, she didn't care that her face was leaving dirty, tear-stained streaks all over it. What did it matter?

After crying until she was spent, she went upstairs to draw a bath. She couldn't ever remember being that angry. *I told Mr. Hill I would surrender to God. I promised I would concentrate on seeking God's righteousness. Look at me, Lord. I have destroyed my marriage and I can't seem to pull myself together. What a mess I've made! I'm so sorry, God. Please help me!*

Later that night, with swollen eyes and a guilty conscience, too exhausted even to sleep, she played the events of the evening over and over in her mind. Mercifully, the Holy Spirit reminded her of what David had said at their last session. *God loves you very much, Catherine.*

A peace she didn't deserve came over her. God seemed to be saying, "I love you, Catherine. Put your cares in My hands and rest, My daughter." The peace only He can give lulled her into a deep, relaxing sleep.

Across town, Steve, sitting on that uncomfortable motel sofa in the dark, was anything but sleepy. Catherine's outburst had shaken him more than he'd like to admit. His hands were actually shaking. Like a pendulum, back and forth his thoughts went. On one end, he felt contrite over his slanderous comment and believed Catherine had a right to react the way she did. On the opposite end, he believed Catherine's morals were suspect, her behavior was tumultuous, and his comment to her was well deserved. Back and forth, back and forth his thoughts swung.

I shouldn't have said that. Catherine slipped that one time. She's always been a good wife and mother. She didn't deserve it. But then again, she has been acting so out of character. First, she has an affair. Then she finds a secret apartment that charges no rent. She must think I'm really stupid to think apartments are free. She's up to something and I bet it's connected to that scum, Austin. To top it off, now she's getting violent! What's next?

Slipping into bed, he started to pray. He had never been a religious man, but things were so out of control in life, he had to do something.

Session 9

Catherine walked into Mr. Hill's office smiling demurely while her body seemed to be dragging. Little bags under her eyes were evidence that she wasn't getting enough sleep. After practically falling into the chair, she looked expectantly toward David for him to start the session.

"I'm a little confused by your look. There's a smile on your face, but your body looks beat. How are things going?"

"I'm sleepy because I didn't get enough sleep last night. Steve and I had a little altercation. I'm tired because I've been packing. I'm smiling because I got the job at the museum."

"Wow! What a week you've had. Why don't we talk about the good news, your job." He learned forward as he always did to show she had his full attention.

"I got the job at the museum, but that's not the best part. In lieu of a salary I'm getting an apartment, with utilities included. It's located right at the museum and it's perfect for me. I'm going to start cleaning it right after our session today."

"What about money? How will you eat and pay for gas?"

"Since it's just a part-time job, I can get another job to supplement whatever money I get from Steve. I should get some money after the finances have been settled between us."

"I'm amazed at how God works. Since your life is a little unstable right now, this is a golden opportunity for you. I can't tell you how relieved I am." His face was beaming.

He really does care, like Christians should. I'm blessed to have him as my counselor.

"That's one of the reasons I'm trying to pack up. Another reason is we have a contract on the house, so things are moving quickly. Maybe a little too quickly."

"In this market, that's incredible. Where is Steve going to live?"

Catherine's smiled vanished. She hesitated before she spoke.

"I don't know and right now, I don't care. That leads me to our fight last night. I hate to tell you, but it got a little ugly last night. I'm sure the Lord was very disappointed in my behavior.

Steve came over unexpectedly, which was really OK with me. He said he needed to talk about the finances. He said there wasn't going to be enough money to buy two houses with the reduced equity we had in our house. I told him he didn't need to worry about that because I already had an apartment. Before I could explain about the job, he accused me of moving in with a lover. I'll admit I liked the surprised look on his face when I told him about the apartment. He's been so cold lately. I wanted him to be a little curious, maybe even a little jealous, but I didn't dream he'd be so hateful.

After he said that about me having a lover, I threw an expensive glass vase toward him, not at him. The explosion it caused startled both us. I don't know who was more shocked, me or him. He got up and left without a word. Of course, I fell apart after that. This morning I had a big mess to clean up, in case the realtor came over.

Everything right now with my job is so bittersweet. I'm happy to have employment and a place to live, but I'm heartsick that it came about because of the divorce."

"Let's talk about last night. What happened when you opened the door to let Steve in?"

"I'm ashamed to say that I thought he came over unexpectedly to have a nice evening with me. It crossed my mind that things had gone too far, and Steve wanted to reconsider the divorce. One look at his face shattered that hope."

"Catherine, I feel like there's a lot of miscommunication between you two. Can you tell me why you think that might be true?"

"Your guess is as good as mine. Steve seems to have turned into someone I hardly recognize. He used to be neglectful, but never hateful. I'll anticipate something good will happen when we get together, but when he arrives, he only gets moody then leaves in a huff. I don't get it."

"Would you consider me being a mediator for you two?"

"You mean to get us through this divorce without hating each other, or worse?"

"I'll be honest. My real desire is for there to be reconciliation. But, if that's not possible, I would like to see you and Steve work together for Zoe's sake. Will you ask him about it?'

"I'll ask, but I'm not going to hold my breath that he'll do it."

"Well, it doesn't hurt to ask, does it?"

"No, it doesn't."

"Do you have any idea why Steve came over so disgruntled?"

"I thought at first it was because of our finances, but then I discovered it was because of the boxes."

"What do you mean?"

"He saw that I had been packing, and he thanked me for helping him. That flew all over me. It seemed he only cared about how convenient it was for him that I was doing all the packing. I told him I was doing it for me. That's when the conversation went downhill.

I'll be honest. I'm really confused about Steve's behavior. I don't have a clue what's he's thinking anymore. Maybe I never knew what he was thinking." The faint glow permeating Catherine when she entered the office had slowly faded away the more she talked about Steve.

"I know you may feel it's too early in your divorce proceedings to discuss this, but I'd like to talk about forgiveness today with you." David steeled himself against the possibility that Catherine would blow her top over the topic of forgiveness.

"How can I forgive him when I'm not really sure what's going on or what he's thinking and planning? Shouldn't we wait until it's all over to see what all I need to forgive him for?" She looked miffed at David.

"You don't wait until you can tally up all their offenses before you forgive someone. Remember, Jesus said we are to forgive people seventy times seven. But we don't wait until we get to 490 before we forgive."

"I've read that in the Bible before and I can't help but think, 'Who keeps a score card on that many times to forgive someone?' It's ridiculous!"

"You're so right and that's the point. We are not to keep up with how many times a person sins against us. We should forgive them each time. Storing up bitterness over what someone's done to us only hurts us, doesn't it?"

"Yes, I guess so." She nodded reservedly.

"We are to forgive someone even when we don't understand why they hurt us. There are three reasons why we should forgive someone. First, we should forgive because Christ forgave us. Do you think we deserved to be forgiven for the things we did? Of course not. He loves us and wants to forgive us, but we must confess and repent. He went to the cross so we could be forgiven. We are to be conformed to His image which means being and living like Jesus. Conformity especially includes having a forgiving spirit.

Second, we should forgive because God commands us to do so. Jesus frequently discusses forgiveness with his disciples. Just as God forgives, it's expected we will, too.

Third, forgiveness gives us freedom. Carrying around bitterness makes us tired. It's a heavy burden. When we forgive, we feel light and free. Even if someone doesn't accept our forgiveness, it's OK. We've done our part in trying to reconcile with that person."

"I can forgive Steve, but it looks like it's going to be a one-way street. I guess I'm bitter over the fact that Steve didn't even want to try to reconcile with me. I know what I did was so wrong, but Steve doesn't even want to forgive me and try to salvage our marriage. It was like all these decades together mean nothing. He acts like we were just roommates and it's time to part ways."

"Remember, we are only talking about you right now and what you need to do. Are you ready to forgive him?"

"I supposed so, but he's not here. Am I to call him or ask him over?"

"Do you think telling Steve face-to-face will help the situation?"

"Not really. He may get mad and say he has nothing to be forgiven of."

"Why don't we try this. I want you to turn your chair and face that other empty chair. Imagine Steve is sitting in it then just speak from your heart."

"To an empty chair? That seems a little silly." When David didn't respond, she turned to the chair. Obviously, he didn't think it was silly.

I feel so dumb talking to this chair, but I'll do it. She closed her eyes and prayed for God to make this feel real. Slowly she began to speak.

"Steve, you've really hurt me. I know I've deeply hurt you and I want to make things right. Even if we never reconcile, I will always love you. I forgive you for not trying to patch things up between us. I forgive you for throwing Austin in my face every time you're mad. I really forgive you."

That does feel good. I feel lighter in my spirit.

"How do you feel? Do you still feel silly?" David wasn't smiling because he knew how important this was to Catherine's spiritual growth.

"Actually, I feel much better. I prayed to God to make it real for me and He did. I'm surrendering the hurt and giving it to Him as of now."

"I hope you mean it. If you rehearse over and over the wrong you've endured, and you want the offender to pay for it, you have not really forgiven them. This isn't the only time you'll need to forgive Steve. I'm sure before this is all over, other hurtful things will be said and done."

"Oh, I can promise you *that* will happen. Steve and I haven't really accomplished anything but putting the house up for sale. We haven't talked in details about finances or splitting up the contents of the house. Of course, there's enough for both of us, so that shouldn't be a problem. Plus, my apartment is so small. I won't be carrying off the lion's share of our things. But, I have a feeling the real anguish will come when Zoe gets involved."

"What do you anticipate will happen when you and Steve discuss the divorce with Zoe?"

"I haven't a clue. Zoe is a very level-headed girl, but she's never really had any major trauma in her life. She always missed her father when he was away on business, but she's always felt loved and secure.

She received a scholarship to study in Paris. She's getting a degree in Art History. Steve sends her money for any expenses that the scholarship doesn't cover. I don't think any of that will change. That's one thing Steve and I have agreed upon. Zoe needs to concentrate on school and not worry about money. She'll have plenty of time as an adult to do that."

"Why haven't you given Zoe at least a hint of the divorce?"

"I don't want her to worry. We're going to tell her when she comes home for the summer."

"You've only got a few months before that happens. Have you and Steve discussed how you're going to broach the subject to her? I would imagine she'll be extremely upset, whether she's leveled-headed or not."

"That's one more thing on my list of things-to-do. Of all the tough things I've been through, this will be the most troublesome. I've centered my whole life around her and I can't stand the idea that she'll be hurt." Catherine reached for a tissue.

"I hope you and Steve discuss this thoroughly before Zoe returns. How you two handle this will determine whether there will be a positive or negative impact upon Zoe's emotional stability. You want to make sure she knows you both love her and are united in her wellbeing. Zoe's going to be shocked, no doubt about it.

By determining beforehand what you will say and do will greatly benefit her and how she'll react to the divorce."

"I guess I do need to call Steve soon and discuss this, if he'll talk to me. He may be a little hesitant to have anything to do with me after I threw that vase at him." Catherine looked a little ashamed.

"Next time we get together I'll be anxious to hear what you and Steve have discussed about Zoe. For now, I think this is a good stopping point for us." David seldom looked at the clock on his desk for fear of giving the message that he was ready for the client to leave. Instead, he had a timer on his watch that vibrated.

"You've given me a lot to think about. I feel better forgiving Steve, but I'm dreading talking to him about Zoe. If he's still angry with me by the time Zoe returns, there's no telling what he'll say about me to her."

"Catherine, I hope for the good of the whole family that Steve uses discretion when Zoe asks why you're getting a divorce. Even grown children don't need to know all the facts when it comes to problems between their parents."

Catherine dialed Steve's number when she got into her car. His voice- mail picked up, so she decided not to leave a message. She needed to actually talk to Steve. Driving home she thought of all she and Steve needed to talk about. Nothing would be accomplished if she acted as she did the previous night. No matter what Steve said, she needed to depend on God to help her act more Christ-like and less Catherine-like.

Steve returned her call right when she pulled into the driveway. She cut off the engine and remained in the car.

"I noticed you called me." He couldn't have sounded more business-like.

"Thank you, Steve. I wanted to first apologize for my behavior last night." She found herself clutching the steering wheel too tightly with her right hand, so she tried to relax by placing it in her lap.

"OK. What else do you want to talk about?" Catherine wanted to ask him why he was acting the way he was, but she knew that would end up nowhere. Steve, like most men, had a hard time expressing his feelings.

"We really need to go through the furniture and our belongings."

"You're right. Since you're already set with a place to stay, I guess I need to hurry up and get my new life going, too."

I don't care how sarcastically he talks to me I won't go for the bait.

"Why don't you come over when it's convenient for you and we'll discuss some other issues, too." Catherine could feel herself getting tense all over. She could tell he wasn't going to make this easy.

"I'll come over tomorrow night around 7:00." With that, she heard the phone go dead. *It would have been nice, Steve, if you had asked if that night was convenient for me.*

Entering the house, it looked so forlorn with boxes scattered around and some of the pictures taken down. *It's looking less and less like a home.* Kicking off her shoes, she grabbed a box to put cleaning products in. She wanted to get started on the apartment early in the morning. After putting the box by the front door, she headed to the basement for some cleaning rags.

After packing some dishes and glasses for her new home, she called Kitty. No matter how irritating she was, Kitty had a wealth of information and referrals related to moving. She would need a mover, even if she wouldn't be taking a whole houseful. Some of her furniture was quite heavy and her days of lifting heavy things were over.

Kitty didn't answer, so she just left a message. Thinking about movers made her recall the move from their apartment to the first house she and Steve owned. Steve was able to put all their belongings in one pick-up truck back then. How far they had come since then. It required two large moving vans to transport all their belongings to this house. And they had bought quite a bit more since that move ten years ago.

All this material stuff had helped make them a comfortable and luxurious home, but now it was like excess baggage weighing her down. Throughout the process of packing, discarding, and recycling, she became increasingly dismayed at all their excess consumption. Had they really needed a house this big? Once you have a big house, you have to stuff it full of things. Couldn't their money have gone to something more worthy than cluttering up a house? Of course, she wouldn't be having this conversation with herself if it wasn't for the divorce. She'd still be living here happy as a clam. Looking at all the rooms she hadn't even touched, she sighed heavily. She'd be relieved when Steve got what he wanted and they put Zoe's belongings in storage.

She starting loading up her car with cleaning products, rags, a broom, and her vacuum cleaner. Cleaning the apartment would lighten her mood and give her a sense of accomplishment. At the house, she would pack one box, only to see so much more that needed to be taken care of. There didn't seem to be an end in sight. She would see instant results from her labor at the apartment since it was so small.

She located the back alley to her apartment. The gate to the courtyard yielded easily to her touch. She opened the door of the apartment and let some fresh air sweep in and replace the stale, dusty funk. The first order of business was to get down all the spider webs. She imagined their displeasure when all the little creatures returned home only to find their webs swept completely away.

Catherine had purchased a squeegee with an extension for the tall windows. Sunlight beamed into the room as the windows were thoroughly wiped clean. Turning around to see the effect of the sunlight on the facing wall, she was shocked to see how stained and dirty it was. This wall would require a good coat of paint. Just washing it wouldn't do. Obviously, the visiting artists hadn't considered cleanliness as part of their stint at the museum.

Catherine worked well into the night to get as much done as possible. She wanted to start painting the next day. Once the paint was dry, the pictures and furniture could be moved in and she'd be all set. She was anxious to actually start her job, but for her own sanity, the apartment had to be in order before she could. She couldn't work knowing her living space was a wreck. Cleanliness and order were important to her emotional well-being. It had always been that way with her.

After a long bath that evening, Catherine laid across the bed. It struck her that she had just a few nights left to sleep on it. Jumping up, she wrote herself a note on her bedside table to remind her to call the furniture store for a queen-size bed. Lying back down, she climbed under the covers and fell into a restful sleep.

The next morning she showered and ate breakfast quickly. Anxious to start painting, she loaded up her brushes and rags then headed for the paint store. A very pale yellow would liven up the apartment, along with a bright white for the baseboards and trim.

Pushing the courtyard gate open, a small, brown rabbit scurried to his home among the weeks. She smiled as she unlocked the apartment. Already the place smelled better. After opening the windows for ventilation, she arranged the painting cloths and started the transformation. Because she had bought an expensive paint, one coat sufficed. No sense working harder than she already was.

By noon the living room was complete. Her back ached from straining with the extension pole on the paint roller, but she wasn't going to let that slow her down. Looking around the room, she was struck by all the light. The shade of yellow she had picked seemed to glow with the sunlight flooding in. That wall alone cheered the whole place up.

Catherine had brought an outdoor chair from her deck to put out in the courtyard. Resting a bit, she looked through the windows and admired the living room from the outside. She had two large lamps that would be beautiful in there. A sense of hope and adventure clutched her heart as she envisioned how the finished apartment and courtyard would look.

The bedroom was next. The same color was going to be used throughout the space. Not having but one window in there, it would take the right lighting to make this room look not so dreary.

Of course, she would be spending most of her time in the living room or courtyard. The bedroom would be just for sleeping.

Before taking another break, she looked at her watch and was shocked. Where had the afternoon gone? Leaving all the paint supplies, she washed her hands and headed out the door. An orange cat silently watched her from his perch atop the gate. Had he made this courtyard his home, too? After locking the door, she turned and found the cat had vanished.

Driving home, she felt bone-tired but satisfied with the work she had accomplished. She decided to stop off at her local deli for an early supper. All she wanted to do when she got home was bathe then wait for Steve. Parking her car in the driveway, she rested her head on the steering wheel and asked for God's blessings on the evening. Looking up, her neighbor was watching her from his yard. She smiled and waved before going in.

I'll bet he'll be surprised when the moving vans show up. I hope nice people buy our house so he'll have good neighbors again.

It always seemed strange for Steve to ring the bell. All those years she would hear his key jiggle the lock open, followed by his familiar footsteps. She answered the door with a smile and led him into the living room.

"I need to apologize for what I said the other night." His head was down when he said it and his repentant tone of voice made Catherine want to run over and envelope him in her arms.

"Thank you, Steve," she said warmly. "That means a lot to me."

"Well, what did you want to discuss specifically tonight?"

"The furniture. My apartment is small, so I won't need as much as you might think. I'm even going to have to purchase a smaller bed."

"Where is your apartment, if you don't mind me asking?" Steve seemed timid nowadays when it came to asking personal questions. It so hurt her that the intimacy between them, even on mundane subjects, was gone.

"Not at all. It's at the western art museum."

"I didn't know they had loft apartments there. How expensive are they?"

"There's only one apartment and it's not a loft. Plus, it's not going to cost me anything. Even utilities are included." Confusion clouded his face.

"What do you mean by a free apartment? What's the gimmick? I hope someone's not taking advantage of you?" Concern was overriding his confusion now. Catherine wanted to kiss him for still caring. How she still loved this man!

"It's unreal how this all came about. I knew I was going to need a job. I applied at the museum. The director was very understanding when I explained my situation. She offered me this apartment in lieu of a salary. Since it's only part-time, I can find another job to supplement the funds I'll get when we divide our assets."

Steve could tell she was proud of this and he didn't want to rain on her parade. But, he was having trouble taking it all in. His wife was starting a new life without him. He suddenly felt like sobbing. Instead, he cleared his throat and retrieved the legal pad he had laid on the sofa.

"Do we want to go from room to room and decide who gets what?"

"That's fine with me. I figured we would have to put Zoe's things in storage until she's graduated. I certainly won't have any space at the apartment to store anything. What do you think?"

"I totally agree. Have you talked to Zoe at all about this?"

"No. Have you?" Steve shook his head slowly. "I'm really dreading that day. I can't stand the idea of hurting her. She's such a good girl." Catherine nodded in agreement.

The size of her apartment dictated many decisions, so the task went quicker than she had anticipated. It wasn't until they got to the bedroom that they got bogged down. They had one whole wall of art that they had picked out together during their many travels overseas. But they weren't arguing over the pieces. It might have been easier if they had. Instead, it was their memories that slowed the process.

"Remember when we were in Spain and went to that funky,

little art shop and purchased this seascape? We were warned not to go down that street because it was known as a tourist-trap. We went anyway and I'm so glad we did. Otherwise, we wouldn't have met Roberto and his lovely wife. Remember how they invited us for dinner after we bought the painting. What a wonderful evening that was!" Catherine's face softened as she was transported back to that time. Steve was caught up in the moment, too.

"I think you ought to have it," Steve kindly offered.

"No, you've always loved boats. I'm sure it would be enjoyed even more at your house. Have you looked for a place yet?"

"Actually, I put a deposit down on a little ranch just a few miles from the office. It's in a quiet, older neighborhood. I didn't need anything large or fancy at this point in my life." His woeful expression betrayed the positive tone of his voice.

Each picture summoned another memory and the mood between them became more and more melancholy as each work of art was discussed. When they looked at the oil of a beach house on the coast of Georgia, a place they had visited on their honeymoon, Catherine realized they needed to stop for the night. She was tired and she wasn't sure if crying in front of Steve was appropriate or not this evening. Who knew where it might lead?

They had become so formal with each other. Her tears could possibly communicate a message she was or was not sending. Who knew what Steve might make of the raw power of her deep sorrow if she released it before him? She didn't want to muddy the waters, especially now that they had come this far. Her sorrow could be dealt with when Steve departed, in the privacy of this lonely, unhappy house.

"I'm tired, Steve. Can we call it a night?" Circles under her eyes validated her plea.

"Sure. I'm pretty bushed myself. Would it bother you if I started moving some of the small things in the next few days? I'll wait and use a mover when the larger pieces are needed. I plan to stay in the motel another week or two."

"I don't mind at all. If any night you want to have supper when you come over, let me know." She was relieved Steve's back was

96

turned away from her overly eager face. Steve's heart was too heavy for him to turn around and answer her. He had to get out of that house before he embarrassed himself by crying like a baby before his wife.

The next day the painting went slower than Catherine had hoped. All the trim work was tedious and she stopped several times to rest her back. The kitchen was very tiny, so she had to contort her body to reach all the little nooks and crannies. She looked into the oven to see how much scrubbing it would take and instantly regretted it. It was disgusting. Obviously, it had never really been cleaned well, if at all. Maybe she would buy a new one and donate it to the museum.

By the late afternoon all the trim work was completed. Stepping back, she surveyed her day's labor and was very pleased. She decided to hunt down Mrs. Talbot and see if she was available to see the apartment, now that all the painting was done. After checking in her office, she began to search the many rooms of the museum for her. It was hard to believe that this stunning building and its exquisite art would be part of her home. Unable to locate her, she headed back to her apartment. It was getting late and she needed to be home in case Steve decided he wanted to eat supper with her.

The water fountain located down the hall from her apartment looked appealing and she bent over for a long, refreshing swallow of cool water. Before she had finished quenching her thirst, a bony finger poked her repeatedly on the shoulder. Thinking it was Ms. Talbot, she turned with a smile, only to be face-to-face with Austin. Jumping back, her smile vanished immediately, while his grin began to span ear to ear.

"I thought that was you when I was crossing the room. It's so good to see you." He had a look in his eyes like he expected Catherine to be pleased to see him, too.

"What do you want?" She couldn't have sounded any colder.

"Well, the last time I saw you, you were running to your car. You never returned my calls. I think your husband got a little miffed with me when I called."

Anger flew up into her face and she was tempted to slap his. *How dare he speak to me! He ruined my life and he's acting like we'll pick up where we left off!*

"Austin, my temporary lapse in judgment and sanity concerning you has cost me my marriage."

"Catherine, I'm so sorry. Of course, now that you're free, that means we can see each other openly and not sneak off to my ranch."

Catherine looked at this man with such a look of disgust that she was surprised he had the nerve to stand there and not run. Anyone else with just one ounce of self-respect would have turned and walked away. His audacity had no limits, obviously.

"Austin, I wouldn't date you if you were the last man on earth. I've started a new life and you will certainly not be in it. Kindly, get out of my way."

"Catherine, you don't know what you're saying. We had a good thing going. I care a lot about you. I have really missed you."

"Save it for another fool. I've got to go."

Austin's hand was quick as he grabbed her arm and held it. Fear and loathing gripped Catherine. How dare he grab her like that!

"Get your hand off of me or I'll call for security, and I mean it!" She hadn't seen a security guard lately and wondered if she would have to scream to get one's attention.

"Listen, baby, I'm not going to leave you. I love you and you're going to be mine." Austin's face had a demonic look that was more frightening than even his physical encroachment.

The museum would be closing soon. Surely a guard would soon be checking each room to see that they were vacated. Catherine saw two visitors out of the corner of her eye, but she didn't want to create a scene if possible. Mrs. Talbot could possibly mistake this incident as commonplace in Catherine's life. She could potentially lose her job and her place to live. Sweat began to roll down her neck as the terror of the situation and its possible repercussions raced through her mind. Closing her eyes, she thought she'd faint, but instead she rallied enough strength and wisdom to change her tactics.

"Austin, I have to go home now. Steve is coming over to get some things. Please let go of my arm. You're hurting me." Amazingly, she was able to smile into his face. Austin dropped her arm, but propped his hand against the wall behind her. He towered over her as she backed up as far as the wall would allow.

"Now, that's better. I understand you've got to go. Will you be staying in your home? I bet I'd enjoy living at your place."

The idea of Austin living with her made her physically nauseous. Also, she wouldn't have her daughter within ten blocks of him. How could she have ever fallen for this guy? Loneliness can drive a person to take some drastic measures, she reasoned. Catherine hoped her sin would not follow her all through her life, but it was apparent Austin wasn't going to take rejection without a fight.

A passerby might surmise that they were having a little romantic encounter by the water fountain. She was smiling up at him and his body language spoke of possession and desire for her. They were talking in soft tones and looked like any typical man and woman in love. Of course, nothing could have been further from the truth. She prayed Mrs. Talbot wouldn't show up unexpectedly and misconstrue this nightmare.

Catherine didn't see the familiar face come around the corner. She missed his whole body shaking as he watched in horror at the scene by the water fountain. Neither did she see him depart, tears blinding his vision as he headed back to the motel. Unfortunately even if she had seen him, Steve wouldn't have believed a word she said to explain.

After jumping into his car, Steve beat the steering wheel with his palms until they reddened and retorted in sharp pain. Pulling into the motel parking lot, he turned off the car and slumped down in the seat. Tears flowed freely as he pictured the scene at the museum. How could he have been such a fool to think she and that man were over? While he had never seen him before, the cowboy boots and his body draped over Catherine's was evidence enough that the man was Austin.

Last night, when she had invited him to come for supper whenever he was over at the house, a glimmer of hope had flickered in his heart. Maybe they could work something out. Some things had maybe gone too far, but they could pick up the pieces and start over. Steve shook his head. What a joke! What a fool he had been! But, no more!

He now was more determined than ever to get moved and get on with his life. When he got into his room he went right to the phone book to look up a moving company. He had thought he'd go over to his house and move a little at a time, thinking this would allow for the possibility of him and Catherine to come to some sort of understanding. He realized now that she had a new life awaiting her and Austin was part of it.

Calling his agent, he explained he needed to move in to his rental house right away. She explained that the cleaning crew had just finished shampooing the carpets and he could move in two days. He would need to call the utility companies tomorrow and get the water and electricity turned on. Boy, what a hassle moving was.

Steve debated calling Catherine and telling her of his plans. But the more he considered it, the more determined he was to have the moving van pull up, load up, and leave without giving her any notice or explanation. If she wanted to be self-indulgent with Austin, he could be self-centered, too.

He couldn't figure Catherine out. She could be so sweet and he would feel he was falling in love all over again. Then she could pull those stunts like at the museum and a feeling of jealousy and hatred would consume him. It would be best for his sanity to get out of her life for good. The move would be the first step in that direction.

The moving company had a 24-hour number to leave a message. Steve explained he would need a large van to move his belongings in two days. He'd have to wait until morning to contact the utility companies.

When Catherine got home her hands were shaking. She instinctively picked up the phone to call Steve. He had always been her rock when she was in trouble. Austin had frightened her so badly that she needed to hear Steve's reassuring voice. He didn't answer and she left no message. This was not something to leave on voicemail.

She began to run her bath water when she heard the phone ring. Running to the phone, thinking it was Steve, she looked at the caller ID and saw it was Austin. *Oh, God, get this man out of my life!* She turned the phone off and went to soak in the tub.

The hot water soothed her muscles and she began to relax. *I bet Steve will come tonight and get some of his stuff. We can talk, then.* She was relieved to know Austin didn't have a clue she was going to be living at the museum. He wouldn't have the nerve to come to her house if he thought Steve was going to be in and out. Slipping down in the water until it came just below her nose she wished she could just stay there until Steve came over. Unfortunately, the water began to cool, so she dried off, put on her clothes, and went to wait for Steve.

She busied herself with making a salad and baking some chicken. Steve had always loved the way she prepared their meals, and this night the food would be just as good. After the meal prep, she went into the living room and waited. After 8:00 she wondered if he was coming. Calling his number, she got no answer again.

"Steve, I've got supper made and I'm waiting for you. I assumed you'd want to get a few things tonight and you do need to eat a good meal. I'll wait for you and we can eat supper together." She tried not to sound too needy and desperate.

She had no idea that Steve had picked up the phone after she hung up, listened to part of the message, and before it was even over, deleted it and cut his phone off.

When 9:00 rolled around, it was obvious Steve wasn't coming. She ate her supper standing up in the kitchen, cleaned up then went immediately to bed. She just wanted to get this day over with. Between the fear she felt at the museum and the disappointment over Steve not coming, she was exhausted physically and emotionally. Her heavy eyes closed for good in the middle of saying her prayers.

The next morning Catherine lay in bed wondering why she hadn't heard from Steve. She called Mr. Hill and cancelled her appointment for this week. Although she was anxious to talk to him about Austin, she felt like she needed to talk to Steve first and get his perspective about everything they were going through. After calling his phone and getting only his voicemail, she got up to begin her day.

Catherine wanted to take a few things over to the museum, but she was a little apprehensive. *What if Austin shows up? What if he starts trouble and I lose my job? What if. . .?* She knew she couldn't live in fear and hide from Austin her whole life. Something had to be done! But, what?

Pulling into the back of the museum, she parked her car and started to unload. She literally ran from her car to the backdoor, always looking over her shoulder for Austin. Of course, why would he look for her in the back? After putting a few pictures up, she cleaned the bathroom well and mopped the floors. The new stove would arrive this afternoon. Mrs. Talbot had already given her permission to purchase it and dispose of the old one. The company said they would recycle the oven themselves, so that was one less thing to worry about.

Stepping into the courtyard, she decided to buy some type of material to cover the rod-iron gate right away. This was to insure privacy from people walking or driving by. The next step would be to have the movers transport her belongings here. As she sat in the courtyard, soaking up the warm sun, she was excited about her new adventure, but also a little downcast. Once she moved her things, the old house would no longer be her home. It would be the final step in dissolving the family environment she and Steve had worked so hard to create. Zoe was going to be shocked and they couldn't put off telling her any longer. She picked up her cell phone and called Steve. *His voicemail, again! What was up with him?*

Just as she was getting a little too comfortable in her chair, the delivery van arrived with the new stove. After they moved the old one out, she mopped the area that had obviously never been cleaned under the oven.

How can people be so disgusting? Well, this new stove will be well cared for and the kitchen will stay spotless.

After they left, she admired the gleaming, white stove and couldn't wait to use it. Sure, there was no comparison to this one and the professional-grade stove she had at home. But, after all, she would only be cooking for one. Well, maybe two if Zoe came over sometime.

After locking up, she drove home and put a few small things in her car for unloading at the apartment tomorrow. She wasn't going to make another dinner for Steve tonight. If he showed up, they could have yesterday's leftovers. She found herself straining to hear if his car pulled into the driveway, but he never showed. Deciding to go to bed early so she could get a fresh start before 7:00 in the morning, she cut off all the lights. She was relieved no one called either. It was a quiet night and she could read a book in bed under the light of her small bedside lamp, then drift off to sleep.

Across the ocean from Catherine, Zoe waited at a sidewalk café for her friend. The sunlight bathed her in a blanket of warmth. Sipping on her tea, she watched the people as they strolled along the sidewalk. Finally seeing her friend approach, she waved to get her attention.

"What a beautiful day in Paris! Zoe, aren't we lucky to be studying here and enjoying all this French culture?" Heather was always so chipper and it was contagious, especially on a day like today.

"I think I could live here forever, but I know I have to go back to the good ol' U.S.A. sometime." Zoe's mouth turned down as she spoke.

"Well, what's going on? You sounded a little urgent when you called me last night."

"I know I said we could spend the rest of the summer here after graduation and we deserve a long, much needed vacation, but I'm going to have to go home. I think something's wrong with my parents."

"Why do you say that? Have they told you something's wrong?"

"No, but it's what they are not saying that concerns me. Dad has always called at least once a week to check up on me, but his calls have become a little sporadic in the last few weeks. When I talk to Mom, she doesn't sound like herself. They both seem very guarded in their conversations, and I'm really concerned. I think they're trying to hide something from me."

"Like what?"

"I'm afraid one of them is very sick and they don't want me to know. My mom has always tried to shelter me. For example, my dad is somewhat neglectful, but mom has always tried to gloss it over. She'd talk about what a hard worker he was and he needed his time alone. She didn't want me to think badly of Dad or think he didn't love me or her. She's just that kind of mom."

"Zoe, don't you think you're reading something into this that just isn't there? You know your parents would want you to celebrate your graduation by traveling throughout Europe. When will we ever be able to do this again? Maybe, never! After summer, I have to get a job and start paying back these student loans. I may have to work until I drop dead, considering all the money I've borrowed, so I may not have this opportunity ever again. Please, don't change your mind! I've been living for this summer. I don't want to travel without you, Zoe."

Zoe felt torn. She was dying to travel and relax, but something was nudging her to return home right after graduation. She felt so unhappy that she was letting Heather down, but her parents came first. Something was wrong. She knew it in her heart. What if one of them had a terminal disease? What if her father had lost his job? She'd never enjoy herself in Europe for worrying about her parents. Right that moment, she made up her mind. She was going home Monday. Graduation was this Friday.

Her parents hadn't planned to come to the graduation, but had told her they'd buy her a new car when she returned home after the summer. They were going to let her pick it out and they'd celebrate her graduation then. Maybe they'd be glad she skipped the summer vacation and came home, especially if something was wrong.

"Heather, I'll make it up to you sometime later. Maybe I could come back in the middle of summer, after I see for myself that my parents are OK."

"Zoe, it won't be the same. What am I going to do in the meantime, while you're back at the States?"

"What about that good-looking teachers' assistant in our class? I've noticed you two have had some in-depth conversations after class. Maybe you two could hang out until I return."

"You've definitely read too much into that situation. He's got a girlfriend. I have been talking to him about the final, that's all."

Zoe couldn't hold back the tears any longer. "Heather, I know I'm disappointing you and that's hurting me so badly. But, I'm so concerned about my parents that I feel like I'm dying inside." She covered her face with her hands and cried like a child. People on the sidewalk slowed down to openly gawk, but some seemed genuinely concerned. Heather wrapped her arms around Zoe and began to rub her back. She was mumbling something, but Heather couldn't understand a thing she was saying because Zoe was crying so hard. She had never seen Zoe like this.

"Zoe, it's OK. I truly understand. I'm disappointed, sure, but I know if I was in your shoes, I'd go home, too. We can vacation together another time. Our friendship is too strong for something like this to destroy it."

Zoe dried her tears and smiled faintly up at Heather. She really was a good friend. She hugged Heather tightly then held her hands.

"Let's finish our tea and talk about plans for this weekend. After all, graduation is Friday and we need to party!" Heather could always brighten the darkest day with her charm and energy.

The girls sipped their tea and discussed various ideas of how they would spend their last weekend together in Paris. Zoe felt better, but a nagging thought kept interrupting her thoughts. *What's going on with my parents?*

Catherine was sleeping soundly when the distinctive beeping of a vehicle backing up aroused her. She thought it must be a delivery truck, but when the sound grew louder and louder, she jumped up and looked out the window. A large moving van was backing into the driveway and Steve was directing it. *What is going on?*

Catherine threw on a robe, jammed her feet into her slippers, and flew down the stairs. About the time she reached the door, Steve walked in. That caught both of them off guard, and for a moment they just stared at each other.

"Steve, what is going on? What's a moving van doing here today?" Catherine's voice sounded too shrill, even to her own ears.

"I'm getting my stuff and moving out today, that's what's going on. Do you have a problem with that?" Steve's voice had such an edge to it that Catherine stopped dead in her tracks.

"You've got your life to live and I have mine. The sooner I move, the sooner I'll get out of your life forever."

"But, Steve, I don't understand why you're acting so angry with me. What's gotten into you?"

"Catherine, I could say so many unkind things to you right now and feel fully justified in doing so. Just go back upstairs and let the movers do their work."

Catherine turned and stormed up the stairs. Hot tears spilled down her cheeks. *Why does he want to hurt me so much? Why can't he forgive me?* After she cried her tears out, she washed her face and got dressed.

Coming downstairs, she just watched as the men loaded up the large pieces of furniture, furniture she had no room for anyway. Steve did everything in his power not to look at her. You could cut the tension between them with a knife. Even the movers looked sheepishly at her when they walked past.

After an hour or so, she slumped back upstairs, her anger totally spent. This really was the absolute end. When the movers came into her bedroom to get the large king-size bed, she slipped into Zoe's room, fell across the bed, and cried. She wouldn't be disturbed in Zoe's room because her things were to be put in storage.

Catherine didn't know exactly when she fell asleep, but when the afternoon sun fell across her face, she awoke. She sat up and listened. Silence. Looking out the window, she saw that the van was gone and so was Steve's car. She began to walk through each room to survey the damage. Steve's office was completely empty. Other rooms had several pieces of furniture gone. One room was entirely devoid of pictures. Once all of Steve's golf course prints had graced its walls.

After loading up a few boxes in her car, she decided to call the storage warehouse to schedule the pick-up of Zoe's belongings. With the house in shambles after Steve's speedy removal of the furniture, she wanted to move out as soon as possible, too. She began to box up Zoe's stuff and clean each room as she emptied it out. A cleaning lady she used was willing to come when the house was completely empty, which was the exact feeling Catherine was experiencing at that moment. That night as she lay in the bed she began to contemplate the near future.

After Zoe finished traveling Europe this summer, she and Steve were suppose to buy her a car and plan a great celebration. Even though Zoe's graduation was a reason for a lot of fanfare, she was having difficulty being excited about anything. Yes, she had the new apartment and the new job, but even these had seemed to pale in the midst of these latest developments. This wasn't a home anymore and she dreaded the moment Zoe would find out about the marriage and the house. What a tragedy for Zoe, after having such a wonderful summer, traveling with no cares in the world, only to return home to nothing. *Zoe, I'm so sorry for the break-up of your home.*

Catherine had shipped a small diamond necklace to Zoe so she would have something to open on her graduation day. She imagined Zoe would be calling her sometime after her ceremony. It was going to take a lot of energy to sound enthusiastic for Zoe, but she was bound and determined to do it.

The movers called and said they'd pick up Zoe's things on

Monday. A local charity was picking up all the belongings she and Steve didn't want. Those things had been put in the garage for easy pick-up. After Monday, all that would be left was Catherine's and she'd have the movers take care of that.

She was a highly organized person, but the fact that everything concerning the move and disposal of all their material possessions was going as planned gave her little cheer. This really was the end of her old life and she felt a deep grief within her soul.

Catherine worked all day cleaning and boxing. Placing a few of Zoe's old toys into the garage finally caused her to suddenly drop to her knees in anguish and despair. She called out to God to help her and comfort her through this whole ordeal. One of Zoe's dolls was still in her hands. Catherine clutched it to her breast as if it was Zoe and cried into the doll's hair. It wasn't until her knees began to hurt from kneeling that she wiped away her tears and went onto the deck for some fresh air.

The sun dipped behind the horizon and the air began to cool. She pulled her sweater off the back of the chair. This would probably be the last time she would watch the sunset from her deck. Tears streamed down her cheeks and she didn't bother to even wipe them away. She was so grief-stricken that she wanted to feel every ounce of the pain and let the tears flow unabated. When her tears finally ceased, she went inside to shower and go to bed.

Monday morning the phone rang around 7:00 a.m. Catherine struggled to wake up and answer. All that crying over the weekend had left her exhausted and puffy-eyed.

"Hello?" *Who is calling me this early in the morning?*

"Catherine, have you heard from Zoe? I thought she'd call me after her graduation, but she didn't and I can't seem to reach her on her phone." Catherine sat straight up in bed.

"No, as a matter of fact, I didn't hear from her either. But let's not panic, Steve. She told me a couple of weeks ago that she and her roommate were planning to celebrate in a big way in Paris after the graduation. I'm sure she's with her friends and she's forgotten all about us in her excitement." *Well, Steve, I guess Zoe will be the only topic of conversation between you and me from now on. Thanks for asking how I was doing.*

"You're probably right. Sorry to wake you up."

The phone went dead and Catherine just stared at it for a moment. *I guess we've even done away with common courtesy, too.* Lying back down, she concentrated on all she wanted to accomplish today. The movers were coming around 10:00. After they finished with Zoe's belongings, she wanted to take a few boxes to her apartment.

After dressing, she ate a small breakfast then started to pack up a box or two. When she'd find something that could go to charity, she'd put that in the garage. The sanitation workers had picked up her garbage Friday so she had several empty trash cans she could fill up. It was amazing how much junk, especially paper, that she had hung onto all these years.

Catherine was taking a water break when she heard the beep-beep-beep on the moving van backing into her driveway. Zoe had the least amount of things so this part of the move would be quick. She had tried to get as much of her things in the living room so the movers could get out as quickly as possible.

After letting them in, she showed the movers all the items that needed to go to the storage warehouse. They must have had a lot of other customers to move that day because they were out of there in record time. She could check that off her list.

Now the house echoed when she walked across the floor since most of the furniture was gone. *I've got to get out of here. It's tearing me up to see our home like this. Home. I guess this isn't home anymore.*

After loading up her car with boxes, Catherine sat down for another water break. While filling up her glass, she didn't hear the car pulling up into the driveway. Sitting down in the living room on a small ottoman that would go to her apartment, she caught a glimpse of someone coming to the door as she raised her glass to her lips.

Across town, Steve had spent the whole weekend trying to sort out his things and get his rental house in order. It didn't take him long to realize that a woman's touch was definitely needed. Catherine had always made their home look so elegant and orderly. Even though the furniture in his house was expensive, his lack of decorating skills made the house look downright pathetic.

Taking a lunch break, he surveyed the kitchen and groaned when he saw all the kitchenware he needed to arrange. It was times like this that made him fume inside because he had been put in this position. He had always been the one to make the money in the family. Catherine kept the home and a landscaping service took care of the lawn. He had no experience with cooking, cleaning, and definitely not decorating. The only thing that was in its proper place was the bed, and it was not made up. Setting up the bed had been his first priority since he had to have a place to sleep after the movers left.

He was just putting his lunch dishes in the dishwasher, when the doorbell rang. *Who could that be?* Even Catherine didn't know his address. Opening up the door, a stunning redhead stood there with a plate of cookies in her hands.

"Hi! I'm Kate, your next-door neighbor." Her smile revealed white teeth and her eyes had that smoky look that can cause a man's imagination to go wild.

Steve didn't know what to say. He felt uneasy and he wasn't sure why. When he still didn't speak, Kate handed him the cookies.

"I thought you and your wife would enjoy homemade chocolate-chip cookies after moving in this weekend." Her eyes looked over Steve's shoulder for the wife.

"Thank you. I really appreciate it. These will taste really good after all that fast-food I've had lately." Steve could tell they had been freshly baked.

"Oh, I'm sure your wife hasn't had time to cook with the move and all." Looking over his shoulder again, Kate could tell the living room was a mess. *I wonder where his wife is? This place looks like a dump.*

"Well, there's no wife. What I mean is I'm getting a divorce, so my wife won't be living here." Kate noticed the pained look that came over Steve's face when he said, "divorce."

"I'm so sorry to hear that. I'm divorced, too." Kate tried not to sound too enthusiastic about this revelation, but her smile did get a little brighter.

Steve kept ogling the plate of warm cookies instead of Kate, much to her chagrin, so she decided to take her leave. She wasn't going to push herself onto Steve, at least not at this stage of the game. She knew exactly when to push and when to pull away when it came to dealing with men. This man obviously still had feelings for his wife and she didn't want to spoil things by coming on too strong. That would send him running away for sure.

"I'm really looking forward to us being neighbors. Why don't you come over sometime and we can have coffee. It's always nice to have someone to talk to when you're lonely." Her voice almost came out as a purr. Kate knew how to work men. Her beauty gave her a power over them, something to which they were completely blind. Her marriage had ended because she just couldn't be satisfied tied to just one man. After all, in her mind, variety really was the spice of life and there were too many men to be charmed.

Steve mumbled, "Thanks," and slowly closed the door. Right away he got a glass of milk and sat down to enjoy the cookies. The more he ate, the more he thought about Catherine and her good cooking. She had been like a gourmet chef, instead of just a cook. Her food had not only tasted good and fresh, but she always presented it in such a way that made it look even more appetizing. He wanted to pick up the phone and call her, but his behavior during his move and his pride kept his fingers from dialing her number.

Kate stood there, looking at the closed door a moment then turned to go home. She smiled to herself, satisfied knowing he was getting a divorce. This was going to be exciting having a good-looking single man next door. *I'll ask him over to eat next time.* Pulling her sunglasses down over her eyes, she walked into her backyard deck to soak up some sun. She wanted to look like a bronzed goddess, now that things were looking up in the neighbor.

All of the men in her neighborhood were married and most of

them were middle-aged and dull. Since her divorce, she had been on the prowl and she had come to realize, that is until Steve moved into the neighborhood, that she would have to look elsewhere for some male attention. Kate had no time or use for the neighborhood women, or any women, for that matter. She had no girlfriends and didn't feel lacking because of it. Her good looks kept many women away and they made sure their husbands kept away, too. It didn't take long for the average woman with an inkling of intuition to size Kate up. She was only into herself. Her own happiness was paramount, and that boiled down to having men worship her. She was self-centered and egotistical, and it would have been very hard for her to understand that her attitude was the really the reason she was never satisfied and never completely content. When restlessness set in during one of her relationships, it was the man who had the problem, not her.

Catherine had seen someone pass by the window and when she heard the door being unlocked, she naturally assumed it was Steve. *Maybe he's come to apologize.* She stood in the foyer, anxious to see Steve.

"What is going on here?"

Catherine couldn't have been more shocked if Santa Clause had opened the door. Instead, it was Zoe! Zoe, looking so sophisticated in her classy, black dress and matching sandals. Catherine couldn't move or speak.

"What is going on, Mom? Why is there a 'for sale' sign in our yard?"

Looking around at all the empty space in the downstairs, Zoe burst into tears before Catherine had even recovered from the shock of seeing her daughter in the flesh.

"I knew something was wrong. I could tell, but I would have never guessed this!" Zoe pointed to the almost empty living room.

Catherine moved toward her, but Zoe was having none of it. She pushed her mother aside and stormed upstairs toward her room. In just an instant, she was back, standing at the top of the stairs and yelling.

"Where is my stuff, Mom? What have you and Dad done?"

Catherine calmly said, "Zoe, come sit in the living room. We need to talk."

Zoe slowly descended the stairs and sat onto the ottoman. Catherine couldn't tell if she was in shock or just tired from her flight from Paris. Zoe all of a sudden looked exhausted and confused.

"Zoe, what are you doing here? I thought you were going to travel through Europe this summer. I wasn't expecting you yet."

"Well, duh! I can tell that by the empty house. Where is everything?"

"Why don't you tell me why you're here first because my story will take much longer." Catherine already felt drained, too, from the shock of Zoe's unexpected arrival.

"Mom, you and Dad have been so strange on the phone lately."

"Strange, how?"

"Either I couldn't get you to answer the phone or when I did talk to you, you sounded so different. It was like you were hiding something, and, boy, I can see now that's an understatement!"

"Your father and I didn't want to worry you while you were finishing up school. Plus, we wanted you to enjoy your last 'free' summer before you begin working. We were thinking of your welfare the whole time. We love you so much."

Catherine found herself tearing up now. She reached for Zoe's hand and Zoe reluctantly complied.

"So, you still didn't exactly answer my question. Why are you here?"

"I was so worried about you two that I cancelled my plans for travel.

I couldn't enjoy myself, wondering if one of you was sick or something worse. I wanted to see for myself what was going on. So I booked the first flight out after graduation."

"Zoe, you shouldn't have. Your father and I gave you the money to travel and have fun. Once you begin working, you won't ever again have a whole summer to goof off." Catherine couldn't hide her disappointment in Zoe's decision.

Looking defiant, Zoe raised her chin and said, "Mom, if you and Dad had communicated with me, this would have never happened. But I feel you left me no choice. I see now that things really are a catastrophe and I was right to come home. Anyway, the spur-of-the moment plane ticket cost a fortune, so I don't have the money I once had to travel Europe. And, this is all your fault!"

Her insolence quickly dissolved when the tears began to flow freely. She reached for her mother and cried hard into her shoulder. The consequences of her snap decision were beginning to dawn on her. Her care-free summer was basically ruined.

"Zoe, I need to explain a few things to you." Catherine rubbed her daughter's back while she contemplated where to begin.

"First of all, this situation started with me." Zoe looked at Catherine like she had lost her mind. Catherine had always been the stabilizer of the family. To think that her mother could have caused this disaster was inconceivable.

Taking a deep breath, she almost whispered, "I had a brief affair."

"What? You, Mom? What do you mean?" Zoe couldn't believe it.

"I'm not going to blame this on your father. There's no excuse for what I did, but your father's business was taking him away from me mentally and physically. He was gone all the time. I was so lonely.

I met a man at the library, and well, we had a very brief affair. Your father just couldn't handle it, so here we are."

"Do you still see this man? Who is he? Do we know him?"

"No. He's a stranger to our family. Zoe, if I could undo what I did, I'd give up everything to erase that terrible sin away." Catherine couldn't hold back the tears. As she cried, Zoe just looked at her dumbstruck.

"So, you and Dad are divorcing?" The pain in Zoe's face was heartbreaking. Catherine could kick herself for the trouble she had caused.

"Yes. I wish we weren't, but I have to face the consequences of my actions. It is a dear price to pay."

"Where is Dad now?"

"He moved out and I'm not sure of his address."

"What about you? Where will you live? Where will I live?" That last question caused Zoe to begin crying so distraughtly that it scared Catherine.

"Honey, please don't cry like that. You'll be taken care of. That's the last thing you need to worry about."

But a little niggling fear began to weigh on Catherine. She had assumed that Zoe would travel all summer, return to the States, and then want her own apartment. After living like an adult in Paris, it never dawned on her that Zoe would want to move back home.

"And where's my stuff?"

"It's all in storage. You don't need to worry about that."

"Mom, where are we going to live?"

"Zoe, I'm going to being living at a museum."

"A museum? What are you talking about?"

"As you know, there's a Western art museum in town. I got a part-time job there, which I will probably start next week, and they offered me an apartment for free. I've been fixing it up and, I'll have to admit, I'm quite proud of all I've accomplished there. I want you to see it and give me your opinion. You always did have a good eye for decorating."

"Mom, why are you getting this free? What's the catch? Is there a man involved in this?" Zoe looked skeptical.

"No, there is no man involved. The director is a woman and she's been divorced. When she found out I had no place to move, she offered the small apartment in lieu of a salary. Since it's part-time, I can find another job to help with other expenses. Plus, your father will be giving me a lump sum of money once the divorce is final." The mention of "divorce" brought both women to tears and there was a small lull in their conversation as they wept.

"What about me? Where do I live? Obviously, I can't live with you in that small apartment? I don't know what Dad's set-up is, so I don't know if that's an option or not." Zoe's pretty face was a picture of sadness and confusion. Catherine felt horrible and would have done anything to bring a smile to her face.

"Zoe, I never imagined you'd want to be living back home. I assumed you'd want a place of your own when you returned. After all, you've been living in another country and look how sophisticated and mature you look."

"Mom, that's true, but I wanted to move back home to get my bearings and decide what to do next."

"Your father and I will help you find a nice place to live, if it doesn't work out for you to live with him. OK? Let's call him right now."

Catherine dialed Steve number and he answered in that business-like tone of voice she hated. After all their years together, he had some nerve talking to her like she was just an acquaintance.

"Steve, Zoe's home."

"What! Why isn't she in Europe? What's wrong?"

"She thought something was wrong with us, so she flew home. I think you need to come over here. We have a lot to discuss."

"Sure. I'll be right over."

Catherine relayed his message to Zoe then leaned over and hugged her strongly. She was still trying to reconcile with the fact that Zoe was home.

"Zoe, I am so sorry about all this. I take the full blame. I wish I could turn the hands of the clock back, but we know that's impossible. I hope you don't hate me." Catherine's eyes filled with tears.

"Mom, what happened between you and Dad?" Zoe sounded so hurt.

"Well, your father was gone so much and when he was here, he was only here physically. His work totally consumed him and he had no time for me anymore. I got so lonely, especially since you were gone. When that man showed me a little attention, I just fell for his charms. I'm not blaming your father, but I wished he would have forgiven me. If he had, all this wouldn't be happening."

"Maybe you don't blame him, but I do! He's been so neglectful for so many years. All he's ever cared about was his business. I wish he would have been more caring. I've felt so sorry for you, Mom." It was Zoe's turn to fill up with tears. She decided she had to change the subject. She just couldn't cry any more.

Zoe told Catherine all about her experiences in Paris. She described her roommate, her school, and the beautiful city. She became quite animated with her story and Catherine was soaking up every bit of it. When the doorbell rang, both women jumped.

"Is that Dad, ringing the doorbell? Why doesn't he just use his key?" Catherine just shrugged then got up to let him in. He brushed past her into the foyer.

"Where's my girl?" Steve looked happier than Catherine had seen him in quite a while. Steve hugged Zoe tightly then held her at arms length just to get a good look at her.

"Zoe, you look beautiful! I'm so glad to see you, but I'm disappointed, too. You're supposed to be living it up in Europe. Baby, you shouldn't have come home. Your mother and I are handling this problem."

Zoe's face turned into a storm cloud. "Handling it? You haven't been handling it at all, Dad. Mom told me what happened. Why couldn't you have forgiven her? Why do you have to be so cold-hearted?"

"Zoe, this is between me and your mother. We need to talk privately so I can give you my side of the story." Steve's face turned red with anger. He shot Catherine a look that could kill. It was an expression Zoe couldn't help but notice.

"Mom has not blamed you for things getting so screwed up, but I do!"

"Zoe, I think you're forgetting that I was not the one who had an affair!" Steve's inflamed face matched Zoe's and Catherine couldn't help but note how alike they were in both facial expressions and temperament.

"This isn't helping, you two. Let's sit down and calmly discuss what the next step is for Zoe, OK?" Catherine sounded serene, but inside a tornado was whirling around in her head. She felt like putting her hands over her ears and just screaming until she collapsed from exhaustion.

Steve and Zoe stopped talking and just stared at each other for a moment. Catherine was worried one of them might start getting physical. Instead of the situation escalating into something more serious, the two hot-heads finally sat down, but across the room from each other. The tension in the room receded a bit as Zoe began to softly cry.

Steve and Catherine went over to her and began to stroke her hair and arms to comfort her. An accidental brush of his hand against Catherine's caused both of them to jerk away. Neither could hide the hurt of that response to each other.

When Zoe composed herself, she looked at her father with pleading eyes. "Dad, I was wondering if I could come live with you awhile; just until I find a job."

"Of course, sweetheart. There's plenty of room. We can have your things shipped to the house right away. I'll arrange that tomorrow."

"Zoe, why don't you plan to spend the night with me at my new apartment. The bed is plenty big enough for both of us."

"OK. Right now I feel I could sleep for a month. Between the plane trip, jet lag, and the drama of you and Dad divorcing, I'm totally exhausted."

"We can leave right away so you can lie down and take a nap."

Steve hugged and kissed Zoe then quietly walked out the door. Catherine gathered her purse, while Zoe retrieved her luggage from the driveway where the taxi driver had left it. After loading up the car, Catherine headed for the museum.

"Mom, I would have rather lived with you if you had had the space. We've been so close all my life. I'm going to feel funny just living with Dad."

"I know, but it won't be forever. When you get a job, I'll help you find and decorate a new place. It will be fun. Just because we're not living together doesn't mean we can't hang out like old times.

Isn't it funny how I said, 'old times,' like it was years ago. I feel like it's been years since life was normal, whatever normal is. Since all this started, I have felt like a feather blown around in the wind. Sometimes I think, 'Who am I? What am I doing? When will I wake up from this nightmare?"

Catherine looked over at Zoe to see if she understood what she was saying. Zoe was fast asleep. Catherine smiled at her sweet daughter and thought about the little girl she once was. Yes, she was grown up, but she would always be her little girl.

When Zoe opened her eyes much later, she was a little disoriented. Not only did she not recognize the room she was in, she hadn't a clue how she got into this bed without waking up. She rubbed her eyes and looked over to see her mother's side of the bed empty. Only vaguely did she begin to recall Catherine putting her to bed. It was just like when she was a child. Catherine's soft kiss on the top of her head was the last thing she remembered before going into a deep, coma-like sleep.

Looking at the clock she realized she had slept all afternoon, all night, and part of the morning. Putting on her robe and slippers, which Catherine had laid out the night before, she slowly shuffled into the living room. The light from all those windows nearly blinded her and she squinted against the glare.

"Wow, all that light will wake up any sleepyhead!"

"Good morning, you're up finally. Come have some coffee and bagels." Catherine didn't look like she had been up too long herself. Her blonde hair was a little tangled and small bags under her eyes showed how deep she had slept, too.

Zoe stood in front of the bank of windows and stretched, while she took in the view of the courtyard. A little chipmunk darted across the walkway. It was all so charming, if it hadn't been so depressing.

"Mom, this is a great apartment. I'm jealous. After I get dressed, I want to look around the museum. I'm really anxious to see which artists are being exhibited here."

"You are welcome to poke around all you want. If someone stops you, just tell them you're my daughter. I won't be able to show you around this morning. I have an appointment." Catherine wasn't ready to disclose the fact that she was seeing a counselor. Not yet.

"I guess you'll need to call your father and see what the plan is for your belongings to be shipped to his house. You haven't even seen his house. Of course, I haven't either."

"Mom, you sound like you want to get rid of me today." Catherine couldn't tell if Zoe was kidding or not since her back was facing her.

"No, Honey, I don't. I want you to take your time, but I will need to be gone this morning. Plus, I thought you'd be anxious to get moved in and settled at your dad's house."

As Zoe turned to face her mother, she made a little face that Catherine couldn't decipher. Was Zoe uncomfortable moving in with Steve? Oh, dear.

Session 10

Catherine's lopsided smile piqued Mr. Hill's curiosity. *What has been going on since I saw her last?*

"Come in, Catherine, and have a seat. It's seems like it's been forever since I saw you last. How are things going for you?" His friendly face always comforted Catherine and allowed her to relax.

"Well, a lot's happened since I saw you last time. I'm not sure where to begin. To put it in a nutshell, Steve unexpectedly moved all his things out, I moved into the museum, Austin accosted me at the museum, and Zoe came home unannounced. There, that's what's been happening in my life!"

"Catherine, how are you handling all this change at one time?"

"I've been praying a lot and trying to be more Christ-like. It's been very traumatic, but I'm making it. I think if this had happened to me before I ever started seeing you, I'd have gone crazy. You've really changed my life."

"I didn't change your life. As you submit to Christ, He changes it. I'm only a guide. Let's talk about Steve moving out unexpectedly. What happened?"

"I really don't know. A moving van backed up to the door early one morning and he was gone. After that, I had Zoe's things moved into storage and I moved into the museum apartment. I'm quite pleased with the way I have decorated it, if I say so myself.

I'll start my job this week, now that I'm all settled in." He could sense her pride in what she had accomplished.

"That sounds great. Now, what is this about Austin?"

"He just happened to be at the museum and when he saw me, he made a beeline toward me. He really acted like we might get back together. When I balked, he got a little aggressive and acted like I was 'his woman.' I was so scared my boss would see that interaction and have doubts about hiring me."

"Does he know you work and live there?" David looked quite concerned.

"No. But, I have an uneasy feeling he'll show up again."

"Catherine, how will you handle that?"

"I think I need to tell my boss about the situation. I'll let her make the final decision of what should be done next. I hope she won't say I need to go because my personal life might affect the harmony of the museum." Catherine began to look forlorn for the first time since entering his office.

"That sounds like a good idea to talk to your boss first. I pray this man is not going to upset your new life."

"I'm going to put it in the hands of Jesus. I have no control over this man. Of course, I think he doesn't have any control over himself either."

"Isn't it amazing how one sin can develop into so many troubles! It's like the sin is an octopus, with arms that can reach out in all kinds of directions. I'll certainly be praying for you about this situation."

"Why did I fall for that man? Look at my life now. I try to put on a brave face, but all this is killing me inside." Tears began to stream down her face as she reached for the tissue box.

"Tell me about Zoe coming home. I imagine that was a big surprise." David decided it was time to redirect her thoughts. Catherine's emotions could capsize what David hoped to accomplish in this session.

"You're telling me. When she walked in the door, I can't describe the look of horror on her face. When she found out what all had transpired, she was both hurt and angry. The divorce, the move, and her not having a place to live were all quite a shock for her."

"That's right. She couldn't live with you in that small apartment, could she?"

"No. She's going to move in with Steve, I think."

"What do you mean 'you think'?"

"She's never been super close to Steve. She and I were little buddies since her father was tied up with business so much. The idea of living with Steve has not set too well with her."

"Had you anticipated where she would live when you realized you were going to move to the small apartment?"

"Really, I thought after she traveled around Europe for the summer, she would want to live on her own in an apartment. After all, it was like she was living on her own in Paris. But, she had other plans. She told me she planned to live at home for a few months while she looked for a job and checked out some apartments. Her coming home early threw a monkey wrench into everything."

"Well, it sounds like she will just have to endure living with Steve long enough to get a job. I'm sure you two can spend quality time together." Catherine nodded in agreement.

"I'd like to pick up where we left off the last time you were here, if that's OK with you."

"To be honest, I don't remember where we left off. My life's been a whirlwind since then, but, sure, we can start where we left off." *I'm tired of talking about Austin, Steve, and Zoe anyway. I really need to hear what spiritual insight Mr. Hill has for me today.*

"We left off in our last session discussing forgiveness. Now I want to talk about living in victory."

"Sounds good, since I haven't felt too victorious lately." Catherine didn't try to hide her sarcasm. She instantly regretted being so negative. David didn't deserve her lousy attitude. Of course, she knew he would want her to be honest with her emotions.

"Because of Christ's sacrifice on the cross, we believers have been set free from the penalty of sin. Jesus paid the debt we owed to God-the debt of sin. Unfortunately, many times we still live under the *power* of sin. Your adulterous act is a case in point. Thankfully, we can be set free from the power of sin, just as we can be set free from its penalty.

When we try to live the Christian life in our strength, we will fail. Many times we believe that following the law, being self-disciplined, or trying to help ourselves, is the answer. We must realize that the victory of living the Christ-like life is not in us, but in Christ. We must surrender to Christ totally in order to live victorious. He wants to live through us and fulfill God's will. Do you understand what I mean by all this?"

"Yes, I do. All my life I've tried to be the good girl. I was actually not depending on Christ to achieve this, only myself. All this started when I was a child trying to earn my father's love. I was trying to earn points with God, too. The very fact that I could so easily fall for Austin shows how I weak I really was."

"Exactly! What's so fascinating about our relationship with Christ is this. As we submit to Him more and more, we desire less and less to sin. God says in Jeremiah 31:33 He has written the law in our heart. It's part of you. Ask yourself, if you gave yourself permission to sin, would you want to?"

"No, not really. After what I did, blatant sinning really makes me feel awful."

"The Holy Spirit within us makes it so that if we sin we won't enjoy it."

"After what I did with Austin, I wanted to throw up. My sin actually made me nauseous."

"I understand. Victory is Christ. It is a gift to us. It's a matter of faith in Him, believing Him to be not only our Savior, but our Lord. Catherine, have you made Christ your Lord?"

"Until all this happened, I would have to say, 'no,' but now I can say 'yes,' and mean it. I still have a long way to go to completely submitting to Him, but I want to relinquish my whole life over to Him."

"What would you say is holding you back?"

"I guess I'd need to think about that for a moment."

David waited patiently for Catherine to collect her thoughts. He knew the question he had posed to her was pivotal to her spiritual growth.

"I guess I'm afraid of turning my whole life over to Christ." Catherine had an apologetic look on her face.

"Afraid of what?"

"Afraid He'll ask me to do something I don't want to do."

"Like what?"

"Like go to Africa or sell everything I have and give it to the poor."

"I'll admit, He does tell some people to do that very thing, but He doesn't tell everyone. Jesus asked the rich, young ruler to sell everything and give it to the poor because the young man had made wealth his god. On the other hand, Abraham was rich. God didn't ask him to sell everything. God calls different people to do different things for Him. I feel I am in God's will and I'm not poor nor have I been called to go to Africa. God has a distinct, individualized purpose for you, too."

"I see what you mean. I guess I haven't found out yet what God wants me to do."

"I think God is purging and molding you for His service. When you're ready, He'll have a plan all tailor-made for you. Right now, I believe God is desiring to humble you and cause you to be more dependent on Him. He wants you to be broken and I think what you've been through lately is part of the process."

"Broken? Why would God want that?" Catherine seemed confused.

"He can't use you if you're not broken. People who are not broken are proud people. The Bible talks a lot about how much God hates pride."

"You would think God would want us to feel good about ourselves. After all, He made us."

"Pride is different from appreciating who we are-made in God's image. I'm going to give you a few characteristics of proud people then I think you'll see what I mean.

Proud people are self-righteous. They look down on others. They want to be recognized and appreciated. They don't want to depend on others; in other words, they want to be self-sufficient. They're always claiming rights. They have a hard time admitting they're wrong or they have sinned."

"I can see why God hates pride now."

"Conversely, broken people esteem others better than themselves. They're not self-righteous. They know there is an unworthiness about them. They know they need others in their lives. They are meek and not pushy."

"I understand now what proud people are all about. I never considered myself proud, but I guess there was and is some pride in me."

"Catherine, we all have some degree of pride. It's a serious attitude to have because of the way God feels about it. We all need to purge ourselves of pride. After all, what do we really have to be proud about? When we compare ourselves to Jesus Christ, who should be our standard of measure, we all fall woefully short. What do you think?"

"You know, I think I always felt I was better than some people. My husband made great money. We lived in an extremely expensive house and drove luxury cars. We were able to send our daughter to Paris to study and live in a nice apartment there. I always felt sorry for the 'little people' who had to struggle to make ends meet and lived from paycheck to paycheck.

I see God has dealt with a lot of my pride, now that I live in an apartment attached to a museum and have no viable means of income. Steve could have been a lot tougher on me about money, especially since I had an affair, but he's been fair. I guess I'm really blessed and a lot more humble than before. Money won't come easy anymore for me.

For example, I'll have to sell my car. The upkeep will be too much for me. A small, economical car will be my next big purchase. I've come a long way from living in the exclusive Piedmont Estates."

David was waiting for Catherine to start crying, but she

only looked a little wistful as she fingered her gold and diamond bracelet.

"I'm sure before it's all over, all the trappings of my former good life will have to be sold. Practicality will replace extravagance. I have no one to blame but myself for all this. But you know, it may sound strange, but when it's all said and done, I might like myself and my life a lot better. What do you think?"

"I think God is doing a good work in you. One day you won't miss all those material blessings you had. Possessions can be a burden. We have to ask ourselves, 'Do I own my stuff or does it own me?' Material things can be a real encumbrance."

"What do you mean?"

"Take, for example, your luxury car. With a car like that, you have to be extra careful where you park so it won't get stolen or dented. All the maintenance on luxury cars is extremely expensive. More effort and time is put in that type of car than an economical one. Never mind the price of insurance. So you see, while you own the car, the car owns a little bit of you. If you analyzed all of your possessions, you would come to realize all the energy and money you put into them really add up. You begin to understand that you're a slave to them."

"I see what you mean. I never thought of possessions like that."

The look on Catherine's face made David ask, "What are you thinking about right now?"

"I'll have to admit. I miss my home and all the trappings that went along with it, but I'm also looking forward to not being so tied down to cleaning that big house. We had a maid, but she only came once a week. All the rest of the week I had to pick up after everyone. The maintenance on a large home is incredible. That small apartment is going to be so easy to keep clean, plus there will only be me to mess it up."

"You're going to be freer that you've ever been as an adult. Without all those possessions to weigh you down, you'll have more time to pursue some of your interests. This will also free you up to serve the Lord more than you've been doing."

Lowering her head, she mumbled something David couldn't hear.

"I'm sorry, Catherine. I didn't quite catch that."

"I said, 'I've never really served the Lord to any great degree.'"

"Is that something you want to change?"

"Yes. I plan to start looking for a church that has a good singles ministry for women my age. We attended church as a family, but we weren't what you call faithful members. Steve was always working, so Zoe and I only attended sporadically. Maybe Zoe might be interested in going with me. We'll have to see."

"That really sounds good. I'll be praying for you about this matter. I'm always praying for you, but I'll add this to my prayers."

"I know you mean it when you say you're praying for me. Those prayers have really paid off. I don't think I could have gone through all I've been through without you lifting me up in prayer. You might say your prayers have kept me from going off the deep end."

"Catherine, we need to give God all the credit and glory. He is moving in your life. He will bring things around for you so you can be more of His good and faithful servant. He loves you and knows what's best for all of us. We're just too stubborn to realize it. If we would quit fighting God and work with Him, we'd be amazed how much of the abundant life we could be living."

"I'm already getting a glimpse of that." Her smile was genuine and David smiled back at her in gratitude for all God's transforming work with Catherine.

"I think this is a good time to stop. I'll be anxious to see what God is going to be doing in your life this week. I look forward to seeing you next week. Let's close in prayer, OK?"

Catherine bowed her head as David prayed over her, her family, her job, and the situation with Austin. She left the office feeling so much lighter.

After returning to her apartment, Catherine decided to check in with Mrs. Talbot. Entering her office, she was surprised to see Zoe there.

"Catherine, come in. I've been having a lovely chat with your beautiful daughter. She was roaming the museum and taking notes, so I wanted to meet this young woman who was so interested in our art."

"Well, she was an art major and has been studying over in Paris." Catherine was beaming with pride as she sat down across from Zoe.

"Mom, since you had an appointment this morning and my things won't be shipped to Dad's until tomorrow, I thought I'd check out the museum. What a fantastic collection of Western art! I'm really impressed."

It was Mrs. Talbot's turn to swell with pride. "We feel we have the diversity and talent that will draw all types of art lovers."

"I came in to see if you wanted me to get started tomorrow. The apartment is all set and I'm ready to work."

"I'm hoping once you get yourself acclimated to the museum, you won't think of your job as work, but as a joy."

"I can tell you I'm already feeling that way. I guess my daughter got a head start on me. I need to start taking some notes on the artists and getting to know their work."

"Mom, why don't we do that today? Together we can make a note of all the artists, then go back to your computer and do some research of each of them."

"I'm sure that can't all be accomplished in one afternoon, but you two go enjoy yourselves and I'll be making an agenda for you, Catherine, for the first school group that will arrive tomorrow. How does that sound?"

"I'm ready!"

Catherine and Zoe left the office and went back to the apartment for a lunch of chicken salad sandwiches. While Zoe was setting the table, she discussed all she saw that morning.

"I didn't even touch the surface of the museum this morning. There is so much to see and experience here. This is going to be a great place to work, Mom. I'm a little jealous."

"Remember, I don't get a salary, but you're right. It's going to be so wonderful working in this environment. I'm excited."

"By the way, I met this strange man this morning. He acted like he knew you, but I've never seen him before."

Catherine felt the blood leave her face and her hands began to shake.

"What did he say to you?"

"He came up to me and said, 'You must be Catherine's daughter. You're the spitting image of her. I told him I was your daughter then I asked him how he knew you. Mom, he got this disgusting grin on his face, but he didn't answer me. He gave me the creeps."

"Did he say anything else?" Catherine started feeling a little light-headed, so she sat down.

"He just said he hoped we'd run into each other again soon."

"Did you tell him I worked at the museum and lived here?"

"No. He didn't ask and I didn't volunteer any information. Like I said, he was creepy. Who is he anyway?" Zoe started to feel on edge because of the anxious look on her mother's face.

"He's nobody and I want you to stay away from him. He's trouble. I mean it, Zoe. Avoid him at all costs."

"Mom, you're scaring me. How do you know him? Has he ever done something to you?"

Catherine hung her head and tears splashed on the plate from which she would be eating lunch. Zoe came over and began to rub her back.

"Mom, what's wrong? I'm sorry I even told you about this guy."

"No, Zoe. I'm glad you told me. I think he's stalking me and now he knows who my daughter is. I can't believe I've brought all this on my family." Catherine's tears fell even harder.

"Mom, we need to call the police. This is dangerous. I'm going to call them right now."

Catherine jumped up and grabbed Zoe's hand, squeezing it until Zoe cried out and jerked it away.

"Zoe, don't call the police. It hasn't come to that point yet. In the future I may have to call them, but not yet."

"Why not?" Zoe was truly scared and becoming a little angry.

"It's a long story. Let's eat our lunch, but we'll skip the afternoon museum tour together. Austin might still be lurking around."

"Austin? Who is he, Mom? Maybe we need to call Dad. What do you think?"

"A hundred times, no! Don't call your father. This thing could get really messy. Please just trust me about this, Zoe. Please!"

"Mom, I'm going to call Dad if you don't tell me about Austin. Also, what did you mean about bringing this all on our family?"

"Zoe, come sit down with me. We need to talk. I am so ashamed to be telling you this. Austin is the man I had the brief affair with. I feel so guilty over what I've done. You'll never know how much I regret it, especially since it destroyed my marriage and it ruined our family. I'm like Humpty-Dumpty. Nothing can ever put the pieces of my life back together again."

"Did you continue to keep in touch with this man after Dad found out?"

"No! After that one time I never saw him again until he saw me in the museum. He came up to me and acted very possessive. I was scared and angry. I thought he'd get the message after I acted the way I did towards him, but obviously I was wrong. Now what kills me is he knows who you are. I have created the most awful mess. Don't ever forget this, Zoe. One sin can ruin your life."

"What are we going to do?"

"*We* aren't going to do anything. This is my problem. I thought I'd mention it to Mrs. Talbot, in case anything came up at the museum. My fear is she'll fire me and not only will I lose my job, I'll lose my home." Zoe saw the fear in her mother's face. It hurt her immensely to see her mother like this.

"Mom, I know you think this isn't my business, but you are my business. I love you and want to help you."

"I love you, too, Zoe. I love you so much it hurts sometimes."

Both women fell into each other's arms and wept. Zoe wept for her mother's pain and Catherine wept over Zoe's love and devotion. After drying their tears, they sat down for a quiet lunch. The whole time they were eating Zoe's mind was working in overdrive trying to figure out a solution to Catherine's problem with Austin.

Because of the emotional upheaval both had experienced at lunchtime, Catherine retired to her bed, while Zoe slumped onto the couch. It didn't take either woman long to fall fast asleep. After a couple of hours, Zoe looked at her watch and noticed it was late in the afternoon. She decided to let Catherine continue to sleep while she took advantage of the silence in the apartment to contemplate the situation at hand. About an hour later Catherine entered the living room, rubbing her eyes.

"Boy, I can't believe I slept so long! All this crying wears you out."

Zoe smiled and patted the seat next to her. Catherine went and sat down beside her and just laid her head on Zoe's shoulder.

"I don't know what I'd do without you, little girl. You bring me so much joy and you always have."

"I feel the same way about you, Mom."

"Let's dress up a little and go somewhere nice to eat tonight. Ok? We need to liven up the mood this evening."

"Sounds good to me," Zoe responded enthusiastically.

The next day Zoe headed for her father's house to await the moving van, while Catherine reported for duty. Mrs. Talbot had the itinerary all ready for her. Catherine would be following a museum volunteer to observe the process of introducing students to the museum and the art displayed. She had an hour to kill before the school bus would arrive.

"Mrs. Talbot, I'd like to have a word with you, if I may?"

"Of course. Sit down. Would you like some coffee?"

"No. I'm already wired from my morning coffee, but thank you."

"What did you want to talk to me about? Are you having problems with the apartment?"

"Oh, no. I love the apartment. This is a personal matter I wish to discuss with you." Catherine felt her face grow warm.

"From the look on your face, this must be serious."

"Well, it is. I have a stalker."

Mrs. Talbot's mouth dropped a little before she spoke. "Who is he? What are you doing about it? Have you called the police?" Mrs. Talbot sounded worried.

"I haven't called the police yet. I didn't feel it had come to that, yet. But, I did see him in the museum. Unfortunately, or fortunately, depending on how you look at it, I know him. He's the man I had a very brief fling with."

"Did he do anything to you in the museum? Catherine, this is a serious matter, indeed. Tell me what happened." A frown crossed Mrs. Talbot's face that made Catherine feel increasingly nervous.

"It was near the water fountain, not far from my apartment, where he ran into me and began to get a little possessive. He somewhat accosted me, but after I told him to get out of my life, he left. This is the part that scares me. He came back the other day and recognized Zoe, since she looks so much like me. He spoke to her, which makes me just shake inside. My fear is that you'll fire me and I'll lose my job and my apartment." Catherine could hold the tears back no longer.

Mrs. Talbot just looked at Catherine. Unfortunately, Catherine didn't have a clue what she was thinking. As she waited for Mrs. Talbot to dismiss her, she clutched her hands together in her lap.

"Catherine, this is a very grave problem. As you know, the museum and the safety of its patrons are my first priority. I'm sure you understand."

"I do. If you give me a week, I'll find another place to live and move all my belongings." Catherine began to feel like she might be passing out from hyperventilating. Her dizziness was starting to affect her eyesight, but she could still see Mrs. Talbot frowning. *Why doesn't she just fire me and get it over with? I need to go lay down.*

Mrs. Talbot's frown began to soften as she said, "Catherine, don't misunderstand me. You are part of this museum. Your safety is just as important as those students that will be arriving soon. You are not the problem; this man is. I want you to give me his name and any information you have about him. I won't do anything at this time, but in the future, if he comes here with any intent other than the enjoyment of the museum, I will call the police. That is a promise."

Without thinking about protocol, Catherine jumped up and hugged Mrs. Talbot's neck, almost knocking her out of her chair.

"Thank you, thank you! You'll never know how much this means to me. You won't regret it. I'll be the best employee you've got."

Mrs. Talbot attempted to regain her composure, smoothing down her hair and straightening the collar of her blouse. Catherine was wiping her eyes and smiling like she had won the lottery.

"I know you'll do an excellent job. That's why I hired you in the first place. Now, prove yourself and go meet that school bus at the front entrance. The children will be excited about their morning at the museum. Have a good day. Come see me after they leave."

Catherine was tempted to hug her again, but she didn't want to push it. Checking her make-up at the mirror by the door, she exited the office and proceeded to the parking lot. Her heart was soaring with joy and relief.

Thank you, God. Thank you for all Your blessings.

The morning went by quickly. She enjoyed being with the first graders. Their excitement was contagious. The volunteer, named Sally, was fun and quite knowledgeable. Catherine took notes, assisted Sally and the children's teacher when needed, and never looked at her watch once. When it was time to load the bus, Catherine couldn't believe the time. It was noon already. She headed for her apartment for a much needed bathroom break and some lunch.

While eating, she caught herself smiling over cute little things the children said. She now knew, without a doubt, that this job was perfect for her. She had never really dealt with children as a group. Zoe was an only child, and except for play-dates with her little friends, she had never experienced such motion and wonder from a class full of first graders. It was wonderful and it made her feel so alive.

Ever since the disaster of her affair and the coming divorce, she had been so depressed and life sometimes hadn't felt worth living. That had all changed in a few hours all because of twenty-two vivacious children. She couldn't stop sending praises heavenward for this new experience and a new lease on life. She had brought such calamity into her life, but God was going to transform it, even if she didn't deserve it. That is just the kind of God He is.

After cleaning up the dishes, she headed for Mrs. Talbot's office. She felt light as a feather and she couldn't wipe the silly grin off her face. *I'm so giddy, she might think I've started drinking!*

Across town Zoe began sorting and arranging things in her bedroom. She realized that there was some junk she needed to throw away and some things that still had some good use she would donate. After living on her own and going to college in Paris, most of her high school mementos and clothing seemed childish and out of style. Next to the outfits that she had purchased in Paris, they looked cheap and unfashionable.

Steve poked his head in the door and watched Zoe busily decorating her room. It was going to be good having her live with him. He had already become quite lonely.

"Well, I see you're making yourself at home. If there's anything I can do to help, let me know."

Zoe looked up and smiled. "I've got it, Dad. A lot of this stuff will be gone by tomorrow."

"Why?"

"Dad, I'm too old for this high school stuff. I've moved on, and I'm going to donate what I don't throw away."

It was Steve's turn to smile. "Too old? Now that you mentioned it, I thought I saw a gray hair."

"Oh, Dad. You know what I mean."

"I do. If you need some money to replace some of your clothes, just let me know. I want you to be happy."

Zoe's smile faded. "Dad, right now, it's hard to be happy while Mom is in trouble." The minute she said it, she could have slapped herself. She promised her mother she wouldn't mention the Austin fiasco with her father.

"What trouble? Is Catherine having financial trouble? I can

help her with that. I don't want your mother to suffer. After all, she is the mother of my one precious child."

"Dad, it's not financial, but I promised Mom I wouldn't say anything to you. I'm sorry I brought it up."

A worried look formed on Steve's face. Zoe could tell he wasn't going to just drop this discussion.

"Zoe, if your mother's in trouble, I need to know. She's been under my care for decades. She's going to need a little assistance until she really gets on her feet. So, what's the trouble?"

"No, Dad. I can't tell you. I promised." Steve saw that Zoe was not going to budge, so it was useless to keep pushing.

"Zoe, I won't pressure you about it anymore. A promise is a promise." *What kind of trouble could Catherine possibly be in? Why didn't she call me?*

Kate had been looking through her blinds off and on all day. She had heard a large vehicle backing up next door and her curiosity got the best of her. She had to know what was going on at Steve's house. She hadn't been over there since she brought him cookies. It was best to give him room and not be too pushy.

Watching the men unload the van, she realized from the furniture that this must be his daughter moving in. That could be problem. Daughters could be so protective of their fathers. Of course, this was not going to deter Kate. She had gone toe-to-toe with protective women before. If Kate set her cap for a particular man, no one was going to get in her way, particularly not some young daughter. She decided to wait a day or two before investigating.

Two days later Steve's car was by itself in the driveway. The daughter's car had left earlier in the morning. Steve was most likely going to work at home today she guessed. This was her chance to see Steve alone. Of course, she needed a reason to get into that house. She wanted to see for herself what was going on with the daughter. Kate decided to make some coffee and halve the cake she had baked the day before. Steve would have to let her in when her hands were full with the things she would bring over.

After applying her make-up, she decided she had to look just right. Steve had shown her that a low-cut blouse didn't really get his attention. She changed tactics and wore a modest dress instead. Filling her arms and hands with the coffee carafe, half a cake, and a bouquet of flowers she had received yesterday from a man she no longer was interested in, she made her way to Steve's house.

Steve seemed surprised to see her at the door. She couldn't tell if he was pleasantly surprised or just surprised, but it didn't matter either way.

"Hi, Steve. I noticed that your daughter, I assume it's your daughter, has moved in. I wanted to bring over a welcome-to-the-neighborhood gift for her, too."

"Come in. Your hands are full. Let me help you."

Kate smiled. Her plan was already working. Thank goodness men were so predictable. She set everything down at the kitchen table. Looking around she noticed the place could sure use a woman's touch, her touch.

"I'm sorry, but I've forgotten your name." Steve looked bashful.

"That's OK. My name is Kate and you're Steve, right?"

"Yes. This is very kind of you. I know my daughter will be touched. She's not here right now, though."

"That's a shame. I was so wanting to meet her. I bought these flowers for her. I do hope she likes them." Kate couldn't have smiled any sweeter.

"I know Zoe will love them. She's always enjoyed flowers."

"Most women do. Is your daughter going to be living with you for a while or is this a temporary thing?"

"I'm not sure. She just got back from studying in Paris. She hasn't really gotten settled in enough to know what she'll be doing."

"Oh, I see. You know young people; they can be so flighty. She may be here one day and gone tomorrow." *I hope.*

"Not my Zoe. She's always been a stable girl. Once she secures a good job, then she'll decide what's she's going to do next."

"Oh, I do hope she finds one soon." *I hope that didn't sound too forward.* "I mean, I'm sure she wants to use her education right away."

"I just want her to find meaningful work. She can live here as long as she wants."

About that time a car pulled into the driveway. Steve looked out the window and saw it was Zoe.

"What a surprise. Kate, you're going to get to meet Zoe after all. She just pulled up."

Kate kept the smile on her face even though she wished Zoe had stayed gone. Now she wasn't going to be able to spend a little time alone with Steve.

Steve opened the door and Zoe walked in with her bundles. When she saw Kate standing there with that fake smile on her face, she instantly got suspicious.

"Honey, this is Kate, our next-door neighbor. She brought some flowers to welcome you to the neighborhood." Zoe could see that her father didn't have a clue what this woman was all about.

"Thank you. That was very nice." Zoe tried to hide the coldness she already felt towards this woman.

"Zoe, you are so welcome. I also brought some coffee and cake. Would you like for me to cut you a piece?"

"No, it's a little early for cake. Plus, I can cut my own piece."

All three just stood there, not knowing what to say next. Finally Kate broke the silence.

"I do hope we can be friends. If I can help you in any way, please let me know. I want to be of any assistance to you and your father."

"My father and I are just fine, but thanks for the offer. It was nice meeting you and I wish you could stay longer, but my father and I have some business to take care of. I'm sure you understand."

"Of course. Well, Steve, I hope to see you soon. I still plan to have you over for dinner, and Zoe, you are welcome to come, too."

Seeing that Zoe wasn't going to budge, Kate departed with a sickening-sweet smile on her face. Zoe wanted to slam the door loudly after her. The minute Kate was out of view, her smile melted quicker than butter on a hot skillet. *She may think she's seen the last of me, but I plan to go over again to get my carafe and cake plate, when she's not there. That young gal is no match for me. I'll see her father whether she likes it or not.*

Zoe turned to her father and just glared. Steve hadn't a clue what was wrong. *Dad is so clueless. I could spot that woman's intentions a mile away.*

"Zoe, what's that look all about?"

"Dad, you just can't be that naïve! Don't you see what that woman is trying to do?"

"Yes, she's trying to be a nice neighbor. What's wrong with that?"

"Nothing, if that was what she was up to. Can't you see she's got her sights set on you?"

"Zoe, you're reading way too much into that little visit. She came once before and brought me cookies. She didn't even come in. I let her in this time because her hands were full. There's really no more to it." Steve wanted to grin, but he knew that would only exasperate his daughter more.

"Dad, how many women have you had in your life?"

"First of all, young lady, that's really none of your business, but I don't mind telling you that the only woman I've ever had was your mother. Why?"

"Because that just goes to show you don't really know women."

Steve did laugh this time. "That's funny. I've lived with two for decades. Doesn't that count?"

"No. That woman is nothing like me or Mom. She's a man-eater. I can tell."

"A what?"

"A man-eater. She's on the prowl for the next man she can charm then devour."

"Boy, you sure saw a lot more in her from just a few minutes than I did. Don't you think you're jumping to conclusions, and, maybe, the wrong conclusions. I'd hate to think that if Catherine had welcomed someone into our neighborhood, she would be accused of being a 'man-eater.'" Steve was just shaking his head.

"Dad, Mom wouldn't act like Kate did. Mom doesn't give off vibes like she's on the make. That's the difference between Kate and Mom."

"Zoe, don't worry about things like this. You know I'll always . . ."

Steve stopped himself. He didn't want to finish his sentence. He was going to say, "You know I'll always love only your mother." But why should he say it, even if it was true. Zoe would have probably shot back, "Then why are you divorcing her?" It was all too complicated and he didn't want to discuss it with his daughter.

"Dad, do you promise not to see her anymore?"

"Zoe, I can't promise that. She's our next-door neighbor, for crying out loud."

"Well, I'm planning on keeping my eye on her, you can bet on that!"

"Zoe, I think you're seeing something that just isn't there, but you do whatever you like. After all, we need to get along since we're roommates."

Seeing how much he relished saying, "roommates," Zoe wanted there to be a complete understanding about this living arrangement. She knew her father was looking forward to them spending as much time as possible together, but she did have a life, one that didn't include her dad as her sidekick.

"Dad, this will not be a permanent situation. As soon as I get a job, I plan to find my own apartment, just like Mom."

"Is her place nice? I haven't seen it yet. Of course, I haven't been invited." Steve was hoping he didn't sound too needy when he said that. He didn't want Zoe to get the wrong message about him and Catherine.

"Mom has done wonders with her place. She described what it looked like before, and it was kind of a dump. You know Mom always had a flair when it came to decorating."

"Your mother always was an excellent housewife."

"Is that all you saw in her-a housewife? Was she just there to cook and clean and raise your child?" Zoe was looking straight into Steve's eyes.

"I've got to be honest. I guess I did take your mother for granted. That would go for you, too. I was so wrapped up in my business that I didn't take the time to cultivate a loving bond with either of you. At the time, I justified it by thinking all my business was for the benefit of the family. Now that my family is broken apart, I can see how much I missed. I could never make it up to you or your mother. I guess that's why she was so easily taken advantage of by that other man."

Zoe saw tears form in Steve's eyes. She dropped hers and just stared at the floor. She had never seen her father so open and vulnerable before and it made her feel a little uncomfortable.

"Dad, I know you're sorry, but we can't do anything about the past. We can only concentrate on the future. Do you think there's any hope for you and Mom?"

Now it was Steve's turn to just stare at the floor. Zoe walked over to her father and he hugged her like he did when she was a child. Both cried softly into each other's shoulders. In the back of each of their minds they thought maybe too much had happened to turn back the hands of time and it broke their hearts.

Zoe went on an interview the next day. While it wasn't exactly what she was looking for, a position with an advertising agency might be fun and challenging. She had left early that morning, looking as sharp as she knew how. Steve had wished her luck and seen her out the door.

He was planning on working at home again today. He seemed to be able to get so much more done at home than in his noisy office. With Zoe gone for the morning, he hoped to really make a dent in a pile of paperwork on his desk. He was just getting in the rhythm of work when the doorbell rang. *Just what I need! An interruption.*

Opening the door he saw Kate. He instantly began to wonder if Zoe was right about her. Another woman in his life was the last thing he needed. Kate was barking up the wrong tree if she was interested in him.

"I wasn't expecting to see you this early in the morning." Steve wasn't exactly smiling at her.

"I'm so sorry to disturb you. I needed to get my cake plate and carafe back. There's a friend of mine who is recovering from a broken leg so I thought I'd cheer her up with some coffee and cake."

"Oh, sure. Come on in and I'll get them for you." *I guess Zoe's wrong about her after all.*

"No, that's OK. I'll just wait here." There wasn't a hint of guile in her face.

"Don't be silly. Come in."

"Well, OK." Kate was smiling in such a way that would have made Zoe want to slap her, if she had been there.

Gathering Kate's things, Steve placed them into her hands. She dropped the carafe by accident, which was only hard plastic, but when they both tried to retrieve it, they bumped their heads. You could have heard the sound across the room. Kate fell sideways across a chair.

"Oh, no! Kate, are you alright?" Steve looked genuinely worried. "I think I've twisted my ankle." Sitting up she rubbed it and tried unsuccessfully to get up.

"Here, let me help you." Steve's strong arms easily lifted Kate into a standing position. She was slender and not very tall so it was no effort at all on his part.

"Do you think you can walk?"

"I'll try." Putting her weight on her ankle caused just a small twinge of pain.

"Ouch! That really hurts. I must have really hurt myself. I'll just hobble back to my house and put some ice on it. Don't worry. It wasn't your fault. I guess I'm just a clumsy fool."

"No, you're not. My head must be harder than even I thought. Let me walk you over to your house. Please."

Steve practically carried Kate to her house, never allowing

her foot to touch the ground. Once inside, he helped her onto her couch.

"Thank you so much, Steve. You don't have to stay. I'm a big girl. I can take care of myself." Kate tried not to look too pitiful. She didn't want to overdo it.

"No, I'm going to put some ice on your ankle then I'll go. Where are your towels?"

Giving him directions to her linen closet and the kitchen, she relaxed on the couch, thinking how this little accident couldn't have worked out better if she had planned it. What more could she want? She had Steve in her home, waiting on her like a doting father. She suppressed a sly smile when he returned with the ice wrapped in the towel. Placing the ice-filled towel gently around her ankle, he stood up and surveyed his work.

"I think that will help a lot. Can I get you something while I'm here?"

"Oh, no. You go back to work. I can manage. I'm sure I can make it to the kitchen to fix a late breakfast. Thanks for all your help."

When he didn't move toward the door, Kate looked at him expectantly.

"I tell you what. I can't cook very well. My wife did all that, but I can run to a fast-food place and pick up something for you. What about that?"

Not wanting him to leave the house, she quickly said, "Oh, no. I'm not much for fast-food. Plus, I wouldn't want you to go to all that trouble. Why not fix me a bowl of cereal? That's all I eat in the morning anyway."

"Sure, I can do that."

He went back into the kitchen and opened and closed cabinet doors until he found the bowls. Next he searched for the cereal. There was a small tray on the counter. After gathering all the things needed for breakfast, he placed the tray on Kate's lap.

"Steve, you have been so nice and helpful. I sure do appreciate a neighbor like you."

"Oh, it's nothing. I'm sure you'd do the same thing for me."

"You bet." *I'd do a whole lot more for you if you'd let me.*

"Well, I better go. Listen, Zoe's going to cook tonight. Why don't I bring you over a plate of whatever she's preparing. If you'd like, Zoe could come, too."

The mention of Zoe instantly spoiled her good mood. "No, that's OK. I'll manage."

"Are you sure?"

"Yes. You go home now and work."

As soon as Steve left, Kate jumped up and threw the soggy towel into the washing machine. She had too much to do around the house to just sit. Hopefully he won't come right back right away or else she'd have to grab the towel out of the washer and lie back on the sofa.

That evening Zoe was busy preparing spaghetti for supper. Steve leaned against the kitchen island and chatted with her about her interview.

"It went fine. I really liked the company and the people seemed extremely nice. The pay would be exceptional."

"Wow. Sounds like a dream job. When will you hear from them?"

"They are going to make a decision next week. We'll see."

"Zoe, you don't sound too enthusiastic about the job. What gives?"

"Dad, I know it would be a dream job, but it may be someone else's dream. I really want to work with art and artists. After all, I did get a degree in art. Remember?"

"I guess you're going to have to keep looking then. What if they offer you the position? What are you going to do?"

"I don't know. Anyway, how was your day? Did you get to the bottom of your stack of paperwork?"

"Maybe not to the bottom, but I got a lot done with the house so quiet."

"Is that supposed to be a hint?" Zoe was giving Steve a mock frown.

"No. I love having you here. It's just that I'm the type of person who does better work when it's quiet, that's all. I did have a little commotion this morning after you left."

"Really? What happened?"

"Kate came over to retrieve her cake plate and coffee carafe."

Zoe immediately stopped what she was doing. "You've got to be kidding! That woman doesn't give up, does she?"

"Zoe, she just came to get her things. She needed them today. When she accidentally dropped her carafe, we both bent down at the same time to get it, bumped our heads, and she fell over a chair. She twisted her ankle and I had to help her home."

"Oh, I'm sure she loved that." Zoe was unsuccessful in keeping the sarcasm out of her voice. "What's her house look like?"

"To tell you the truth, I didn't notice. It was clean. I had to wrap her ankle in ice, so I really only got a good look at the kitchen."

"Wait a minute! You actually rendered first aid to her? I don't remember you being so compassionate with Mom."

Steve shrugged. "I thought I'd take her a plate of spaghetti after supper since she's hurt her ankle."

"Dad, I'll take it over there. You two have spent too much time together today."

"Zoe, you're being silly." Steve knew there was no use arguing with her, so he dropped it. He didn't care if Zoe took the food to Kate's.

After supper Zoe proceeded over to Kate's house, while Steve cleaned up the kitchen. Zoe noticed he seemed to be fine with Zoe taking the food instead of him. That certainly made her feel better.

After knocking on the door, Kate looked through the peephole and groaned. She had expected Steve to come with her supper, even though she told him not to bother. She opened the door with a bright smile, which Zoe didn't return.

"Come in, Zoe. I wasn't expecting anyone at this hour."

Zoe wanted to laugh in her face, but she held back. *I imagine this woman gets visitors at all hours.*

"Dad told me you had injured your ankle so we thought we'd

bring you some supper. This way you can stay off your leg. It seems like you're not as injured as Dad thought. That's good."

"Your father was so nice. I guess he told you what happened. The ice pack really did the job. I bet your Dad really pampered your mother."

Zoe had no intention of discussing her parents' relationship with Kate. While Kate took the food in the kitchen, Zoe looked around the living room. Yes, it was very clean, but her taste leaned toward the tacky. The art work was cheap and so was the furniture. *There is no way my father could think this woman is anything like Mom. She has no taste and she's too forward.*

When Kate returned, she motioned for Zoe to have a seat on the couch. Zoe would have just as soon sit by a cobra.

"No, I really have to go."

"I hope we can become good friends, Zoe. I'm sure we have a lot in common."

This chick is out of her mind. I have nothing in common with her. I've got to get out of this nuthouse before I say something I'll regret.

Since Zoe didn't respond to Kate, she walked over to the door and opened it. Once Zoe was out of sight, Kate rolled her eyes and closed the door.

Boy, is she rude! I bet she's just like her mother. No wonder that sweet Steve and his wife are getting a divorce.

Walking into her house, she called for her father, but he was watching television in his bedroom.

"I'm back from the hussy's house. By the way, she's doing just fine," Zoe said loudly. Steve got up and came into the living room.

"Zoe, I think you're being mean. But, I'm glad she's better. Kate seems very nice, but you never know who's going to sue you. We need to be as friendly and helpful as possible to her for awhile."

"Well, if she sues us, she can get some new furniture and pitch that tacky junk she owns into the landfill." Before he could respond, Zoe was heading to her own bedroom. It had been a long day.

The next day, after Catherine loaded the last group of students onto their school bus, she noticed Zoe sitting in her car in the parking lot. Zoe waved, got out of her car, and approached her mother.

"What's going on? I didn't expect to see you today." Catherine never ceased to enjoy spending time with her daughter. She smiled brightly, even though she was quite tired and her back ached. She had taken four groups on tour today and her whole body suffered from it.

"I thought I'd surprise you and take you out to supper."

"Zoe, I know you don't have a job yet. You can't afford to be taking me out to eat. You need to save what money you do have."

"Mom, I got some spending money from Dad. He told me to take a friend to supper if I wanted. Since you're one of my friends, I selected you. No more arguments. We're going out to eat!"

"I'm really tired so this is a special treat. I don't have to worry about fixing anything tonight. Let me go get my purse."

Zoe accompanied her mother to the apartment. As she was walking, she wondered if her mother ever got scared living alone in this big building at night.

"Mom, do you get scared at night here? I mean, it's a large, deserted building after 9:00 p.m."

"No, not really. Actually, there is a night watchman here from nine to six in the morning. I feel secure with him here."

"That makes me feel so much better. I do worry about you, Mom." Catherine put her arm around Zoe and marveled at having such a caring daughter.

"I love you."

"I know you, too, Mom."

Catherine applied some more lipstick and put it into her purse while Zoe looked out at the courtyard. She noticed there were quite a few lights from the street that shone into the courtyard. Because of light, there were no dark corners or shadows where someone could hide. She was beginning to feel much better about her mother's living conditions now.

Both were chatting away as the security guard unlocked the

front door for them. They walked hand in hand toward Zoe's car. Several other vehicles were also parked in the same vicinity, such as three small vans and one large bus, all belonging to the museum. After buckling up, Zoe started her car and they sped off toward a new restaurant Zoe had discovered. They never saw the blue truck wedged suspiciously between the bus and one of the vans.

After getting settled into their booth, Catherine noticed that Zoe wasn't looking like she was too happy to be there.

"What's wrong, honey? I thought you were excited to try this new restaurant. The menu has a wonderful variety. I'm in the mood for some fish tonight. What do you think you'll order?"

"Mom, I didn't know this place was going to be so noisy. I wanted us to be able to relax and talk. That's the only thing I'm disappointed about. I saw a waiter taking some pasta dish to another table. I might try that."

"Well, did you have anything specific to talk about or did you just need some girl talk?"

"Both." Zoe stopped talking when the waiter came up and took their orders. Catherine waited for him to walk away.

"I'm all ears now. What do you want to talk about?"

"It's about Dad."

"What about Steve? Is something wrong?"

"Oh, it's nothing like that. He's fine. It's our neighbor I'm worried about. She's a real hussy."

"Really? Do you think your father is interested in her?" Catherine could feel a lump forming in her throat.

"You know Dad. He doesn't have a clue what this woman is up to. He thinks she's just a friendly neighbor, but I've seen the way she looks at him. She makes every excuse in the book to come over.

The other day she fell in the kitchen and supposedly hurt her ankle. He had to help her hobble back to her house. She's so transparent. I plan to keep my eyes on her. Dad doesn't need to get involved with anyone, but especially her. Your divorce is not final yet. Plus, I don't see Dad as the kind of man that will be fast on the trail of another woman. Do you?"

"I don't think so, but what do I know? I didn't think we'd ever get a divorce. I really thought he'd forgive me and we could work things out." Catherine's voice sounded like she was going to cry and she hated that.

"Mom, I'm sorry. I shouldn't have brought this up. It's just that this woman makes me so mad and I wanted to talk to you about it. I'm sorry." Zoe sounded like she might start to cry, too.

"Boy, we're a mess! We came here to enjoy each other and some good food. Why don't we change the subject and talk about you? Do you like the house your father lives in?"

"It's alright. It's not like our home at all, but the neighborhood seems nice and safe. It doesn't matter anyway. I don't plan to live there too long."

"What are your plans?"

"As soon as I find a good job, I'll be moving. You were right, Mom. After living abroad and having my own apartment, I'm not going to be happy living with Dad. I really don't think I want to live with anyone right now. I want to enjoy my freedom as long as I can."

"What do you mean as long as you can?"

"I mean until I get married. You know what I mean."

"I'm afraid I do know what you mean and it makes me a little sad. Zoe, marriage isn't like prison, but that must have been the message either your father or I gave you since you believe marriage takes your freedom away. Am I right or wrong?" A pained look crossed Catherine's face as she thought how she and Steve may have poisoned their daughter against marriage.

"To be frank, marriage is a drag for the woman. Dad pretty much did whatever he wanted, but you were stuck taking care of a child and the home. You seemed to have had the most work dumped on you, while all Dad did was go to his job. I know I've simplified that some, but that is my honest assessment of your marriage."

"Zoe, if we gave you that impression, then I need to ask for your forgiveness. Marriage was never a prison sentence for me. I didn't work because I wanted to stay home and raise you. Yes, your father was gone a lot on business, but, believe me, it wasn't all fun and games for him to be away from his family.

I think in his mind he really thought by working his way up the ladder of success, he was doing the best thing for his family. Of course, I believe he might see it a little different, now that we're getting a divorce."

"Mom, I always felt you were a little unhappy with Dad. Am I wrong?"

"What I was unhappy about was that your father was gone so much. I got very lonely without him. It's not a valid excuse for my behavior, but I had that short fling because of the loneliness. It was the biggest mistake I've ever made and it has cost me so, so much."

Zoe reached over and squeezed Catherine's hand. They finished eating their supper with only a little small talk. Talking about Steve and Kate had caused the evening to lose some of its luster. When they got back into the car, Zoe looked extremely grieved.

"What's wrong now, sweetie?"

"This was supposed to be a treat for you, but I feel like I made you uncomfortable and depressed. I'm sorry, Mom. I should have been more discreet and not dumped my worries about Dad on you."

"There's nothing to be sorry about. I loved the dinner and spending time with you." Catherine gave Zoe a light kiss on the cheek while Zoe started the car.

Pulling into the museum parking lot, Catherine told Zoe not to park. She'd ring for the night guard and go straight to her apartment. She didn't like Zoe to be on the road too late at night. Zoe didn't argue with her mother and drove off when Catherine had reached the museum door.

"Did you have fun tonight?" A familiar voice carried across the night wind. A chill ran down Catherine's spine and the hair rose on her neck. Catherine, in her fright, pushed the buzzer repeatedly. Looking over her shoulder, she saw no one, but she knew who was hiding in the shadows. She was almost ready to call 911 when she saw the night guard sprinting over to the door.

When he saw it was Catherine, he dropped his scowl and smiled as he unlocked the door.

"Where's the fire? You don't usually ring more than once or twice. I was all the way in the back of the museum. That's why I took so long to get here."

Not wanting to divulge the reason for her fright, she thanked him and walked as fast as she could to her apartment. Once inside, she fell across the couch in tears. That voice from the dark scared her like no horror flick ever could. *Why is he stalking me? What am I going to do? Should I quit my job and move? Should I call Steve? God, help me to know what to do.*

After calming down she realized she had let Austin put her into a panic. Although she was scared of him, he was not going to run her off. Besides, he could follow her to wherever she relocated, so why run.

Tears of regret and sorrow spilled down her cheeks when she thought about the safety of her old home and her old life. None of this would be going on if she had just been satisfied with what and who she had. Why had she been so weak to fall for a crazy man? She cried herself to sleep that night, right there on the couch with her clothes still on.

Waking up several times in the night, she would lie there listening for any sound. She was startled once when she heard a voice outside her courtyard. Listening intently, she eventually realized it was a drunk out on the sidewalk talking to a companion. She fell back into a fitful sleep.

When the sun finally rose, Catherine was exhausted. One look in the mirror told her she would not be the freshest looking tour guide today. Dark, puffy circles under her eyes made her appearance look old and tired. A long shower, numerous cups of coffee, and extra cosmetics were going to hopefully make her look and feel a little bit more human.

Kate was up bright and early for her ritualized morning beauty treatments. She never went a day without pampering her face and body in the hopes of looking young as long as she lived. After she fixed her hair and dressed, her appearance in the long mirror on the back of the door affirmed that the time spent was worth it. Blowing a kiss at her image, she walked into the kitchen to fix breakfast.

The phone rang, but upon seeing who was calling, she ignored it. Kate was bored with all the men she had dated lately. She was going to put all her attention on Steve. He didn't seem like a loser like the other men did. He had a steady job and was quite nice looking. She decided to skip breakfast. Watching her calories was so important the older she got.

Seeing his car alone in the driveway, she determined this would be the day she'd invite him for supper. After knocking on the door, she saw Steve pull back the curtains to see who it was. He opened the door a little cautiously. *I bet Zoe's tried to discourage her father from seeing me. I'll show her.*

"Hi, Steve. I came over to invite you over for supper tonight. Of course, Zoe's welcome, too. I thought I'd make a meatloaf. Do you like meatloaf?" Her face looked as innocent as a child's.

"Sure. I haven't had homemade meatloaf in a while. Let me call Zoe to see if it's convenient for her." Her smile never left her lips while he dialed Zoe's number. Inside she had a deep desire to slam down his phone in Zoe's ear.

"Zoe, Kate wants to know if you and I would like to come over tonight for meatloaf. I was calling to see if you had other plans."

Kate could just imagine what Zoe was saying on the other end. Steve was patiently listening to her talk then abruptly said his good-bye. He looked sheepishly over at Kate.

"She said she's already gotten a headache. She was just planning on coming home and going to bed. I hope she's not getting sick."

"Well, if she goes to bed without supper, what are you going to do? If she can't come, you could come over and eat, then later take her a plate. She might feel like eating later." *Who could argue with that logic?*

"I don't know. I'd feel a little funny leaving Zoe at home when she's maybe coming down with something."

"Oh, I know how it is to have a bad headache. You just want to curl up in your bed and be left alone. The quieter the house, the better."

"I guess I could come over for a little while." Kate saw him wavering.

"Then it's settled. I'll see you at 6:00." She walked away before he could answer, grinning all the way to her front door.

When Zoe arrived home later that day, she trudged into the house, playing the part of a woman with a massive headache. Steve took one look at her and led her to her bedroom.

"Honey, I want you to get in bed and rest. That will be the best thing for that headache. Can I get you some aspirin or something?"

"No, Dad. I'll just rest. Maybe later I'll feel like fixing you something to eat."

"You don't need to worry about that. I'm going over to Kate's at 6:00 for a quick meal then I'll bring home a plate for you."

Zoe could feel her blood boil. This was not going the way she had planned. She thought Steve would stay with her if she was feeling bad.

"Dad, do you really need to go over there? Can't we just spend a quiet evening together, just the two of us?"

"That would be great, but I'm sure Kate's already prepared the food. It would be rude for me not to go."

Seeing that her father wasn't going to budge, she asked him for some aspirins and lied across the bed. She kept her eye on her bedside clock. Around 5:40 she rose to freshen up then walked into her father's office. Steve looked up and smiled.

"You look like you feel better. Do you?"

"Much better, Dad. I think I'll go with you over to Kate's, if that's OK with you?" *I'm not letting you go to that vulture's house alone.*

"That's great. Let me make one quick phone call then we'll leave."

Kate had been periodically checking to see if Steve was walking across her lawn. The last time she looked, she saw Steve and Zoe. Disappointment and a little bitterness rose up in her, but she answered the door with a big smile.

"I'm so glad you both could make it. Zoe, your father said you were sick. I'm surprised to see you." *Surprised and irritated.*

"I'm feeling much better and I couldn't let my father come here alone. It might have made him feel awkward, you know?"

"I don't know about that. Your father and I have become fast friends."

Steve was just looking around the living room, basically ignoring the conversation. His mind was on the great-smelling meatloaf. He could hear his stomach start to growl. Zoe and Kate stopped talking and were just sizing each other up, when Steve started walking toward the kitchen.

"Kate, that meatloaf smells wonderful. I can't wait for us to eat."

"I hope it tastes as good as it smells. The table is all set. You two go sit down in the dining room and I'll bring out the food." Zoe noticed it was set for only two. When she heard dishes rattling in the kitchen she knew Kate was getting another place for her.

After taking a few bites, Zoe reluctantly had to admit, only to herself of course, that the food was really delicious. There was no way she would encourage Kate by complimenting her. Steve might add his admiration for her cooking then Kate would assume she was making headway in her plans for Steve.

Later in the meal, when Kate purposely brushed up against Steve while serving dessert, Zoe saw red. Kate had tried to ingratiate herself to Steve all through the meal. It was sickening. Zoe had had enough of her little feminine wiles and she wasn't going to remain quiet anymore.

"Kate, I wish you would quit running after my father." Immediately, the silence was deafening in the room. Kate stared with mouth ajar at Zoe then shot a glance at Steve to see his reaction.

"Zoe, that was extremely rude of you, especially since we are guests in Kate's home. I think you ought to apologize." Steve looked as angry as he sounded, but Zoe only lifted her chin in defiance.

"Zoe, what do you have to say to Kate?"

"You don't want to hear what I'd like to say to Kate!"

Kate realized that this could be her shining moment since Steve was so upset with Zoe. Although Zoe's words really only made her mad, she decided to play the wounded victim. She burst into tears and jumped up to run into her bedroom. After slamming the door, she put her ear up against the door to hear what the repercussions of her actions would be.

"Zoe, you need to leave right now. I can't tell you how ashamed I am of you at this moment. I have never seen you so rude. Go home now!"

"But, Dad, she is trying to get her claws in you. Why can't you see the obvious?" Zoe hated for her father to be so mad at her. Angry tears began to roll down her cheeks as she stormed to the front door.

After she left, Steve walked to Kate's bedroom door and knocked softly on it. Kate had to quietly move back so he wouldn't know she had been eavesdropping.

"Kate, can you come out? I'd rather not talk to you through the door."

Kate, with tear-stained cheeks, slowly opened the door. Steve took her hand and led her back into the dining room.

"I can't apologize enough for Zoe's behavior. I don't know what's gotten into her. Maybe it's the divorce. She and her mother are very close."

The touch of Steve's hand sent a shiver down her spine. She dropped her head so Steve wouldn't see the gleam in her eyes.

"It's OK, Steve. I forgive Zoe. She's probably so mixed up about the divorce that she doesn't know how to control her emotions. I guess the evening's ruined. Maybe it would be best if you went home, too."

"I don't mind staying and helping you clean up."

"No, you go. I'm sure you and Zoe have some things to discuss."

"You bet we do. But, listen, Kate. I want to make this up to you in some way. Maybe I can take you to dinner."

"That won't be necessary." While Kate had a downcast face,

inside she was jumping for joy. *Thank you, Zoe. Just look what you've done!*

"No, I insist. We'll go out sometime this weekend, if you're not busy."

"I'll have to check my calendar, but I think I might be free."

Steve walked to the door, turned around, and said, "The food was delicious. Thank you so much for having us over."

"You're welcome." Kate's voice sounded as sorrowful as possible without being overly dramatic. When she closed the door, she felt like she could have turned cartwheels.

Steve entered his home and slammed the door. Zoe was watching the tube in the living room, but she jumped to her feet when Steve blew into the room like a tornado.

"Zoe, what was that all about?"

"Dad, I was just asking Kate a legitimate question. She is running after you and I don't like it."

"First of all, Zoe, I think you're wrong about Kate. Second, even if it's true, it's none of your business. I'm a grown adult and I don't need my daughter watching over me. I'm not some senile senior citizen! I can handle myself and my relationships without any help. I want you to drop all of this immediately. Do you understand?" Zoe had never seen her father as mad as he was right then. She decided to back down for now.

"Sure, I won't say another word about what Kate is trying to do, but if you get tangled up with her, I feel sorry for you."

Steve didn't even respond, but went straight to his bedroom and slammed the door. Zoe sat back down and starred at the television. She wasn't really watching it anymore because her mind kept playing back what Steve said, over and over. She began to wonder if she could stay much longer in this house. She refused to watch her father make a mockery of himself with that woman. How he could not see Kate's devious ways was beyond her. Men could really be blind when it came to sly, little vixens like Kate.

Zoe picked up today's newspaper off the coffee table and began to search the want-ads. She just had to find a job soon and move out.

Session 11

Catherine walked into David's office with a slight frown on her face. After seating herself, he looked intently at her, waiting for her to start.

"Well, it's been another eventful week. Since we got together last, Austin approached Zoe at the museum. He didn't really let her know who he was, but I'm sure he knew she would tell me about the encounter. He wanted me to think he could invade any part of my life. One night recently, he waited in the parking lot for me to return to the museum. I was coming home after dinner with Zoe and when I walked to the museum door, he called out to me. I am quite concerned and frightened about his stalking."

"And you certainly should be. This man could be dangerous. Have you spoken to your boss yet?"

"I did. I was so afraid she'd let me go, but instead, she is very supportive of me. Mrs. Talbot told me if he comes around the museum to harass me, she's calling the police."

"Did you call the police when he was waiting in the parking lot?"

"No. I guess I should have, but I never saw his face. He could have denied he was there. I'm just glad the museum has a night watchman. I'm sure Austin has figured out I live there."

"Have you told Steve?"

"No! I told Zoe not to say a word to him. The last thing I need is Steve being involved. Anyway, although officially we're still married, in so many ways he's not my husband anymore. I can't ask him to defend me, especially against my ex-lover!"

"Catherine, I have mixed emotions about that decision of yours. I understand what you're trying to do, but I also know that sometimes we need to ask for help, even from people we are hesitant to ask.

Austin is obviously a man who has no respect for women. Sometimes that type of man will only listen to another man, especially if that man is assertive towards him and lets him know he means business."

"I hadn't thought about that. I tell you what. If this thing with Austin escalates, I'll get Steve involved. Will that make you feel better about my safety?" She was grinning over his fatherly protectiveness.

"Yes, but Steve needs to be careful, too. This Austin could be a loose cannon. It may require police involvement before it's all over."

"Why doesn't he just leave me alone?"

"There could be numerous reasons. He may be so out of touch with reality that he thinks you really desire him and need to be man-handled a little to see things his way."

"Boy, if he thinks that, he really is out in left field."

"I want you to keep me posted on this, and don't hesitate to call me if something occurs between sessions."

"I will. I promise. Right now, I'm happy at the museum, but I wonder what the will of God is for my life. Maybe this situation is a warning to move."

"I can tell from that statement that the Holy Spirit is certainly working in your life. That's the very topic we were going to discuss today."

"What is?"

"The will of God. Many people think the will of God is something hidden and we must search and search for it. They think if they don't find it, they are out of God's will and will have to settle for second best in their lives."

"Now that you mention it, I think that's what I believe."

"Let me ask you this. If you wanted Zoe to do something as a child, would you have made it difficult for her to know what you wanted done?"

"Of course not."

"God is the same way. Colossians 1:9 states that God has the responsibility to let His will be known to a believer."

"If that's true, then why is it so hard to discover it?"

"Because we are not to seek His will, but Him. When we find Him, He will disclose His will. As we have intimacy and enjoyment in the Lord, He will reveal what He wants us to do. The will of God is surrendering our life to Christ and letting Him live His life in us. It's really that simple."

"Boy, I never thought of that. I have slowly been loosening my grip on my life so Christ can live in me, but it's hard."

"It's hard because you are not fully surrendered. It would be like driving with one foot on the gas and one on the brake. That expression, 'Let go and let God,' is really a little nugget of truth. We need to take our hands off the steering wheel and let God take us where He wants us to go. He doesn't need a co-pilot."

"I know in my heart you're right. I've got to let Him have the reins."

"Also, we often feel our sin nature will prevent us from knowing God's will so we strive to be perfect. We wrongfully believe we have to get our spiritual house in order before we are useful to God. Believers forget that they are holy and righteous already, but not because they've done anything holy and righteous, but because Christ and His holiness and righteousness reside within us. We can't do anything holy in and of ourselves. Just read Isaiah 64:6."

"I know in my mind that is true, but I feel so dirty because of Austin. These feelings are a real hindrance to my spiritual life."

"Have you repented and asked for forgiveness?"

"Yes, I have."

"God knows your heart. If you have done these two things, then you are forgiven indeed. You just need to claim God's promises, like the one in 1 John 1:9."

Catherine wrote that verse in the little notebook she always brought to her counseling sessions. She liked to look up the verses at home and ponder their meaning before she went to sleep at night.

"Catherine, you need to remember that Satan wants you to feel defeated. Don't give in to his temptations."

"Temptations?"

"Yes, temptations. He is tempting you to feel worthless and dirty because he knows you'll act like you're defeated if you feel defeated. He's whispering in your ear that God couldn't possibly forgive a person as sinful as you."

"You know, that's exactly how I have been feeling, but I'm going to memorize this verse in 1 John and use it against Satan."

"That's good. Also write down James 4:7. That will be helpful, too. Now, let's go back to our discussion of knowing God's will. Don't be paralyzed because you don't know God's will. Walk in faith and He will close and open doors as He sees fit.

Another thing is, don't tell yourself that if you desire to do a certain thing, it can't be God's will. Of course, I'll not referring to sin. Many people think God always wants them to do what they don't want to do. That's just not true. He wants you to enjoy serving Him. He may give you the desire to do a certain thing because that's what He wants you to do."

"That's what I've been thinking. I really love my job and I sometimes feel a little guilty because I do. I guess that's silly, isn't it?"

"It's not silly, it's just wrong thinking. It's especially incorrect to think God is mean and wants us to always suffer through life. While He tells us we will suffer, that's not because He likes for us to endure pain.

I'll tell you in a nutshell what is God's will: Surrender your life and allow Christ to live through you. That's it, but I'll break it down a little more for you, if you'd like."

"Yes I would. I feel I can use all the spiritual guidance I can get."

"Write down the verses that go with each point I'm going to make. I have seven points concerning the will of God.

First, He wants everyone to be saved. Not everyone will accept His Son, Jesus Christ, as Savior, but that's His desire. Write down 2 Peter 3:9. Second, He wants you to surrender to Him and be transformed. Romans 12:1. Third, walk in the Spirit. Ephesians 5:17-19. Fourth, submit to the authorities over you. Ephesians 6:5-8. Fifth, live a holy life, one not conformed to this world. 1 Thessalonians 4:3-5. Sixth, rejoice in the Lord, always giving thanks. 1 Thessalonians 5:16-18. Seventh, if you are suffering because you are in God's will, remain faithful to the Lord and do good. 1 Peter 4:19. Do you have any questions?"

"Not at this time. I plan to read all those verses, then meditate on these seven points and implement them into my life."

"Please, remember this: you can't do these things in your own strength. You must daily ask the Lord for His strength and power. As you allow Christ to live in you, these things will become part of your everyday walk with Him."

"I think I do have a question now. I don't want to wait until next time we get together. What does it really mean to walk in the Spirit?"

"Basically, walking in the Spirit is living out the will of God. Like I said before, when we surrender daily to Christ and allow Him to live through us, we will be in the will of God. I'll give you a few verses to write down and study later. Ephesians 5:8-10, Colossians 1:10-12, and Romans 8:3-4. We should let the Spirit guide and control us, avoiding sin as we live our lives.

Galatians 5:16-26 gives some practical advice on what to avoid and what to embrace. I think if you study these verses I have given you, you'll have a pretty good idea of what it is to walk in the Spirit."

"All the Bible knowledge you share with me means so much. Before I started coming to you, I was little more than a nominal Christian. We saw how that worked out for me, didn't we!

Even though in some ways my present life is just a shadow of my former pampered life, I feel more fulfilled and content than I ever have. The only big problem I have right now is Austin. I'm going to turn this situation over to Jesus and see what He wants done with it."

After discussing the problem of Austin for a while longer and deciding various actions to take, Catherine left Mr. Hill's office feeling more secure and a little less like a victim. She planned to highlight those verses David gave her in her Bible when she got home.

Saturday evening Zoe left home to go to Catherine's to spend the night. She couldn't stomach seeing her father take Kate out on a date, even though he kept emphasizing that it wasn't a date. Steve told her she had been rude and he was going to make it up to Kate. Zoe had a hard time understanding why he had to make it up to Kate. That woman's feelings hadn't really been hurt. She just acted pitiful that night to get Steve's sympathy.

When Steve picked Kate up, he noticed she was a little under-dressed for the restaurant in which they would dine. He thought about saying something to her, but decided against it. What if she got offended? It's so much easier when a guy is married. He doesn't have to worry about such things. Wives just seem to naturally know what was appropriate to wear.

Kate's skirt was a little too short and her blouse was a little too low. He thought he'd try one tactic that might help his dilemma.

"You might need a sweater. It can get chilly in some of these restaurants." *Maybe a sweater would hide some of that exposed skin.*

"You're so sweet to be concerned about my comfort. I think I'll be fine. I'm always a little hot anyway." Steve decided to leave that comment alone.

The only thing Steve could think about talking about with Kate was the weather. After a few pleasantries, they rode in silence to the restaurant. When Kate saw where they were going to dine, she started clapping her hands together like a child.

"I've been dying to eat here. Most of my previous boyfriends were too cheap to take me here. Steve, you must be rich!" Steve felt his cheeks redden in embarrassment from her inappropriate comment.

Once inside it was clear from the other patrons' clothing that Kate was not dressed appropriately for this restaurant. While the hostess led them to their table, he fully expected Kate to become alarmed and want to leave. Instead, she acted like she was in her element. She couldn't stop smiling, in spite of people, especially the women, giving her disparaging looks. Steve felt a little uncomfortable, but he never frequented this place anyway, so he figured he wouldn't ever have to see these people again.

From the way she ordered her meal and what she ordered, he knew Kate was used to fast-food and take-out, contrary to what she had said earlier. When she asked for catsup with her steak, he almost audibly groaned. She was a beautiful woman, but had little knowledge of social etiquette. He found himself feeling deeply sorry for her.

After eating supper, he hoped they could slip out without much notice from the other customers. Surely, she wouldn't order dessert. Most women didn't since they were always watching their weight.

"Steve. I can't tell you how much I've enjoyed this meal. This is the nicest meal I've ever eaten. I'll remember this as long as I live. I don't want the evening to end. Can we order some dessert?"

When he saw her excitement over this occasion, he wanted to kick himself for thinking such harsh thoughts about her. She couldn't help it if she had been raised without proper social training.

"Certainly, we can order dessert. I'm glad you're enjoying yourself. I hope this makes up for Zoe's behavior."

"It more than makes up for it! Steve, don't be hard on Zoe. She's just a kid." *Maybe I'll score points with Steve if I act sympathetic to his kid.*

"She's in her early twenties. She's more than a kid, but I know what you mean. She's got a lot to learn about life and about people."

Kate knew that being critical of Zoe would backfire in her face. She had to appear as if she was an understanding ally because blood is thicker than water. If it came down to it, Steve's allegiance would naturally be with Zoe. He didn't have to know the truth that she couldn't stand even the sight of his daughter. Oh, how she wished Zoe would move away, and soon.

When they drove home, Kate wondered how she could make the evening stretch out a little longer. Her conceit would never allow her to think that Steve might just want to go home and go to bed. When it came to women, she felt he was a little shy, that's all. After all, he had been married for quite some time. He was out of practice. Kate just needed to be patient and let things between them blossom slowly, as she just knew they would.

Pulling into her driveway, she let out a contented sigh. She wanted Steve to know she was putty in his hands. Of course, she knew she would have to make the first move.

"Was that a yawn I heard?" Steve was smiling at her.

"No. I was just reliving our dinner together. It was so special. I hate to see the evening end."

"Well, as they say, 'All good things must come to an end.'"

"I know." She sighed loudly again.

"I guess I'll see you around. I'm glad you had a good time."

Steve just sat there, waiting for her to exit his car. She debated leaning over and giving him a small kiss, then decided against it.

"Thank you, Steve. I'll have to have you over again soon."

"That's not necessary. I think we're even now."

Reluctantly she opened the door of his car and got out. When she got to her door, she turned around and waved good-bye. He returned the wave and backed out of her driveway. Kate went inside feeling a little defeated. Why couldn't he see what a catch she really was?

Catherine and Zoe were eating supper at the apartment, enjoying their meal and as well as each other's company. Catherine had fixed all of Zoe's favorite foods and was really enjoying watching her eat every last bite.

"Mom, that was delicious as usual. It's amazing that you can still fix gourmet meals in that little kitchen. It's a far cry from your kitchen back home."

"Well, I do have to improvise sometimes, but the secret to

good cooking is not the size of the kitchen. My mother had a small kitchen and she was an excellent cook. She believed, as I do, in using only fresh ingredients and just the right spices."

"I vaguely remember her, since she died when I was only six, but I do remember her homemade cookies. They were delicious!"

"Yes, they were. By the way, how's the job search going?"

"It's going. I'm sending out resumes everywhere. I never heard from the advertising agency where I had an interview. It's just as well. That really wasn't what I was interested in. I'd love to do something art related, but those types of jobs are scarce, even when the economy is good. Of course, Dad is in no rush for me to move, but I've got to get out of there."

"Really? What's wrong? Are you and your father not getting along?"

"Oh, it's nothing like that. It's our neighbor."

"That woman you mentioned that is attracted to Steve?"

"Exactly. She had us over for dinner the other night. She was brushing up against Dad in such a suggestive way. It was sickening. I finally asked her why she was running after my dad."

"You're kidding? What happened?" Catherine was shocked that Zoe could be so bold, but a tiny part of her wanted to praise her for it.

"Dad demanded I apologize and Kate ran into her bedroom crying. She is such a drama queen. I left and went home. Dad was really mad at me, but I didn't care. I told the truth and I didn't feel I had anything to apologize for."

"That was rude of you, Zoe." *I feel like a hypocrite because I'm truly happy Zoe acted ill-mannered toward that woman.*

"Not you, too, Mom? She had it coming."

"We need to be polite in someone else's home. I thought I taught you better than that." Catherine's tone was far from condemning, but Zoe felt a little chastised.

"Mom, let's don't argue. We've had a nice evening. I don't need a lecture. You don't have any idea how this woman is acting toward Dad. He only took her out to eat this evening to make it up to her, but I bet she's reading a lot more into it. She was probably so ecstatic that my rudeness turned into a dinner date."

"They went on a date tonight?" Catherine felt like someone had stabbed her in the heart. It was taking all her effort not to bust out crying.

"He kept saying it wasn't a date, but I don't know what you'd call it when a man takes a woman to an elegant restaurant."

"Your father is a gentleman. Maybe he was trying to just make it up to her since she had her feelings hurt."

"First of all, he could have just sent her flowers as an apology. Second, I bet her feelings weren't really hurt. She's one tough, little cookie. She's a schemer and I'm sure she's used to getting what she wants." Catherine didn't know how to respond to Zoe's last comment. The thought of Steve out with another woman made her feel so depressed, but she didn't want to ruin the evening. They had really been enjoying themselves. Zoe didn't seem to realize how much it hurt Catherine to hear about Steve's little date, so Catherine attempted to keep the mood upbeat.

"Let's talk about something else, why don't we?"

"Sure, Mom. I'm sure this makes you mad and I don't blame you."

Oh, Zoe, if you only knew how this news cuts me to the core. What's worse is that I'm to blame for things getting to this point. If I hadn't had an affair, I'd be home with Steve right now.

"How's your job going? You haven't run into that man anymore have you?"

Catherine tried to keep her face straight and not alarm Zoe by telling her about Austin stalking her in the parking lot. This was Catherine's problem and she would deal with it.

"No, I haven't seen him. The school children are so precious. I just love to introduce them to the wonderful art we have here. Of course, a few of them act bored, but most really enjoy looking at all the different types of art we have. We even have a little scavenger's hunt. The children have to look for certain things in each painting in a particular room. The child with the most correct answers gets a little prize. It's so much fun watching them go from painting to painting, filling out their little scavenger sheets. Mrs. Talbot has made the children's program here so educational and fun."

"I'm so glad you're enjoying yourself, Mom. You deserve it. You were and are such a good mother, I know the kids must really like you."

"Well, I don't want to brag, but I've had teachers send me little thank-you notes from some of the students. Would you like to see them?"

"I'd love to read them."

The topic of Steve and Kate never came up again that evening or the next morning, to Catherine's relief. She needed to be alone in order to process the idea of Steve going on a date.

Kate decided to wait a few days before she made another move on Steve. She didn't want to spook him by being too aggressive. While some men might like that type of woman, she could tell Steve did not. She couldn't help but notice he hadn't picked up on the fact that she was attracted him. Much to her annoyance, he just didn't seem too intrigued with her.

The thought that he might still have feelings for his wife was like a pesky fly that she had to keep brushing away. Of course, to her thinking, he couldn't be that much in love with her since they were getting a divorce, unless his wife was the one wanting the divorce. Steve had never given her any details of their troubles. She would have to try another tactic with Steve. She had to think of a way to get his mind off his wife and onto her.

There was one bit of hope. It had seemed to really bother him that Zoe had insulted her. That alone had resulted in their little dinner date. What could she do to make that happen again? Certainly, Zoe wouldn't cross her threshold anymore. Her opinion of Kate was far too low. It had to be on their turf this time. But, what could she do to make Zoe insult her again? She smiled wickedly as an idea started to form.

Zoe was usually gone during the day, mostly going on interviews. This little plan would have to take place in the evening when Zoe was home. Plus, sometimes Steve worked away from home and didn't come home until after six. She made it a point of always keeping tabs on all their comings and goings. Consequently, Kate's little scheme would have to be at night.

Getting in her car early Tuesday morning, she headed straight for the big flea market across town. Parking at one end, she planned to scour the whole place until she found just want she wanted. It could take all day, but she was willing to make the effort.

"Can I help you? Are you looking for something in particular?" The man with the five o' clock shadow and grimy t-shirt grinned at Kate, hoping she would be his first real customer of the day.

"Actually, I am. I'm looking for anything that has to do with Paris. Do you have anything like that?"

"I've got a miniature model of the Eiffel Tower. It's $10."

"I don't know. I was wanting to buy several items and I've only got $20." She had more, but he didn't need to know that.

"I'll let you have it for $7 since you're so pretty."

Smiling radiantly at him, she handed him the $7, then took the package back to the car. As it worked out, it did take all morning to find exactly what she was searching for. When the last item was purchased, she drove home and proceeded to wrap each one. All four gifts were wrapped in beautiful paper and topped with bows. Looking in her closets, she finally found the perfect basket to fit them all in. If Zoe's reaction to her gifts was what she anticipated, she could almost bank on another date with Steve.

Thursday evening Kate noticed that Steve and Zoe were both home. This was her chance to try to wedge herself into Steve's life again. After double-checking the bows on the gifts, she left her house and walked over to Steve's. After knocking on the door, Zoe looked out the window, saw who it was, and yelled, "Dad, there's somebody here to see you." When Steve opened the door, Kate saw Zoe leave the living room in a huff.

"Come in. What have you got there? Christmas is a long time away."

"Oh, this isn't Christmas and it's not for you either. It's for Zoe."

"For Zoe?" Steve got a look of relief on his face. He didn't want to start exchanging gifts with her.

"I just feel like I've gotten off on the wrong foot with her and I want to try to make amends. I spent all day Tuesday shopping for some things that I think will remind Zoe of her days in Paris." The basket was getting heavy so Kate placed it on the coffee table.

"Zoe, Kate's here to see you." No response.

"She might be on the phone. Let me go get her."

Knocking on her bedroom door, Steve elevated his voice some so Zoe would hear him. Still no answer. Kate pretended she was admiring a piece of artwork on the wall while Steve attempted to get Zoe to open her door. Finally he just opened her bedroom door and went in. Because he closed the door tightly after him, Kate couldn't understand what was being said, but she could imagine. A minute later Steve returned to the living room.

"Kate, Zoe will be out in a minute. She's getting dressed. Have a seat." Kate could tell that Steve was feeling a little uncomfortable about Zoe's behavior in her bedroom. There was no telling what she had said.

"That's OK. I know all about wanting to get spruced up for company."

Steve didn't reply because Zoe was definitely not getting herself "spruced up" for Kate. There was no telling how she would look when she came out.

"Oh, Zoe. It's good to see you. I have some presents for you."

"What for?" Zoe didn't try to hide the contempt in her voice.

"I feel we've gotten off on the wrong foot and I wanted to make it up to you. I shopped all day, searching for things I thought you'd like."

Zoe started opening up the gifts. She could tell none of the items were new and all of them looked cheap and tacky. After opening the last one, she just stared at Kate. Kate could feel a blush coming up on her face.

"I don't know what to say. Really."

"Oh, you don't have to say anything. I just hope you like your gifts."

Zoe looked at Steve and rolled her eyes. She wasn't fooled one bit by this little charade. Kate was up to something, that much she did know.

"I really don't have any room for these things."

Steve's mouth dropped. He couldn't believe his ears. Was this discourteous young woman really his daughter?

"Zoe, I'm sure we can find some place to put these things. What do you say to Kate?"

It infuriated Zoe to be talked to like a child. She glared at Steve, then over at Kate.

"Thanks, Kate. If you don't mind, I need to take care of some things in my room." She left the gifts and wrapping on the floor, like they were yesterday's newspaper.

"Sure. Zoe, I was just trying to bring back memories of your time in Paris. I'm sorry if I messed up." Kate wanted to get up and slap Zoe across the mouth, instead she smiled sweetly.

Steve didn't know what to say. Zoe's behavior was out of line, but she was an adult. He couldn't make her like Kate. He didn't understand it. Kate had been so nice and Zoe had misinterpreted everything she had done. Kate was no threat to her. What was the big deal anyway?

"Kate, again, I apologize. I hope Zoe has not hurt your feelings again." Steve's face was a picture of disappointment and hurt. "Maybe you just need to give Zoe some time and not try to push yourself on her."

"Oh, I wasn't trying to be pushy. If that's how I came off, I truly am sorry."

"Maybe 'push' wasn't the right word. I guess what I'm trying to say is, 'Just leave Zoe alone for awhile and I'm sure she'll come around.' She's never acted like this before in her life, but she's never seen the break-up of her parents' marriage, either."

Kate sat there wondering what to say next. She felt that tears at this point might be a little overly dramatic. She wasn't sure what her next move should be.

"Kate, why don't I walk you home? It's late and you don't need to walk alone at this time of night."

Kate stood and let Steve open the door for her. She walked

slowly to her house, wondering what she could say to get him to come in.

"How about some coffee? I have a fresh pot I brewed just before I come over."

"Not tonight. I have a big day tomorrow and I need some sleep."

As he entered his house, Steve decided to leave Zoe alone for now. The more he talked to her about Kate, the less productive it became. He'd just let things be. He understood that she was hurt just as much as he was about the break-up of his marriage. That could be the only explanation for her behavior lately.

"Dad, are you alone?" Zoe's tone had a defensive edge to it.

"Of course." He wanted to say, "Do you really think Kate would come back here after you were so rude," but he didn't want to press the issue.

She came out of her bedroom and Steve could tell she had been crying. His heart ached for his little girl. This whole situation was hard on everybody.

"Dad, I really don't appreciate you talking to me as if I was a child."

"Zoe, it's late and I don't want an argument with you right now. I need to go to bed. I've got an early morning meeting. Can this wait?"

"I guess it can. I just want to say that I don't want Kate to come between us."

"Between us? For crying out loud, Zoe! She's just a neighbor."

"She considers you to be more than a neighbor. Women can tell these types of things."

"Zoe, go to bed. Quit worrying yourself. As far as I'm concerned she's just a neighbor and that's where it ends. Period."

Zoe went over and lightly kissed Steve's cheek. She hadn't done that type of thing in a while. He returned her affection with a big bear hug. Steve didn't want anything to come between them either.

Meanwhile, Kate cut off all the lights and went to bed. She

needed the house to be dark and quiet so she could concentrate. Steve was going to be a bigger challenge than she had anticipated. He never had shown any real attraction to her. All his overtures had been strictly neighborly and platonic. There was no spark to ignite this relationship into a flame. What could she do to rectify that?

Sometime during the night as she tossed and turned, an idea formed in her head that was a little risky, but if it turned out the way she anticipated, it would be so worth it. Cutting on her stand lamp in the wee hours of the morning, she reached for her address book. After a little search, she found his name, Randy. Yes, he was coarse, aggressive, and a little crazy, but he just might fit the bill. She hesitated before dialing his number, remembering how she was so glad to get this man out of her life over a year ago.

Before she lost her courage, she punched in his number and waited for him to pick up. Yes, it was early, but she didn't care if she woke him up or not. After five rings she was ready to hang up, then he answered, sounding either very sleepy or very drunk.

Swallowing hard, she said, "Randy, this is Kate."

Coming alive, he said, "Boy, this is a surprise hearing from you. If my memory serves me correctly, you dumped me last year. What's the problem, you can't get 'randy Randy' off your mind?" His disgusting laugh made Kate want to slam the phone down, but her determination to see this plan through kept her on the line.

"I have to admit I do miss you, Randy." She made a face like she was going to vomit. It was a good thing he couldn't see through the phone.

"Well, when do you want to get together? You want to come to my house now. I'm still living in the same trailer off Etowah Drive. Come on over and we can have a few beers and get reacquainted."

There was no way she was going to that dump again. Besides, her plan involved Randy coming to her house.

"No, thanks. It's a little early for beers, wouldn't you say?

Why don't you drive over here this evening and I can fix some supper?"

"Actually, my car got repossessed. Can you pick me up?"

Kate was ready to throw in the towel and tell Randy to forget she ever called, but he was the perfect man for the job. She'd have to bend a little to make this work.

"I'll pick you up around 5:00. Is that good for you?"

"Sure. It's not like I have anything else to do. I'm between jobs right now." That didn't surprise Kate one bit. What a bum!

Kate hung up and looked out the window. The sun was just coming over the horizon. Steve's car was already gone. She hoped he'd be back before dark tonight. She wanted him to see that another man was at her house. She knew it was going to take an extraordinary event to get Steve's attention.

While driving up to his trailer later that day, old memories of this place almost caused her to turn the car around. Randy was abusive and repulsive. While he was good-looking, that didn't compensate for his bad manners and aggressive ways. When she parked beside his trailer, he came immediately out, like he had been watching for her. It looked like he hadn't shaved in several days and his jeans looked like they hadn't been washed in weeks. Kate smiled and waved for him to get into her car. *I bet he smells, too.*

"Hey, Baby. You're looking fine as usual. I can't wait to get back to your place to rekindle that old flame we had."

"Randy, let's just take it slow, OK?"

"It's never been slow for us before. Why should it be now?"

She didn't have an answer, so she just continued to drive, eyes on the road. Randy was unpredictable and she had to handle him with kid gloves, otherwise, this whole idea could blow up in her face. Keeping her focus on the goal of getting Steve made this whole ordeal palatable. Kate knew she was going to have to get Randy a little tipsy to get him to react the way she wanted. Of course, that would be quit easy. Just offer Randy alcohol and he was like a pig with slop; he wouldn't know when to stop.

When they entered her house, Randy immediately started to

make his move on Kate. She wasn't having any part of it, but she had to be careful not to anger him too soon.

"Let's have a few drinks first, OK?" Kate cooed.

She walked into the kitchen and poured him a strong one. Knowing he would want her to drink, too, she poured ginger ale in a tall glass for herself. After gulping down a few drinks, Randy wanted to get a little romantic and lead her to the bedroom. Kate had to be very cautious. Randy was a mean drunk. Just one wrong look or word would send him into a flying rage. The time for that was yet to come. Glancing at her clock, she realized Steve should be home any minute. Then it would be "show time."

Putting on some soothing music seemed to keep the lid on Randy's behavior. She had to get him drunk, but not so drunk he passed out. Watering down his drinks would do the trick.

Pretending she wanted to close the blinds for privacy, she peered out to see if Steve's car was there and it was, thank goodness. She hadn't heard his car pull into the driveway for the music playing in the living room. Everything was set. Now the trick was to get Randy to play his part, unbeknownst to him.

"Randy, let's go out in the yard." She walked to the front door, wanting him to follow. Nightfall would be in an hour or so.

"What for? I'm perfectly happy here."

"I want to show you something. Please."

Randy was getting that look on his face that she knew from experience meant trouble. But he needed to be in the yard for her plan to work and there had to still be some daylight.

"Well, I'm taking the drinks outside. You can just sit in here by yourself." She opened the door and exited without looking back. He reluctantly followed.

"OK. Now what?"

"I'd like for you to move some of my yard art around. I want you to rearrange it for me because it's so heavy."

"You've got to be kidding! I'm not your yardman. I'm going back in."

"You better do it. I didn't bring you over for nothing." She gave him a defiant look and put her hands on her hips to show she meant business.

"Kate, you better shut up and quit that sassy talk right now."

Kate went over to grab Randy's hand, but he pushed her away and sent her flying to the ground. When he ran over to her, not knowing his intentions, she kicked violently at him. Randy grabbed her by the hair and began to drag her toward her front door. Screaming at the top of her lungs, Kate desperately tried to pull her hair free from his hands by scratching them as hard as she could. This only made Randy get more violent with her.

Steve had just sat down to watch television when he heard a woman screaming. At first he thought it might be someone just playing around in the neighborhood, but when the shrieking continued, he jumped up. Looking out his front window he witnessed something like you'd see on some reality show. Kate was being violently jerked back and forth by her hair. She was covered in dirt and the man assaulting her looked like he was demon-possessed. Steve expected to see him foaming at the mouth he was so crazy.

Running into the yard, he yelled for him to stop, but Randy was too caught up in the moment. Randy's actions reminded Steve of someone trying to wring a chicken's neck. Without hesitation, Steve raced across the yard and hit the man broadside, like a football player. He and Randy hit the ground with a hard thump. Without a moment's hesitation, Randy jumped up and pulled a knife, while Kate lay motionless in the grass.

Without any thought of his own safety, Steve kicked high and knocked the knife out of Randy's hand. A neighbor must have called the police because a squad car raced up Kate's driveway and two officers leaped out of their car. One checked on Kate while the other yelled for Steve and Randy to get on the ground. Steve complied instantly while Randy lunged at the officer after retrieving his knife. A shot rang out and Randy was dead before he hit the ground. The momentary silence was deafening. Steve laid on the ground face down in shock and disbelief.

The officers jerked Steve to his feet. It was only after explaining the situation and neighbors verifying his story that they released him from their grip. Steve ran over to Kate to see the extent of her injuries. She was crying, bruised, and dirty, but no permanent damage had been done. Her hair looked like she had been in a cyclone, so Steve bent down and smoothed down her hair as much as possible while he comforted her with soothing words. She reached up and stroked his cheek, giving him a broken smile.

Two ambulances came, one to transport the body to the morgue and the other to take Kate to the hospital to be checked out. At first she protested, but Steve convinced her to go. Reluctantly, she allowed them to place her into the ambulance. Steve waved good-bye and told her he would check on her when she returned. The ambulance doors were shut and off they went.

Steve never saw the smile of satisfaction that spread across Kate's face as the doors were shutting. What a day! For Kate, there was no grief or despair over Randy's violent death nor for the part she played leading up to it. Kate saw this as a win-win situation. She reasoned Randy was permanently out of her life, which was a relief, and Steve's concern for her condition was a sign he just might be falling for her. Sore head or not, she was feeling good!

Zoe and Catherine met on Saturday for lunch at a little café near the museum. Little tables with umbrellas were scattered around the courtyard, making it a perfect place to eat when the weather permitted.

"Mom, I just love this place. It reminds me of Paris. There are so many outdoor cafes like this over there. This restaurant puts me in such a good mood."

"Great. I did notice that little frown you had earlier is gone now. Is everything OK?"

"It's Kate again," Zoe stated sarcastically.

"Who?"

"Kate, our next door neighbor. The one who has eyes for Dad."

"Oh, her. What's going on?" Catherine always felt a little pain in her heart when Zoe mentioned that woman.

"Well, she is nothing but trash."

"Zoe, that's not a nice thing to say about anyone. People are made in God's image, so no one is trash."

"Mom, you've changed. There was a time you would have said the same thing about a woman like her. Now you're getting all preachy on me."

"Zoe, Christ has changed me. I'm submitting more and more to Him and letting Him live through me. Consequently, the old Catherine is gone."

"I kinda liked the old Catherine." Seeing the look of hurt in her mother's eyes, she quickly added, "But, I like the new one, too."

"I love you, too. Now, tell me about Kate."

"Oh, yeah. She had some trashy man, oops, I mean bad man over at her house who roughed her up a bit."

"That's terrible. Is she OK?"

"She's got a few bruises and she told Dad her head is very sore from being pulled across the lawn by her hair. She was at the hospital only for a few hours, so nothing serious is wrong with her. The thing that's got me upset is Dad."

"What's he got to do with this?" That pain in her heart sharpened.

"He tried to break it up. The police came and ended up shooting the man dead. It had the whole neighborhood in an uproar."

"Your father didn't get hurt, did he?" Panic began to rise in Catherine.

"Oh, no. He did tackle the guy, but Dad didn't even get a scratch."

"That sounds like your father. He can't stand to see anyone being hurt." *Except me.*

"Since then, Dad is checking up on Kate every single day. I'm afraid he's going to get attached to her. I certainly don't want her as a stepmother."

Catherine sat stunned by the news. The idea that Steve might fall in love with someone else made her physically ill. She just sat there, unable to look at Zoe for fear of crying her eyes out.

"Mom, are you OK?" Zoe saw that the color had left her mother's cheeks and she wasn't smiling any more.

"Yes, I'm OK. It's just hard to hear about your father being involved with someone else."

"Don't worry, Mom. If I have anything to do with it, she won't get entangled in Dad's life or mine. I can't stand her!"

Catherine smiled, knowing Zoe was trying to be supportive and loyal. How the tables had turned. She was the one who had always lifted Zoe up in the past. Now her daughter had to be the strong one.

"I think the reason your father is being so solicitous is because of his sister. She was beaten up very badly by a boyfriend when she was a teenager. Steve always blamed himself because he introduced them to each other. I'm sure that's the only reason."

"I never heard this story about Aunt Connie before. You're probably right. Dad's only being overly kind because of his past, not because he really cares for Kate." *Please, God, let that be the reason.*

Catherine's explanation made perfect sense and Zoe sighed with relief. She had gotten extremely worried that a relationship was forming between Kate and her father. Maybe she could stop being so tormented about Kate now. Sitting there in the sunlight, it began to feel as if the sun was shining a bit brighter. Zoe smiled and felt the burden of Kate begin to ease.

"If that woman had a man in her life that would resort to the type of violence you described, I can't imagine she and Steve having anything in common. Your father has always liked peace and calmness in his life. His business had enough confusion. He didn't want to bring that home, although he sometimes couldn't help it. His home was his sanctuary."

Catherine was thinking back when Steve's business phone would ring off the hook some nights when he was home. He didn't like it, but what could he do? That was just the nature of his work.

"Kate is one ball of confusion if you ask me. She's conniving, a sneaky little fox. I wish she'd move. I want to move, but part of me is afraid if I leave, Kate will go all out trying to get her hooks into Dad."

"Zoe, don't worry. Your father has a fine head on his shoulders. I think you can trust him to make the right decision about Kate." *Oh, I wish I could really believe that!*

Kate was tidying up the kitchen that evening when she heard that familiar knock on the door that always set her heart beating a little faster. She ran to the living room and sat in the recliner. Except for a sore head, she was fine, but Steve couldn't know that. She was going to milk this situation down to the last drop.

"Come in," she said weakly. The door was unlocked because she was expecting Steve to make his nightly visit to check on her.

"Well, you're looking better. I bet you feel better, too." Steve tried to sound as encouraging as he could. It broke his heart to see Kate still so affected by her ordeal.

"Thanks. I feel a little better. I don't know what I would have done without you. You saved my life, you know." She smiled sweetly and hoped Steve would feel like a hero. Men always loved to be knights in shining armor. Making him out to be a hero could only endear her to him.

"Actually, the policeman stopped that man dead in his tracks. I just knocked him down." Steve always felt a little uncomfortable when people attributed praise to him that rightfully went to someone else.

"What have you got in your hand?" She had noticed he had brought in a white bag. Like a child, Kate loved little surprises.

"I stopped by this little deli near my office to get you one of their delicious sub sandwiches. I figured you wouldn't feel up to fixing anything for supper." He handed it to Kate and she reached for it like an invalid. To Steve it appeared as if it took all her strength just to stretch out her arm.

"Thank you, Steve. You've got to stop spoiling me. I can fend for myself, although at times it is difficult. My head throbs so much. Sometimes I just have to lie down and rest from the pain." She sighed loudly for effect.

It never dawned on Steve that she seemed to be able to keep her house so clean for someone who was convalescing. Neither did he consider that her well-coiffed hair always looked like she had spent a lot of time on it. While she would have never fooled any woman, she banked on Steve being a typical man and not noticing details like that. Her mother used to say that housework was only noticed when it wasn't done.

"Well, I've got to get back to the house to do some paperwork. Have you been back to the doctor?" Steve looked genuinely concerned.

"Yes," she lied. "He told me I'd need to take it easy for at least three weeks. I don't know what I'll do if I have to recuperate for that long."

"Don't worry. I'll be checking in every day. Do you need someone to help you with the housework?"

"No!" she said a little too quickly. She was afraid he'd suggest Zoe.

"I can manage. It's just me here, so the house doesn't get dirty that much. But, Steve, that is so sweet of you to be so concerned."

"Any good neighbor would do the same, especially after all the trauma your body has gone through."

Kate was wondering how she could get Steve to think of her as more than a neighbor. She wanted their relationship to be much more personal. If she could marry a man like Steve, her worries would be over. She was sure he could provide handsomely for her. Of course, Zoe would be a problem, but she could handle her once she was her stepmother.

"If there's nothing else I can do for you, I guess I'll be heading home."

"I'll walk you to the door."

As she got up from her feet, she did feel a little light-headed. This was her opportunity to get Steve to stay a little longer. Falling forward to the floor, she made sure she didn't hit her head on the coffee table. Her head already was so sore that just brushing her hair was somewhat painful. Steve heard the crash and instantly ran to her side. She knew she couldn't fake being unconscious, but she could act a little dizzy.

"Are you OK, Kate? Let me help you up."

His capable arms lifted her up easily as he guided her back to her seat. It felt so good with his arms around her, only she wished it was for a more romantic reason.

"Do I need to call an ambulance?"

"Oh, no. I just need to sit here awhile and clear my head. I'm so sorry I fell. You run along now. I'll be fine."

Steve looked intently at her while he debated going home or staying another hour or so to make sure Kate was really OK. He needed to get back home and make some phone calls, but he'd feel terrible if she fell again and worsened her condition. Kate looked so pitiful, so he decided he could postpone his phone calls for an hour.

"I think I'll stay another hour, just to make sure. Is that alright?"

Kate wanted to shout it was more than alright, but she gently nodded her head and settled back into her recliner. It would be heaven if Steve would stay all night, but she didn't want to push it. If he could only stay another hour, she'd have to accept it and be satisfied, for now.

Steve cut on the television and started watching some ball game. It irritated Kate that he wasn't paying any attention to her, but at least he was there and that's what counted. Having him close was a comfort.

The whole time Steve was engulfed in the game, Kate watched him, like a cat patiently watching a mouse. She was going to make him hers if it was the last thing she did. The pity card couldn't be played much longer or he'd tire of looking after her. She had to come up with another plan, but what?

After the game was over, Steve stood up and stretched. He looked down at Kate and realized she had fallen asleep. Taking the afghan off the sofa, he draped it across Kate and tiptoed out. When he closed the door, the sound woke her up. She had only been taking a little cat nap, so she was wide awake in an instant. If felt so good to have Steve wait on her. How could she keep his attention?

Stepping into his living room, he saw Zoe was working on a crossword puzzle. He loved having her live with him. It made the house seem less depressing and a little more like a home. Smiling at her, he took a seat on the sofa next to her. Knowing she wouldn't be interested in hearing about Kate, he decided the topic of Catherine would be more than acceptable.

"How was your lunch with your mother?"

"Fine. We found this great little café near the museum. What have you been doing tonight?" Zoe knew he had been over at Kate's.

"I was checking on Kate." He always felt uncomfortable talking to Zoe about Kate, seeing as she disliked her so much. Since she brought up the subject, he'd go along with it.

"You were gone quite a while." Zoe's voice had a hint of condemnation.

"When she got up from her recliner, she fell and I thought I better stay a little longer. I think being dizzy made her fall."

"Oh, she's dizzy alright or should I say ditsy."

When Steve didn't say anything, she continued, "I take that back. She's not ditsy, she's very calculating and she thinks she's got you fooled."

"Fooled, how?" Steve felt himself getting a little defensive now.

"She's not as hurt as she let's on. She's going to use her injuries to keep you running over to her house. She's no fool."

"I think you're wrong. If you had seen how that creep manhandled her, you'd be singing another tune. I'm surprised he didn't break her neck."

"I'm not saying she's not sore. I'm saying she's not in such bad shape that she needs a nursemaid over there all the time."

"Zoe, as usual, you're not seeing the real picture. I'm just being neighborly. I'm sure she'd do the same for me."

"Oh, I don't doubt that for a minute. She has her sights set on you. Wonder what her next move will be when she's healed?"

Monday morning Steve called his attorney. He hadn't heard from Catherine and could only surmise that she had begun her new life in earnest. It was good that she and Zoe had a good relationship and he would do all he could to encourage that. Unfortunately, his relationship with Catherine appeared to be over and he didn't see any point in putting off the divorce. In the beginning, he hadn't been in any rush to get one because in the back of his mind he thought they might reconcile. Obviously, that wasn't going to happen. He was ready to get on with his life. He had been feeling like he was living in limbo. Of course, he told himself, this decision had nothing to do with Kate. After all, she was just a neighbor.

His attorney advised him to get with his own financial advisor to discuss his financial situation then he would draw up the divorce papers. He knew his financial stability wasn't all that great. It was hard to believe that there wouldn't be as much as he thought there would be to divide with Catherine. He wanted to be fair to her. She had been a good wife and mother all those years, but he had to live, too.

His advisor could see him right away. He had had a cancellation and would be happy to fill it. Steve gathered what paper work he had at home and drove to his office. After reviewing all the graphs, bank statements, and such, Steve discovered he was in worse shape than he imagined. The slump in the real estate market had forced him to sell the house at a deep discount. After paying off the mortgage, there was less than $50,000 left in equity.

His stocks had taken a big hit, also. The financial reward for all that hard work those many years had almost evaporated. It was like the clock had been reset for twenty years earlier. Boy, he hated to tell Catherine the hard truth. He never wanted her to hurt financially, but what could he do? It wasn't his fault the economy had gone bust. He picked up the phone and called her number. She answered immediately and sounded glad to hear from him.

"Catherine, we need to talk." His voice told her this was not going to be good news or a friendly chat.

"Ok, let's talk." She had hoped he was calling to get together with her, but no such luck. He was sounding much too business-like.

"I think it needs to be in person." Steve tried not to sound so negative, but he couldn't act cheery, not when there was little to be cheery about.

"I guess you're calling to tell me there's someone else in your life, right?" Catherine felt the tears starting to well up in her eyes.

"Good grief, no. This has to do with financial matters." He knew Zoe had filled Catherine's head with who-knows-what concerning Kate.

They decided to meet later that day at her apartment. She told him to park in the back, next to her little courtyard. Arriving on time, he got out and surveyed the courtyard's beauty. He could tell everything had been recently cultivated. The flowers were beautiful and abundant throughout the area. He was quite impressed with all she had done in such a short time. He started thinking about how she had made their home such a showplace and his heart started to ache.

Knocking on her backdoor, he hoped the pain he was feeling wasn't registering on his face. Catherine opened the door and he was struck anew by her beauty. The last few times he had seen her were under stressful circumstances, but in this casual meeting he realized how much he still really loved her. Of course, too much water had gone over the dam in their relationship. He believed they had come to the point of no return.

Once inside, Steve was amazed at all she had done to decorate the apartment. The colors she had chosen were so tasteful and vibrant. She really knew how to make even a humble abode a place of charm and style.

"Would you like something to drink?"

"No, thank you. I just ate."

Steve sat down and began to place papers all over the coffee table. Catherine realized this was going to be a serious meeting. She had hoped they could relax and chat awhile, but Steve was acting like he was preparing for a board meeting. She tried to mask her disappointment.

"I want to come right to the point, Catherine. I talked to my attorney about getting the divorce rolling and he suggested I meet with our financial advisor first."

At the mention of divorce, Catherine closed her eyes momentarily to force the tears not to fall. This was it. The beginning of the end.

"We are not in very good financial standing. We made very little on the house and our stocks have plummeted. There will be very little to divide, but we will divide equally what is left."

"That's fine." Catherine's voice was not much louder a whisper.

"I had hoped there would be enough for both of us to buy a house each, but that's going to be impossible. It's nice that you have a permanent set-up here. I guess I'll just continue to rent the house I'm in for now. I'll have the attorney draw up the divorce papers and when we sign them, I'll have a check made out to you for your half."

Catherine just nodded. Her voice caught in her throat and it was all she could do not to cry out, "I still love you! Don't you love me?"

If Steve had made up his mind about the divorce, Catherine was not going to contest it. Although she was deeply hurt, she deserved this divorce because of her infidelity. Pain would be the consequence of her actions.

"I think that's more than fair, Steve. Just let me know when the papers are ready and I'll sign them." She smiled faintly to let him know she was not upset, although deep inside she was dying.

"Catherine, I'm so glad you've moved on and made a life for yourself. It makes me feel better about this whole divorce thing. I won't have to worry about you now."

Unable to hold back her tears much longer, she stood up and motioned Steve toward the door. She refused to break down in front of him. It wasn't pride. It was more a fear that she'd lose all control and Steve would be at a loss at what to do or say.

Picking up all his papers, he walked out the door and headed to his car. When Catherine saw his car pull away, she burst into tears, sobbing uncontrollably. Little did she know that Steve had to pull over into a shopping center nearby to shed his own tears.

Austin had watched the man, who he assumed was Catherine's husband, leave the courtyard. The fact that Steve was carrying a briefcase let Austin know this had not been a romantic meeting. Smiling to himself, he watched Catherine's apartment to see if she would come out, too. He had put two and two together and realized she was living at the museum. Obviously her marriage must be over, so this opened the door to romance Catherine.

After an hour he decided she wasn't coming out. This might not be the best time to knock on her door and let her know he knew where she lived. Not knowing the nature of her encounter with her husband, it might be best to leave her alone today. He could wait. He had all the time in the world to make her his own.

Meanwhile, Catherine washed her face and reapplied her makeup. She had a lot to do today and she didn't want to look like death warmed over. It broke her heart that Steve wanted to finalize the divorce. Had Kate been a factor in all this? He had denied any romantic feelings toward her to Zoe, but he could have been lying.

After a few jagged sighs, she walked into the museum. A school group would be coming after lunchtime. She had lost her appetite so she could utilize the time she would have been eating to check on the agenda for this group of children. She squared her shoulders and headed for Mrs. Talbot's office to pick up today's itinerary.

Kate decided to make Steve something delicious to thank him for all he had done for her. Getting out an old cookbook that belonged to her grandmother, she searched for the perfect meal. After some time, she settled on four recipes that any man would love-Maryland fried chicken, beaten biscuits, green bean casserole, and a triple-layer chocolate cake. That was southern eating at its best. Looking in her pantry and refrigerator, she discovered she had very few of the items she needed. A trip to the grocery store was in order. She didn't want to wait another minute. These recipes would take some time to prepare and she wanted the food to be ready for Steve's arrival home in the evening.

While she was gone, Steve arrived home early, both tired and depressed. His life seemed like a farce right now. He had been so sure that he wanted to divorce Catherine when she had that affair, but now he felt torn. He realized he didn't really want a divorce, but what about Catherine? She hadn't even flinched when he discussed the matter with her. He felt neither married nor single because he still loved Catherine, yet they were separated on so many different levels. From her actions, she had obviously moved on and he might as well, too. Yet, he wondered how a wife could move on when her husband was still emotionally anchored to her.

The idea of sitting inside his empty house after such a depressing day seemed like torture. Fresh air just might invigorate him. He went around the back of the house, pulled out a chaise lounge from the storage building next to the house and began to relax in the warm afternoon sun. It wasn't long before he was sound asleep.

Kate brought the groceries in and placed them on the counter. The cake should be prepared first, then the chicken. She hummed to herself as she baked the cake, fried the chicken, and rolled out the dough for biscuits. She couldn't wait to see the look on Steve's face when she presented her authentic Southern supper to him.

After all the food was prepared, Kate put everything in the nicest containers she had. Looking out the window she made sure Steve's car was still there and it was. Putting the containers in a large basket, she headed for his front door.

Ringing the bell and knocking on the door produced no response. A little part of her wondered if he was deliberately ignoring her. Anger began to stir her soul when she thought of all the time and expense she put into this meal. But before she blew her top, she decided she'd go around the house. Maybe he was on his back deck. When she walked around the corner of the house and saw him sleeping so hard out in the yard, she felt a little guilty about thinking he would deliberately not answer his front door.

Maybe she'd wake him up in a special way. Quietly she tiptoed to his side, leaned over, and kissed him lightly on the lips. Instantly, his eyes flew open. She had so startled him that in an attempt to jump up, he had flipped the chair on its side, which caused him to fall face first in the grass. Kate couldn't help but giggle. Unfortunately for Kate, Steve didn't find it amusing at all.

"Hey, what's going on?" Steve's angry expression immediately stopped Kate from laughing.

"I'm sorry. I didn't mean for you to fall out of your chair. I just wanted to wake you up and give you your supper." Kate gave him a winning smile.

"Supper?" Confusion sounded in his voice. He wasn't sure he was fully awake. What other explanation could there be for him not remembering that Kate was supposed to bring over supper? Or was she?

"Yes, I wanted to thank you for all you've done for me since I was attacked. You've been so kind and this is the least I could do."

"Well, that is very nice." After a few moments hesitation, Steve asked, "Why don't we eat it together?" He had no desire to eat by himself this evening. He was depressed enough.

"Sure, let me go set it up in your dining room. OK?"

Before he could answer Kate was walking swiftly toward his backdoor. Maybe she was afraid he'd change his mind. The aroma of the food trailed her and Steve's stomach began to growl. Jumping up off the ground, he brushed himself off and followed her.

Once inside, he noticed Kate had emptied her basket and was putting plates on the table. After washing his hands, he sat down and watched her at work. She really was a sweet woman and he wished he felt more attracted to her. Maybe when he was over Catherine he could find room in his heart for her. Yes, she was a little uneducated, but she was pretty and had a real knack for cooking. She would make someone a good wife.

Sitting down, she smiled as he scooped large quantities of food on his plate. It had been a while since his last home-cooked meal. As a matter of fact, Kate had prepared that one, too. Catherine was a great cook, but her cooking was more low-fat and healthy. Kate was a country cook. Her meals stuck to your ribs. Unfortunately, they also stuck to your stomach, hips, and thighs.

Kate nibbled at her food. She didn't want to gain an ounce of fat, so she had to monitor her food intake. Her chicken was delicious, if she did say so herself, but she didn't eat all she would have liked to. It was so satisfying seeing Steve wolf down his food. He must have been famished. This was one of her joys in life-seeing a man enjoy her cooking.

"That was delicious. I don't think I could eat another bite."

"What about dessert? I made a triple-layer chocolate cake."

"Wow, that sounds good. Why don't we let our supper settle, then we can have dessert?"

"That's fine with me. Why don't I clean up and you go watch television?"

"Are you sure? I can help you with the dishes."

"No. Go relax and I'll join you in a minute."

"Whatever you say. I'm too stuffed to protest."

After Kate finished the dishes, she went into the living room and sat next to Steve. Not sitting too close for fear of scaring him, she leaned back and relaxed for the first time that day. It wasn't long before Steve looked over and saw she had fallen asleep. It was too warm to cover her up, so he just let her rest as she was.

About an hour later, Kate awoke with a start. She hoped she hadn't been drooling or, worse, snoring. She touched her lips just to make sure they were dry.

"I'm sorry. I didn't realize how tired I was. I better go on home."

"You don't have to rush off. It gets lonely here sometimes. Zoe is out and won't be back until late. I'd enjoy having your company, unless, of course, you need to go."

"No, not at all. I'd be glad to stay for awhile. You know, I get lonely, too, living by myself. At least you have Zoe. I have no one."

When he had asked her to stay, her heart leaped for joy. He had never acted like he really wanted her company before and she hoped this was the beginning of a real relationship between them.

Steve didn't talk while his show was on. Only during the commercials did he engage her in conversation. It was only light conversation, but she didn't care. She was here with Steve and that's all that mattered.

"Have you tried that new restaurant they just advertised?"

"No, I don't like to eat at restaurants by myself."

"When I traveled a lot, eating alone was a way of life. It was always so good to come home and eat a home-cooked meal with Catherine and Zoe."

Kate wanted to steer the conversation away from his family, so she suggested they try the new restaurant together some time. Steve nodded, but didn't pursue the topic, so she let it drop.

After a couple of hours of cop shows, she had had enough. Quite bored, she decided to go home. She had hoped for a little romance tonight.

"I've got to go, Steve. I'll see you later."

"Sure thing. I want to thank you again for the delicious supper. Don't forget your leftovers."

"Oh, I put all that in some of your plastic containers and stuck them in the refrigerator. You can have leftovers tomorrow, if you like."

"Thanks. I really appreciate all the effort you went to."

Walking to the door, Kate wished he'd kiss her. She turned and faced him, but he just smiled and thanked her again. Disappointed by his lack of attraction to her, she smiled back and left feeling a little empty.

Catherine had an appointment with Mr. Hill the next morning. She could see that their time together was drawing to a close. She felt spiritually stronger than she had ever felt. The more she submitted her life to Christ, the more she was at peace with herself and the world. No, she was still melancholy over Steve, but she had accepted the fact that she would be divorced, no matter how much she loved him.

She couldn't imagine ever loving any man other than Steve.

Dating was not going to be an option for her. The rest of her life would be devoted to the Lord, Zoe, and her work at the museum, in that order. Getting on her knees, she cried out to God to help her with the chronic pain of losing Steve.

"Dear Holy Father, I praise you for all the good things You have put into my life. Thank You for the many years I had with Steve. Thank You for the wonderful daughter You gave me. Thank You for the apartment and job I now have.

Although I have been unfaithful to Steve, which means being unfaithful to You, too, your faithfulness to me has not wavered. You are so good and merciful to me, a sinner saved by your grace. I don't deserve all the good things You have given me over the years.

Please protect me from Austin. Remove him from my life and may he never harass me or Zoe again. Forgive me for my adultery and help me to accept the consequences of my actions. Please take the sting out of the hurt I feel. Help me to reconcile myself to a single life. I ask all of this in Jesus' holy name. Amen."

Rising to her feet, Catherine felt better and was ready to have her session with Mr. Hill. As she got into her car, she failed to notice the blue truck parked a block away. Austin followed her at a safe distance to see where she was going. When she pulled into the parking deck of the office building, Austin drove past, deciding not to follow her there. He headed back to the museum to wait.

While she was unbuckling her seat belt, her phone rang. Recognizing the number, she answered on the second ring.

"Mom, Dad's at it again."

"What do you mean, Zoe?" Catherine glanced at her watch. She couldn't talk long because she didn't want to be late for her appointment.

"Kate brought him supper last night while I was out, and he kept raving about her delicious cooking this morning. I'm so scared he's going to be blinded by her domestic charms." Her last phrase was spoken with as much sarcasm she could muster.

"Domestic charms? That's a new one. Zoe, I can't talk right now, but I'll call you later. Love you."

Session 12

Catherine walked into Mr. Hill's office beaming, even though her short conversation with Zoe had taken a little of the glow out of the morning. After taking her usual seat, he shut the door and sat down behind his desk.

"Well, you're all smiles today. Things must be going well for you."

David noticed Catherine's whole demeanor had changed and for the better.

"Actually, nothing has changed concerning my circumstances since I saw you last. I'm smiling because I'm content."

"Great! What brought about this contentment? Are things working out with you and Steve by some chance?"

"No, we're getting the divorce very soon. He brought the papers over to my apartment and he's ready to get it finalized."

"I'm really sorry to hear about that. I have prayed that there would be a reconciliation between you two."

"I know you've prayed about it. I have spent many hours begging God to soften Steve's heart, but to no avail. Steve has a free will and God's not going to force him to forgive me. Also, nothing has happened lately with Austin, but that doesn't mean it won't. You see, I'm relying on the Lord more and more. He's my Shield and Protector. I've quit worrying about Austin."

"Catherine, you've come a long way from the woman who first entered my office months ago. I can see you took it seriously about surrendering to Christ and letting Him live through you. I'm so proud of how far you've come. So, what did you want to talk about today?"

"Actually, I've come to say this will be my last session with you. You'll never know how much you've helped me. Although my life is turned upside-down, I'm more content than I've ever been. I can truly face the future with optimism. Who knows what the Lord has in store for me!"

"You know, I've been thinking you were about ready for our sessions to end. I don't say that often to my clients, but I can honestly say it to you. You're really living the victorious life."

"I'm hoping I can get Zoe to come to you. She really needs counseling. Our break-up has really affected her. Another thing that is causing her emotional distress is Steve's next-door neighbor."

"What about his neighbor?"

"She has her sights set on Steve and Zoe thinks she's a gold digger. This woman, Kate, has bent over backwards to try to get his attention. So far she hasn't succeeded, but she's not giving up."

"I would be glad to have Zoe come see me. Just have her give me a call and we can set up an appointment."

"I'll try. She's a little stubborn, but aren't we all at some time or another. Just like me being stubborn with God and trying to live my life my way. We see how well that worked out. I don't think Zoe has accepted the fact that we're getting a divorce. I think she's afraid Kate will interfere with our possible reconciliation. While I know this woman is attracted to Steve, I haven't gotten the impression the feeling is mutual.

Zoe also has this fear that Kate could turn out to be her step-mother. I can see why that would worry her. Since Zoe is living with Steve, she really doesn't have her own life yet. I think once she gets a job and a steady boyfriend, she'll be too occupied to be worried about Steve's love life."

Catherine's laugh at this point was a little hollow. David wondered if Catherine had some of the same fears Zoe had.

"Catherine, how would you feel if Steve formed a relationship with someone else?"

"I'd be lying if I said it wouldn't hurt me. It would kill me inside, but I would never make a scene or make things uncomfortable for Steve. After all, my actions caused this divorce in the first place.

I'll just have to lean more on Jesus, that's all. That's what He wants me to do anyway. I can't ever see me wanting another relationship, but what Steve does is his business."

"I believe you're serious about that. Don't you see how spiritually strong you've become. Your strength isn't from you; it's from the Lord. He's giving you the ability to handle all this. Write down Philippians 4:13 and study that daily. It will encourage you when things get more difficult."

"You mean things will get worse?" Catherine teased.

"We all have mountain top experiences, then we descend into the valleys. There's no one immune to trouble. Even Christians, as Jesus said in John 16:33, can expect hardships in life."

"Mr. Hill, that is one of many things I admire about you."

"What's that?"

"You really know your Bible. How can I be like that?"

"It didn't happen over night. One way to know the Bible is to read through the whole Bible once a year. Memorizing key Scriptures is vital, too."

"I'm going to start this evening reading through the Bible. I want to be able to quote Scripture as well as you."

"That's a great goal, Catherine. Studying your Bible is one of the spiritual disciplines that all Christians should be engaged in."

"Spiritual disciplines? What are those?"

"Spiritual disciplines are practices from which we can grow spiritually. For example, there are the disciplines of prayer, fasting, meditation, and several others."

"The word *discipline* sounds regimented, like God wants to put us in spiritual boot camp."

"I can understand what you mean, but actually you should discipline yourself to faithfully practice these things, not because God is forcing you, but because you want to get closer to Him."

"I see and you're right. I do want to get closer to God."

"Some people practice the discipline of simplicity. They unburden themselves from having so many material things. It's very freeing to live this lifestyle. Being frugal is not a burden when the goal is to be free to serve the Lord and enjoy the truly beneficial things in life."

"I just read a magazine about getting the clutter out of your life. Is that what you mean?"

"It's more than just making your home clutter-free. Having fewer possessions allows one to pursue intangible things, like prayer, study, and helping others. I don't believe people truly understand how 'things' weigh them down. Now I'm not talking about being homeless. I'm talking about having only those things that are necessary."

"You know, I'll have to admit that since I moved from that large home into a small apartment, it has been freeing. I didn't realize how much time I spent with maintenance alone on our home. You're right about it giving you a sense of freedom."

"We have to ask ourselves: do we own our possessions or do they own us?"

"My large home used to own me, that's for sure. So much money and time went into it. Steve was gone so much of the time, so we really didn't need to have such a large house. But we got caught up in the American dream. You know, the bigger the better. Praise God I don't think that way anymore. Even if I ever get another house, it will be small. I'd say extra small because it looks like it will only be me living there."

"I challenge you to keep your life simple from now on. The Lord has plans for you and you don't need to be tied down to material possessions. Stay free, just as you are now."

"I can't believe it wasn't that long ago that I talked about missing all the trappings of the good life. I really have grown, haven't I?"

"Yes, you have and you'll continue to grow as you submit more and more of your life to God."

"I have you to thank for my transformation."

"No, I was only your guide. Transforming people is God's work.

Second Corinthians 3:18 tells us that the Holy Spirit is the agent of transformation. He is changing us into the likeness of Christ."

"Well, I thank you so much for being my guide. God put you into my life. I know it was no accident."

"Well, I want you to know that if you ever need to come back, I'll be more than happy for you to return."

"To be honest, I hope I don't have to come back. That's no reflection on you. It's just that I hope to be in an even better place as time goes by."

"I know what you mean. You don't have to apologize. It's healthy to want to move on. I worry about my clients that never want to leave. It means they're too attached to me or they're not growing. If they're not growing after a few months, it's apparent they have not put the work into their spiritual and emotional health that they should have. Counseling is hard work. It's not just about sitting in a chair and talking, as some would like for it to be or imagine it to be."

"You've got that right. These last few months have been a mental workout for me. But, just like exercise, I can really see the results. Submitting to the Lord is hard. Of course, just like exercise, the more you do it, the easier it becomes. Once you trust Jesus Christ with your life, you can let go of most of your worries."

"Not all?" David grinned.

"You know what I mean. Not worrying about anything is the goal. I haven't gotten there yet."

"The Christian life is a journey. All believers have traveled different distances along the road to conformity to Christ. One person may just be getting started. Some are very far along the path. Of course, perfection won't happen until we're with the Lord."

"I want all this for Zoe. She seems so bitter now and again. I am not sure whether she's saved or not. She was raised in church, but we weren't active like we should have been. That's my fault."

"Actually, it's Steve's fault, too. Husbands and fathers are to be the spiritual leaders of their home. Unfortunately, many men don't lead. Ephesians 5:22-33 speaks of the family hierarchy. Of course, if the man won't lead spiritually, the mother is left with the responsibility, but that is not God's design.

But, let's not put all the blame on Steve. Since you were the one who had to be the spiritual leader, you may not have done all you could to raise Zoe in a Christian home. Am I correct or not?"

"Unfortunately, you're correct. We went to church, but that was about all. It was as if we were Christians on Sunday morning, but the rest of the week God didn't cross our minds very much. There was no family Bible study or prayer. I didn't even get Zoe in the practice of saying a blessing at meals or praying at bedtime. I guess I really messed things up for Zoe and for me. Zoe's spiritual malaize is my fault and I feel so guilty about it." Tears began to well up in Catherine's eyes.

"Catherine, God can take our mistakes and use them. He is a powerful and creative God. Don't act like Zoe's spiritual upbringing was all on your shoulders. God was and is still interested in Zoe becoming a Christian woman. He's not thinking that because you and Steve dropped the ball, in a manner of speaking, that Zoe's future is ruined and there's no hope for her. In addition, now that Zoe has become a young woman, she alone has to answer to God for her spiritual condition.

One thing you can do is pray for Zoe's spiritual condition and allow her to see what changes God has made in your life. Zoe needs to see you reading your Bible, praying, and especially living out your Christian faith. Some people say that religion is a private matter, but that's not true. Jesus was very public in ministering to people, praying, and teaching about God. He died a very public and humiliating death on the cross for us. The only thing He spoke of us doing in private was having quiet prayer time with God. Even Jesus went off alone to pray.

We are not to call attention to ourselves when we are praying or helping others. We want God to get the glory, not us. Do you understand what I mean?"

Catherine had dried her tears and she managed to smile before saying, "I do understand. Thank you for that word of encouragement. I felt like for a moment I was going to break down in tears. I couldn't stand the thought that I had completely spoiled Zoe's chances of having the abundant life in Christ I now have."

"God's not through with any of us. All believers have to go through the narrow gate and begin their journey on the narrow road that Jesus speaks about in Matthew 7:13-14. God's going to lovingly guide us to that gate. He won't force us to go through it, but if we do, He'll lead us on our journey to heaven."

"That's very comforting. We need all the help we can get."

"Well, I think we've covered all the bases today and I want to remind you again that you are welcome to come back anytime. My door is always open."

"Thank you so much, Mr. Hill. I hope I don't need to come back, but if I do, I won't hesitate. My next mission is to get Zoe to come for counseling. What advice do you have for persuading her to come?"

"Catherine, I would discuss with Zoe how much counseling has done for you. Explain that counseling is for people that need to work some issues out in their lives. She needs to understand she's not crazy. Some people think that a person must be insane if they need to go to a counselor. That's not true at all. It's like our need for certain medicine. Sometimes we need help to feeling better. Counseling is the same. Just about everyone could use it at some time or another. It's certainly nothing to be ashamed of. Be sure to get that point across to Zoe."

"I will."

Catherine got up from her chair and shook David's hand. He gently squeezed hers and walked her to his office door. She began to feel a little sad, knowing she probably wouldn't be seeing him again. He had helped her so much and she was so grateful to him. It was a bittersweet moment for her.

After Catherine left, David went back to his desk and began to pray. He asked the Lord to guide and direct Catherine. Zoe's willingness to come to his office was his next request. Because

God can do the impossible, he also begged Him to bring Catherine and Steve back together. This family needed to be reconciled.

After getting into her car, Catherine reached for her phone to call Zoe. Before she could connect with Zoe, the phone began to ring. She saw it was Zoe calling her.

"Hey, Sweetie. I was just about to call you. What going on?"

"Nothing really, Mom. I just called to see if you wanted to have lunch with me."

"I'd love to. I was going to suggest the same thing. Where do you want to go?"

"I'm craving a burger. Why don't we meet at that little burger joint near the museum? I love that place."

"That sounds good to me. What time?"

"Well, it's twelve o'clock now. Why don't we meet at one?"

"That would be perfect. See you then."

Once Catherine and Zoe got settled into their booth at the restaurant, they focused on their menus and waited for the waitress to arrive. After giving her their orders, both leaned backed and relaxed against the cushioned booth.

"How's your day been, Mom?"

"Well, I've hit another milestone. Today was my last day with Mr. Hill, my counselor."

"How does that make you feel?"

"Now you're starting to sound like a counselor." Catherine giggled and smiled at Zoe.

"You know what I mean. Are you happy or sad that this was your last day?" Zoe seemed genuinely interested.

"To tell you the truth, I'm both. I'm sad because I may never see Mr. Hill again, but I'm happy to know I've come so far. I'm ready to face the world relying on Jesus alone. So, you see, it's a little bittersweet for me."

"What do you mean relying on Jesus alone? I thought you had been doing just fine on your own." A little frown formed on her lips.

"The fact that I had an affair, no matter how brief it was, is proof positive that I was not doing a very good job running my life.

Had I been walking closely with the Lord that probably wouldn't have happened."

"Mom, you've been a wonderful person as long as I've known you. I blame Dad a lot for the affair. He was quite neglectful when it came to you and me."

"I have no one to blame but myself for the affair. Let's not throw any blame on your father. I wasn't forced to do what I did. I did it willingly and it was my own sin."

"Mom, you didn't use words like *evil* and *sin* until you started going to Mr. Hill. He changed you." Zoe's expression gave the impression she didn't approve of the change.

"Mr. Hill didn't change me; Jesus did. Mr. Hill only guided me to the truth and the truth was that I was just a nominal Christian."

"What's a nominal Christian?"

"It's a person who says she's a Christian, but she doesn't really have a relationship with Christ. She's a Christian in name only. In other words, she's a hypocrite and a phony."

"Mom, you've always been good. We went to church most Sundays. Doesn't that mean you're a Christian?"

"No, it doesn't. As Jesus said, 'You must be born again.' Just being good and going to church is not good enough. The Bible says all have sinned and fallen short of the glory of God. That means none of us are good enough to live eternally with God. Mr. Hill taught me to understand the Bible better and to apply what it says to my life."

"Mom, why don't we talk about something else?" Zoe was looking a little uncomfortable.

"Before we go to another topic, I want to say two things. First, I want to apologize for not being a true Christian mother."

"You have nothing to apologize for, Mom."

"Yes, I do because you're not the person God wants you to be and part of that is my fault."

"Well, thanks! I thought I turned out to be pretty good, especially compared to a lot of girls my age. You should see what they do."

"Zoe, if we just compare ourselves to others, we can always find people we are better than, as far as behavior goes. But, when we compare ourselves to Jesus Christ, we see how sinful even the best of us are."

Zoe realized at that point that her mother was right. Compared to Jesus she was very sinful. She began to feel convicted and it made her squirm a little in her seat.

"The second thing I wanted to say is I think you would benefit a lot from seeing Mr. Hill."

"Oh, great, now you think I'm crazy!"

"Am I crazy? I went to him because my life was in such turmoil. He helped me see the reality of who I really was and why I was so unhappy."

"I'm happy enough. I don't need to see a shrink." Anger briefly crossed Zoe's face.

"Mr. Hill is a Christian counselor, not a psychiatrist. Zoe, I feel you have a lot of pent up anger about the divorce. It would do you good to go to him."

"I'm not thrilled about your divorce, but I'm not suicidal about it, if that's what you mean." Zoe's flippant attitude seemed to raise its ugly head more and more these days. She didn't like talking to her mother like that, but all this talk of going to a counselor was putting her in a bad mood.

"I know you're not suicidal, but would you just consider getting some counseling?"

"I'll think about it, but I'm not making any promises."

"Fair enough. Now, let's change the subject. How's your job search going?"

"It's not going very far, that's for sure."

Catherine could tell that Zoe was still upset about the previous topic of conversation and drawing her out was going to take some effort. When Zoe was angry or upset, she tended to shut down.

"Have you had any offers?"

"No."

"Well, I know something will come along."

Their food arrived and Zoe concentrated on eating instead of conversing. Catherine took the hint and let her daughter quietly sulk.

Steve hadn't seen Kate in several days and he wondered what was going on. It wasn't so much that he desired her, but there were days that seemed more lonely than others and she could be a pleasant diversion. What he especially missed was her home-cooking. All he had managed to master was the microwave and his small charcoal grill. That grill was a joke compared to the one he had at his old house. With several gas burners and a warming tray, it had been a state-of-the-art grill, fit for a chef. Oh, well. He's only grilling for one, so what does it matter.

On his days off he caught himself looking out the window at Kate's house several times a day. Most of the time she was home and he wondered why he hadn't heard from her at all. He thought they had had a nice evening together when she was over last time. Catherine had always enjoyed sitting on the sofa with him and watching his shows so he just assumed Kate would, too. Maybe Steve had been married so long that he didn't know how to entertain like a single man anymore. On the other hand, maybe Kate was just busy and hadn't had time to come over.

To make things even more depressing, Zoe kept to herself when she was home, which wasn't often. Steve knew she was going on interviews and spending time with her mother. Other than that, he didn't have a clue what she did with her time. She was a little too old for him to give her the third degree about her whereabouts. Their relationship was strained enough without him making matters worse. He just wished she desired to spend more time with him. He wanted to have quiet evenings with Zoe, eating dinner and watching television together. Maybe that was too old-fashioned for her.

Getting up from the sofa, he looked out the window for the third time that day and saw Kate's car in the driveway. It wouldn't hurt to go over and just say hello. After knocking on her door several times, Steve saw her look out the window. For a brief moment he wondered if she was going to open the door.

"Hello, stranger. I haven't heard or seen you in awhile and I thought I'd come over for a minute. Of course, if you're busy, I can make it another time."

Kate smiled and opened the door. She wasn't her usual vivacious self, but she didn't act like it annoyed her that he came over either. Sitting on the sofa, she motioned for him to join her.

"Can I fix you something to drink or eat?"

"No. I'm fine. I just came over to see how you're doing."

"Things are going well. Nothing new is going on in my life right now. How about you?"

"Nothing new here either."

For a while the conversation just dragged. Kate was wondering if there wasn't too much to Steve after all. He seemed a little boring. Of course, he did have money, which was more important to her than his charm or lack thereof. She knew how to act interested, even if she was bored out of her mind with a man.

"I wish you'd let me fix you something to eat. When was the last time you had a good home-cooked meal?" Kate knew that Steve loved her cooking and this may be the only way to snare him.

"The last time I had a good meal was the last time you fixed it. The grill and microwave seem to be the only way I know how to prepare food. But, I hate for you to go to any trouble." Kate could tell he really did want her to go to the trouble.

"It's settled. You sit in the living room and watch television and I'll whip up something good for a late lunch." Steve rewarded her invitation with a big smile.

Later, after the food had been cooked and eaten, Steve and Kate settled back in their chairs in the dining room. Steve was stuffed and feeling a little sleepy. He wanted to go back home and take a nap, but that would be extremely rude. Noting his sleepiness, Kate suggested he stretch out on her sofa and relax. He took her up on the invitation and it wasn't long before he was snoring.

Kate watched Steve as if he was a specimen under a microscope. What could she do to get this relationship to go to the next level? He seemed very relaxed around her, after all he was sleeping like a log on her sofa, but maybe he was too relaxed. He almost acted like they were an old married couple, in other words, in a rut. They didn't ever do anything exciting or different. She cooked and he ate. This was getting very old and it needed to stop.

After about an hour, Steve opened his eyes, stretched, and yawned. It took him a moment to realize where he was.

"How long have I been sleeping?" he asked sheepishly.

"Not long," she lied. "You were tired and I'm glad you could get a little rest. You must work really hard to get so tired." She tried to look concerned.

"Not really. Business has been a little slow. I think I'm tired because I'm bored."

The minute those words passed his lips he knew he had made a grave error. Kate's eyes flashed with anger.

"Well, I'm just as sorry as I can be that you're so bored here. Forgive me for being such a lousy hostess!"

"Kate, no! I'm not bored with you. I'm bored at home and maybe even with my life. What I said had no reflection on you. You're a wonderful hostess and woman."

Giving him a look that said, "I don't believe you," she put her head into her hands and began to cry. Steve blamed himself for her anguish, so reaching over he put his arms around her shoulders. Without warning or forethought, Steve leaned over and kissed her. Her crying ceased immediately and she kissed him back passionately. When Steve felt Kate responding so enthusiastically to him, he quickly pulled back. Kate's eyes flew open and she noted his look of shock.

"I'm so sorry. I shouldn't have done that. You were upset and I just wanted to comfort you. Please forgive me, Kate." Steve looked so ashamed she thought he might start to blush.

"That's alright, Steve. You don't need to be ashamed about anything. I've been wanting you to kiss me."

Feeling extremely uncomfortable now, Steve looked away and said nothing. Kate felt rejected and could feel her anger rising, but this was no time to blow her stack. Instead, she did the one thing that almost always touched a man's heart-she began to cry again. Not touching her, he caressed Kate with his voice.

"Don't cry, Kate. I think you're just overly sensitive and I've hurt your feelings by mistake. I'm sorry."

"What do you mean I'm overly sensitive?" She narrowed her eyes.

Steve began to think he couldn't say anything right any more to her. Things were so much easier with Catherine. She certainly wasn't as complicated as Kate. At least, he didn't think she was.

"Kate, I better go home. I can't seem to say anything without getting you upset. That has not been my intention at all. I'll go so I don't do any more damage."

Kate realized she was getting ready to lose Steve. If he walked out right now, it might be a long time before he ever came back. He was not the kind of man to be easily manipulated. She had to handle him carefully.

"Please don't go. I'm OK now. I guess you're right. I must be too sensitive. Let's just watch a little television. What do you say? There's a good ballgame coming on soon." Even though she despised any kind of sports, or anything else that took a man's concentration off of her, she'd endure a baseball game for Steve.

"Are you sure? You might need to rest after being so upset."

He must think I'm some kind of hot-house flower. He doesn't have a clue how tough I really am, but maybe that's a good thing.

"I'm fine, Steve. Just come over here and relax, while I fix you a drink." At that moment angels in heaven couldn't have smiled any sweeter than Kate.

While Kate was fixing some sweet tea and slicing lemon wedges to put in the glasses, she heard Steve's cell phone ring. Putting her knife down, she listened intently to hear what he was saying.

"I'm over at Kate's for a little while. . . . yes, I'm coming home for supper. . . .Zoe, we'll talk about this when I come home. . . . Honey, I said we'd talk when I come home. . . Bye."

Kate made a face when she heard Zoe's name. What a pest! Bringing the tea to Steve on a pretty lacquer tray, she pretended she hadn't heard his phone ring. She couldn't help but notice the guilty look on Steve's face.

"Is everything OK, Steve? You look a little funny."

Steve tried to rearrange his face in more friendly lines. It wouldn't do for Kate to suspect he got a blistering call from Zoe, complaining about him being at Kate's house and calling her a few choice names.

"The tea looks great. Unfortunately, after I'm finished, I've got to go home."

"Oh. Is everything alright?"

"Sure. I just need to get started on some paper work, that's all."

Kate watched Steve drain his glass in record time and she tried not to look too bothered about it. Kate had come to realize that when Zoe said jump, Steve jumped.

"Would you like another?"

"No. I really need to shove off. Thanks for a lovely evening."

"You're very welcome. Please feel free to come over anytime. My door is always open for you."

She quickly looked down in her lap to avoid looking at Steve's face. Sounding a little too anxious and forward, she didn't want to see if her comment struck a negative chord with him. After he left, Kate closed the door and fumed. If only Zoe would find a job in another city and move. What a relief that would be!

Zoe was waiting at the door. The look on her face made Steve want to get in his car and drive off, but he returned her scowl with a bright smile.

"Hello, Sunshine!"

"Sunshine, my foot. Dad, why do you have to keep going over to her house? I don't think you're really interested in her, but you're sure giving her the green light by all these frequent visits."

"Zoe, I haven't been over there in awhile. Please stop worrying about nothing. On a whole other note, what do you want to do for supper?"

"Let's go out. Kate might want to pop over for supper."

"Zoe, you're silly, you know?" Steve just rolled his eyes and wondered how he'd eat another bite after the big meal at Kate's.

Zoe went over to peck Steve's cheek as a way to make up. Upon closer inspection, Zoe saw lipstick on Steve's lower lip. Reaching up, she wiped it off and held her finger up for Steve to see.

"What's this?" Zoe wiped her finger on her jeans.

"Oh, that. Kate was upset so I gave her a little kiss to cheer her up." He couldn't have looked more like a little boy caught with his hands in the cookie jar if he had tried.

"Oh, sure. You know what? You make me sick!"

Without warning, Steve slapped Zoe's face so hard she saw stars. While she was trying to get her bearings, Steve grabbed her and hugged her so tightly she could hardly breathe.

"I'm so sorry, Zoe. I don't know what got into me. Please forgive me, please, my precious girl. I don't know why I hit you like that!"

Tears filled Steve's eyes, while rage filled Zoe's. She pushed him away with all her strength.

"Don't you touch me! You've never hit me like that, ever! I knew this would happen. She's come between us and I'm sure she would be delighted to know it. Why don't you go back over there and tell her I'm moving out!"

"Zoe, don't. Please, Honey, I'm so sorry. Please forgive me. I don't know what got into me. Please forgive me. It will never happen again, I promise."

Steve was shaking he was so upset. Zoe ran into her room and slammed the door. Jerking her suitcase out of the closet, she crammed her clothes in it without a thought of folding them or packing in an orderly manner. Steve started knocking on her door, but she ignored him. Grabbing a bag, she swept all her make-up from the vanity into it. Realizing she would have to pass Steve to get out the front door, she quietly raised her window, threw her things on the ground, slid out then ran.

It wasn't until Steve heard her car start up that he stopped knocking. Running to the front door, he caught a glimpse of her tail lights. He fell to his knees and cried out to God. Sobs wracked his body until he was too weak to continue. Getting up, he fell across the sofa in despair.

What am I going to do? What will Catherine say when Zoe tells her all about this? God help me. My life is falling apart.

Kate had been taking in the night air on her back porch, when an unusual noise caught her attention. She watched as Zoe threw her things out of the bedroom window then climbed out herself. Zoe quickly ran to her car, clutching all her possessions then sped off in a cloud of dust. Kate was relieved Steve couldn't see the devilish smile on her face. He would have been shocked if he knew how much she hated Zoe.

Zoe sped down the highway to her mother's apartment. Tears were streaming down her cheeks and her face ached every time she touched it. Flipping her visor down, she looked in the mirror and saw how red and slightly swollen the right side of her face was. Pushing harder on the gas pedal, her speed began to exceed eighty miles per hour. She couldn't get to Catherine's fast enough.

About a mile from the apartment, the siren and the flashing lights of a police car startled Zoe. He appeared as if out of thin air and was right on her bumper. It wasn't until she looked at the speedometer that she realized how fast she was going. Pulling over on the shoulder, she reached in her purse for her driver's license with one hand and dried her tears with the other.

"Lady, I clocked your speed at eighty-five miles per hour. Can you explain to me why you were going so fast?" His gruff voice started the tears afresh.

"I'm sorry, Officer. I'm trying to get to my mother's place."

"Is this an emergency?"

"Yes and no. My mother is fine, but I need to tell her what my father did to me." *Why did I tell him that?*

"Why don't you step out of your vehicle?"

In the glare of the officer's flashlight, Steve's handprint was embossed upon Zoe's cheek. The officer looked intently at Zoe's face.

"Is this what your father did?"

"Yes, sir, but it's no big deal."

"When did this happen?"

"About fifteen minutes ago."

"Did you attack your father?"

"No, of course not."

"I'm going to need to look at your driver's license."

Handing it over, Zoe began to wonder what the officer had in mind. He hadn't even written her a ticket for speeding. All she could do was stand by the side of road and try to avoid the looks of people driving by.

"Is this your correct address?"

"No, my family moved and I live with my father now."

"I'm going to need your father's name and address, please."

He wrote all the information down then called radio dispatch using police jargon Zoe didn't recognize. It wasn't until he relayed Steve's address that she got a funny feeling in her stomach. What was the officer doing?

"Do you need medical attention?" he asked with little compassion.

"No. I'm fine. Officer, what's going on? I heard you give the dispatcher our address."

"You don't need to worry. I've issued an arrest warrant for your father. He won't be bothering you any more today."

"Arrest warrant! What for?" Zoe felt a little faint.

"Assault."

"Sir, it was just a little slap. Everything's OK. Please don't do this."

"I'm sorry. You have visible signs of abuse and you've admitted your father did this to you today."

Zoe slumped against her car. Nothing made sense any more to her. Between her father slapping her and now his subsequent arrest, Zoe felt dizzy and sick to her stomach. What had she done!

"Are you sure you don't medical attention? You look a little sick."

"I just need my mother right now. Am I free to go or did you want to issue me a ticket." At this point she didn't care what the officer was going to do, as long as he let her go.

"I'm going to let you slide this time because of what you've been through. But if I ever catching you speeding again, I'll throw the book at you. Do you understand?"

"Yes, sir," she said meekly.

He turned to get into his squad car, while Zoe almost fell into her front seat. She only had a short distance to go, but she wondered how she'd make it without fainting or throwing up. Slowly she pulled her car out into the street and drove to Catherine's, keeping an eye on the rear view mirror.

Once she got there, Zoe stumbled out of the car and headed for the courtyard. Catherine just happen to be watching the stars on this warm, clear night when she turned and saw Zoe. The street light revealed that Zoe's face was white as a sheet. Running to her, Catherine helped her daughter into a chair. For a minute Zoe said nothing.

"Zoe, what's happened? Are you sick? What can I do for you?"

"Mom, something terrible has happened and it's all my fault!"

Catherine had never seen Zoe so upset. For some crazy reason her mind jumped to Austin. What had he done?

"Calm down. Just tell me what happened." Catherine tried to speak calmly, but irrational thoughts were racing through her mind, which made it so difficult.

"I got Dad arrested! Oh, Mom. What am I going to do?"

"Arrested! What for?" Catherine's calmness seemed to be spilling out, while panic rushed in.

"For assault! What am I going to do?" Zoe looked so frightened.

"Assault! Who did Steve assault?" Austin still kept popping up in her mind. Who else could bring Steve to such action?

"Me!"

At this point Zoe broke down into what seemed like a thousand tears. Her shoulders were shaking so hard that Catherine was having trouble holding on to her.

"Zoe, Steve hit you? Are you sure?" *What a stupid thing to say; of course, she's sure.*

"I told Dad he made me sick and he slapped me across the face as hard as he could." Catherine could now see the mark on her face.

"So you called the police?" Catherine was careful not to sound judgmental or partial to Steve. If she did, Zoe would completely shut down.

"No, I didn't call the police. I was stopped on the way to your house for speeding. The officer asked why I was in such a rush. I told him I wanted to hurry to you and tell you what Dad had done. I'm such an idiot! I don't know why I told him what occurred at Dad's house. I was just trying to get out of a ticket. Now, look what I've done. Could my life be any more screwed up?"

Catherine sat quietly while her mind whirled like a top. What's going to happen to Steve? How will this affect the family? How will Zoe ever get over this? The questions just wouldn't stop pecking at her brain. Zoe looked at Catherine for comfort and advice. Her eyes were pleading for a motherly solution. Catherine led Zoe to the sofa into the living room and then sat at the other end.

"Let's calm down a little and discuss why your father hit you. That's just not like him. Could you tell me what led up to him hitting you?"

"It's all Kate's fault!"

"What has Kate got to do with this?"

"Dad came home from Kate's with lipstick on his lips. I told him he made me sick then he slapped me. Mom, I was so wrong to say that. He said he was just trying to comfort her. I blew everything out of proportion."

Catherine's swirling thoughts stopped abruptly. "Lipstick on his lips," started to play over and over in her mind like a tape on a reel. A sadness came over her like a dense fog. She really had lost Steve, hadn't she? The image of him kissing another woman formed before her eyes until she no longer saw Zoe, tear-stained and pathetic-looking.

"Mom?" Catherine took a moment to clear her head before responding.

"Yes?" She had to shake that image of Steve out so she could focus on Zoe.

"What am I going to do?"

"I guess we need to go down to the police station and explain the situation. Maybe they'll release Steve when we clarify things to them."

Steve was sitting like a zombie on the sofa, overcome with guilt and grief, when someone started banging on the door. *I'll bet that's Zoe. This must be her way of showing me how mad she is.*

When he opened the door, he was surprised to see two officers standing on his porch, neither looking like they were there for a friendly visit. Sweat began to form on his forehead. *Please, Lord, don't let there be anything wrong with Zoe. I hope she didn't get into an accident.*

"Are you Steve Russell?"

"Yes. Is everything all right with my daughter?"

"Yes, no thanks to you."

"I'm afraid I don't understand. Was she in a car accident?"

"Mr. Smith, you are under arrest for assaulting your daughter. Turn around and put your hands behind your back."

Before Steve could react, one officer twirled him around and twisted the handcuffs onto his wrists. They each grabbed an arm and roughly walked Steve to their squad car.

"Officers, there must be some mistake. I admit I slapped my daughter, but there was no assault. I can't believe she called you to have me arrested."

"She didn't. She was stopped for speeding. Your daughter explained why she was rushing to her mother. The officer who stopped her called the incident in. Watch your head getting into the backseat."

Steve was wondering which neighbor might be watching this whole nightmare play out like a B-movie, when his question was answered. Kate was running down her steps toward the squad car.

"Steve! Steve! What's going on?" Kate looked dumbfounded.

"You need to step away from the vehicle" the younger officer growled. Kate wanted to stick her tongue out at him, but she didn't.

"Kate, I'll talk to you later. It's all a misunderstanding. I'll let you know when I'm released."

Kate stood speechless while the car pulled out of Steve's driveway. *I'll bet that Zoe has something to do with this. What a wretched little brat!* She ran into her house and grabbed her keys. Realizing she might need to look her best, she put them down and ran a brush through her hair, applied new lipstick, and sprayed her best perfume behind her ears. Some policemen could be charmed by a good-looking woman and she was going to do her best to get Steve out of this jam.

Steve stood in shock and disbelief in the police station, afraid to move or speak. He had never been in this situation before and was ignorant of the procedures and policies. The older arresting officer was filling out some paperwork. The younger one had disappeared out the front door.

At the same time, Catherine and Zoe were climbing the steps of the police station. Catherine didn't have a clue what to do to get Steve released. She figured she'd go inside and ask the first officer she encountered. Immediately finding a friendly face, she stopped the officer and explained the situation. He directed her down the hall. It wasn't long before they spotted Steve, handcuffed and staring at the floor. They were about to approach him, when a woman pushed past them, nearly knocking them down. When Zoe's mouth flew opened in shock, Catherine instantly realized just who this rude woman was.

"I can't believe she's here. What business does she have with this? The nerve of that woman!" Zoe was so incensed she felt like walking over and slapping Kate.

"Who is that, Zoe?" Catherine said, knowing full well who she was.

"That is the root of all my problems, Kate. I can't stand that woman!"

Zoe and Catherine watched Kate walk over and reach for Steve. The arresting officer gave her a look that made her hand instantly retreat to her side. Kate's back was to Zoe and Catherine and her body blocked Steve's view. He had no idea his family was standing not fifteen feet away.

Kate became very animated with the officer sitting at the desk. Steve looked at her then back at the officer. After about five minutes, Steve was led away, but not before Kate stepped aside, giving him a clear view of his wife and daughter. If someone had asked Catherine to explain the look on Steve's face when he saw them, it would have been impossible. Catherine wanted to run over and hug him, but, instead, she stood in the same spot she had been in since entering the room, like a deer in the headlights. The whole scenario was surreal. Catherine seemed unable to move or speak.

When Kate turned to leave, her eyes fell upon Catherine and Zoe. She felt like just walking past them, but decided against it.

"Zoe, this must be your mother."

"What are you doing here?" Zoe's voice was laced with venom.

"I came to see what I could do to get your father out of jail. Do you know why he's here? This must be some kind of big mistake." Kate's voice dripped with honey, and she even smiled at Zoe, like they were friends. Catherine felt so awkward, but she knew she needed to extend a Christian handshake. After all, this woman hadn't done anything wrong, except fall in love with her husband. And, they were getting a divorce, after all.

"Hello, my name is Catherine. I'm Steve's wife." She reached for Kate's hand, but Kate kept hers by her side.

Kate cocked one eyebrow up and said, "I thought you were getting a divorce."

Jumping in before Catherine could say another word, Zoe, speaking a little too loudly, said, "They're still married because they're not legally divorced yet. So, you see, he's not available right now."

Kate didn't bat an eye at Zoe's rudeness. It seemed to have

energized her, in fact. An unattractive smirk came upon her lips before she spoke, enunciating every word.

"They're not living together, so they might as well be divorced."

Catherine could see this woman was trouble. She decided to put her arm around Zoe and lead her out the door. Nothing could be gained from sparring with Kate. Zoe was no match for her, even if she thought she was. Before Kate or Zoe said could say anything else that would cause further trouble, Catherine decided the best offense was a good defense. In this case, just exiting the building without another word was going to be the best move.

"I hate you! Stay away from my father!" Zoe's face was beet red.

"Zoe, hush. Let's go. Don't start anything, especially here in a police station. Do you want to get arrested, too?"

People were already staring expectantly at them, hoping a cat fight might erupt. While Kate might like that, Catherine was having no part of it, and neither was Zoe. Catherine was so glad Steve hadn't witnessed any part of this side-show. It was all too trashy.

Kate turned and left by another exit. She didn't need to get Steve's wife *and* daughter against her. Two against one. Those were not good odds. If both women were set against her, Steve would most likely take their side. She didn't want to give him any reason to reject her.

Zoe stormed out of the building with Catherine almost running to keep up.

"Whoa! Zoe, you're walking too fast. My heels won't let me run. Please wait up."

Zoe turned around and Catherine could see tears streaming down her face. No wonder she was running. She probably didn't want Kate to see her tears of shame. Catherine wrapped her arms around her daughter and let her sob, right there on the sidewalk with people walking around them and staring. It didn't matter because her daughter was hurting so badly. When Zoe finally raised her head from her mother's shoulder, the tears had stopped, but the pain in her eyes remained.

"Mother, please let me move in with you? I know it's cramped, but I just don't think I can live at that house anymore. Between the pain I've caused Dad and Kate's smug attitude, it would be a living hell to stay there. So, please let me move in with you. It won't be permanent. I'll find a job and get my own place soon."

"Zoe, we'll go get your things and put them in storage in the morning. All you really need is your clothes and toiletries when you stay with me. It's late and I know you've got to be as exhausted as I am. Let's go home."

Zoe's weak smile squeezed Catherine's heart. In the harsh streetlight she looked like Catherine's little girl again. Catherine just wanted to embrace and protect her all she could at this moment.

The next morning, after leasing a storage unit, they rented a small truck and headed to Steve's. Zoe didn't even glance in the direction of Kate's house. She had seen her car, so she knew she was home. If Kate had the nerve to come out and speak to her, she wasn't sure if she'd be able to hold back her anger. *Kate, if you know what's good for you, you'll stay put in your house.*

Zoe left some of the larger pieces of furniture in her bedroom. She wouldn't need them right now, plus they were too heavy for Zoe and Catherine to lift. Steve wouldn't mind those things staying at his house. After all, if she took everything, the room would look so barren. Steve could use her bedroom as a guest room for now, if he ever had a guest stay over. If Kate moved in she surely wouldn't use the guest bedroom. The thought of her father and Kate sharing a bedroom made her stomach turn.

Kate watched discreetly behind her drapes as Catherine and Zoe made several trips back and forth to the truck. She felt like dancing, knowing Zoe would be gone! *I wonder how Steve will take it when he finds out Zoe's moved out?*

After everything that they could physically manage was put on the truck, Catherine and Zoe headed back to the small storage unit. Both were quiet as they neatly placed Zoe's possessions in the unit. It wasn't until they returned the truck to the rental agency and got into the car that they spoke.

"Thanks, Mom. I really appreciate this."

"You're welcome. After all, that's what mothers are for-to lend a helping hand to their children." Catherine smiled warmly at Zoe.

"I'm starved. Can we stop somewhere to eat?"

"Sure. Just let me know where you want to go. After we eat, let's go home and rest. My back is killing me."

Steve was released on bail the day after his arrest. The bail was low enough for him to pay it right out. Because his car was still at his house, he had to call a taxi company to come pick him up. As he was getting into the taxi, he caught a glimpse of himself in the reflection on the car window. With his hair uncombed and a five o' clock shadow on his face, never mind the wrinkled clothes, he looked like a bum and smelled like one, too. He fully expected the taxi driver to order him out of the car, but the cabbie never looked in Steve's direction. Getting the address, the foreign-looking driver concentrated on the road.

Once home, he literally ran into the house. He didn't want to see any neighbors and he prayed they wouldn't see him. He really didn't want to see anyone for awhile. His answering machine was blinking, but he ignored it, too. Before he did another thing, he was determined to wash that jail house funk from his body.

After a long, hot, soapy shower, Steve wrapped up in his robe and fell across his bed. He hadn't slept a wink the night before. Being in a group jail cell, he kept one eye open all night. Some of those guys looked like they might beat the stuffing out of you if you so much as looked in their direction. Steve had just sat quietly in a corner, minding his own business. The whole time he tried not to think about what filth was on the floor. He planned to dispose of all the clothes he had worn in jail. They'd never be clean enough for him to wear ever again.

After dozing for a few hours, Steve opened his eyes and just stared at the ceiling. He began to play back the scene in the police station lobby with Zoe, Catherine, and Kate. The vastly different looks on their faces was the only scene his mind kept rewinding, over and over. Zoe had a look of anger. Was she still mad at him or was it directed toward Kate? Catherine seemed to be in shock. It was almost as if she didn't know where she was or what was happening in front of her. She was probably only at the station because of Zoe. Kate's expressions of concern for Steve and aggravation toward the police had oscillated back and forth the whole time she had been at the station.

While he would have given anything for Catherine or Zoe to have shown him some semblance of love and support, it was Kate, his neighbor, who had expressed more solicitude. Mixed feelings ran through him as his mind weighed the pros and cons of where his allegiance should now lie. Catherine and Zoe were his family. Unfortunately, the way he reckoned, it was Catherine who had rejected him briefly for another man and Zoe had had him arrested. It was difficult not leaning toward Kate for the loyalty she had displayed. She was the only one in the world who seemed to worry about him now.

Getting up from the bed, Steve dressed and walked over to Kate's. When she saw him climb her steps, she wondered if this was good news or bad. Maybe she had upset Steve by showing up at the police station. Possibly the fact that she and his family were there together caused him to become unnerved. Could it be that he actually was glad she came? The questions kept coming, but she'd never know the answers if she didn't hurry up and answer the door.

"Kate, may I come in?"

"Of course, Steve. Have a seat." She caught his fresh scent as he walked by. Thankfully, he had showered before coming over. She had smelled men fresh from jail and it wasn't pretty.

"I just wanted to thank you for coming to the police station. I was able to get out on bail and I hope I never have to go through that again. There will be a court date in a few weeks. I can't imagine how that will go.

I just appreciate your support so much. My family has obviously turned their back on me. I saw them at the station, too, as you probably did. I'm not sure why they were there. I never got to talk with them. It was crystal clear that you were there to secure my release and I can't thank you enough."

Tears began to stream down Steve's face. The sadness he felt was mainly over the perceived betrayal of his family, after all the years he had loved and supported them. It was really hard to take in. What a shame that the biggest show of support came from his neighbor. What did that say about him as a husband and father?

Kate sat quietly by his side, then reached over and put her hand over his. His raised her hand to his lips and kissed it softly. After wiping his tears with his handkerchief, he leaned over and wrapped his arms around Kate. Kate hugged him back and waited for him to make the next move. Instead of kissing her, like she expected, he moved back and took a good, long look at Kate. She really was pretty. Besides that, she was so sweet. She had done so many thoughtful things for him and Zoe since he had moved next door. Zoe didn't like her, but he was sure Zoe wouldn't like anyone who tried to get close to him.

"Kate, I hope we can get to know each other better. I'd like to start dating you, if that is alright with you."

Kate wanted to jump into the air. Instead, she smiled and told him she'd like that very much. Kate was glad Steve couldn't read her mind. Now she was absolutely sure she had him. The hook was set. All the hard work she had put into pursuing him had paid off. Zoe was out of the picture and Kate was free to interact with Steve whenever she wanted. She was dying to know why he was arrested, but she'd find out later. This was no time to bring up any subject that might spoil the mood.

It wasn't until Steve returned home that he realized that Zoe had moved out. He sat on her bed and looked at the naked hangers in her closet. The drawers of her dresser were pulled out and empty. He could tell Zoe had packed in a hurry. The realization that he now lived all alone again made the ache in his heart increase. Getting up he closed the closet door, pushed in the dresser drawers, and picked up a few bits of trash left on the carpet. Shutting the door to her bedroom, he felt the weight of his loneliness setting in.

He toyed with the idea of calling Zoe, but what was he going to say that hadn't already been said. He was terribly sorry for hitting her and he had asked for her to forgive him. Zoe wouldn't come home anymore, that he was sure of. It might be best to let the dust settle and hope to repair the relationship after all her hard feelings had subsided.

Meanwhile, Zoe sat on the sofa at her mother's apartment and stared at nothing in the courtyard. She kept thinking about her father at the police station. He looked so pitiful. Steve had always seemed to her a tower of strength, but in that environment, he had been reduced to a mere shell of himself, fragile and helpless.

Slapping her had been wrong, but, in a way, she had deserved it, and it didn't warrant her father going to jail. She wondered if he was out yet. Catherine hadn't said a thing nor had she attempted to locate his whereabouts at that time. It wasn't that her mother was unfeeling about the situation, it was more she was in shock. Violence, jail, and the police had never been part of their lives, ever. It was all too revolting and confusing to take in. Catherine had taken to her bed for the rest of the day. She couldn't take another crisis in her life.

Zoe was tempted to pick up the phone and call Steve's number, but the thought that her father may be furious with her for putting him in this quandary kept her from calling. This situation could escalate into something far uglier than it already was. Maybe she should let sleeping dogs lie. Getting off the sofa, she decided to walk around the museum instead.

The beauty of the art and the silence in the museum had a calming effect on her nerves. She slowly walked through the different rooms she had become so familiar with since her mother started working there. Mrs. Talbot was walking quickly through the lobby and just had time to wave to Zoe.

Zoe really liked her and hoped she could be more involved with the museum in some capacity in the future. Not only did she have warm feelings for her because she had helped her mother, but

Zoe appreciated Mrs. Talbot's love of museum. That they had this common adoration of art seemed to form a bond between them. Also, Mrs. Talbot was the only uncomplicated person in Zoe's life now.

Catherine stayed in the bed, although she slept very little. She couldn't decide which was more upsetting to her-Kate at the police station or Steve at the police station. She wanted to have harsh feelings toward Kate, but somehow she couldn't. Every time she felt a twinge of anger and jealousy rise up, the contrite feeling that she had brought all of this on herself pushed those negative emotions down. It was her fault, not Kate's, that she was no longer part of Steve's life.

Steve had seemed so helpless and lost when he was being arrested. Never in all of his life had he been in such a predicament as far as she knew. To make matters worse, his hitting Zoe had escalated into this unbelievable nightmare. She couldn't get over the fact that her one sin was the origin of all these transgressions her loved ones had committed. Several Bible verses popped into her head about the consequences of sin, which included shame, trouble, separation from God, reaping what you sow. The list could go on and on. Even though she had received forgiveness for her sin, the consequences were still being played out and would probably continue all her life.

God in His infinite wisdom lets us suffer the consequences of our sin. If He didn't we wouldn't learn. But it's so hard when our sin affects others who had nothing to do with it. Oh, Lord, I am so sorry that my adultery has not only divided my family, but has led ultimately to my husband being arrested. Please, Lord, help us!

Catherine cried softly into her pillow. She didn't want Zoe to hear her and get worried. She had caused that child enough anguish. After wiping her tears away, she decided to get up and see what Zoe was doing. It had been awfully quiet in the apartment the last hour.

Zoe was nowhere to be seen. Even though it was getting dark, Catherine wasn't overly concerned. She fixed a small snack, then started reading a book she had barely touched. Stretching out on her sofa to get more comfortable, she thought she caught a glimpse of a beam of light out in her courtyard. Her heart began pounding as she slowly slipped onto the floor and crawled over to the window. The gate to the courtyard was locked and there was no way anyone had just accidentally stumbled into her backyard.

There was no moon that dark night, so she was unable to discern who was out there. Crawling over to her living room floor lamp, she attempted to cut it off without rising up completely. After several attempts, she finally jumped up, extinguished the light, then slithered slowly back to the window. The light was gone, but whether the person holding the light was gone remained to be seen.

Sweat popped out on her skin and she began to worry in earnest about Zoe. Where was she? She didn't even leave a note, which wasn't like her. The thought of Austin being somehow involved with the light in the courtyard caused Catherine to panic. She needed to get to her cell phone. Before she could retrieve her phone and turn all the lights out in the apartment, a scratching sound at the door caused the hairs on the back of her neck to rise. Someone was jiggling the door knob.

Putting her hand over her mouth to stifle a scream, she slid over to the front door, stood up to kill the overhead light, and put all her weight against the door. Hearing the lock click open, she exerted all her strength to prevent the door from opening.

After several attempts to force the door open, Zoe screamed, "Mom, let me in! What's going on in there?"

Relief poured over Catherine as she swung the door wide, causing Zoe to fall into the room and onto her hands and knees. Before Catherine could reach down to pick her up, Zoe scrambled up and darted over to the light switch. Catherine's look of relief and joy at seeing Zoe safe and sound was met by her daughter's scowl and crossed arms.

"What is going on in here, Mom? Why did you try to keep me out?"

"I'm sorry, Zoe. I thought you were someone else. I saw

someone in the courtyard then you started scratching on the door. I was terrified!"

"I was not scratching at the door. The light outside our door is burned out and I was trying to get my key in the lock."

"Oh, I see. I'm sorry I upset you." Catherine reached over and rubbed Zoe's shoulder.

"What drama! So you didn't recognize who was in the courtyard?"

"No. I only saw a light, but when I went to the window to get a better look, the light was out."

"It could have been someone looking for their lost dog or cat, you know."

"I'm afraid not. The gate to the courtyard was locked. Someone had to climb the wall to get in. I'm going to talk to Mrs. Talbot about getting a bright security light out there. I'd feel much safer. By the way, why don't we change that burned-out light bulb right now."

Catherine found the bulbs and handed one to Zoe. Zoe went out the door with a flashlight. Instantly she was back inside, furiously locking the door.

"What's wrong? Did you change the bulb that quickly?"

Zoe's face was white as a sheet as she said, "Mom, the bulb wasn't blown. Someone had unscrewed it." Catherine's hands began to shake as Zoe handed her the unused bulb to put back into the box.

After sitting down on the sofa, Zoe noticed how worn her mother looked. They had both been through a lot lately, but Catherine was older, so stress was going to affect her more.

"Where were you? I was so worried. You didn't leave a note."

"Mom, I was just strolling around the museum. You were in your bedroom and I got bored. I thought I'd see if any new artwork had come in. I'm sorry. I didn't mean to worry you. I really thought you'd still be in bed when I got back. You need to remember that the security guard is out there patrolling the halls. It's very safe."

Zoe's naivety was both charming and heart-wrenching. She

had no idea how dangerous the world was, especially since Austin had become a stalker of sorts and invaded their world. Determined evil-doers had a way of masterminding their way past security into the lives of unsuspecting victims. Catherine wondered if she'd ever feel safe again.

It was funny how she had always felt protected by Steve, even when he was out of town. Yes, they did have the latest security system, but it was more comforting knowing Steve would have dropped everything if there had been an emergency at home. When she lost Steve, she lost so much more than her life partner. Without realizing she was doing it, Catherine inhaled and sighed loudly. Zoe shot her a questioning glance, but Catherine just yawned and stretched to hide from Zoe her feelings of regret.

"Tell me about your walk through the museum. Did you like our new display of genuine Native American pottery and baskets? Those are on loan from a museum in New Mexico. We've had a lot of interest from the public and attendance has increased significantly since we acquired them."

"Mom, you are starting to sound like an infomercial for the museum."

Catherine returned the jest with one of her own when she said, "Well, I guess you've become the night stalker at the museum, roaming the halls looking for new art." The second she said "stalker" Catherine felt a lump form in her throat. Zoe noticed the change in her facial expression.

"Mom, you're worried about that man who spoke to me in the museum that day, aren't you?"

"Yes, but I'm worried more for you than me. I didn't use to worry when your father was around. I just need to turn these cares over to God."

Zoe rolled her eyes and got up to get some water. Her mother's new faith was a bit irritating.

"Zoe, I don't think Mrs. Talbot will have any problem with you staying here, but you know this is not a permanent solution. Have you given any thought to what you'll be doing in the future?"

"Mom, with all that's gone on with you and Dad, do you really think I've had the frame of mind to really look for a job. It's been a zoo since I returned from Paris. Please don't pressure me!"

"Honey, I'm not pressuring you, but you need to realize that the longer you don't get a job, the longer it will be before you get settled in your own place. I think when you find the right apartment you will start getting some peace of mind. I also think you need to find a good church which has a good singles program. That would be a good place to meet people your age."

"Boy, you've got my life all mapped out, don't you? Before you try to straighten out my life, why don't you start with your own?" The second those words left her lips Zoe was grieved. Why did she have to say that? Her mother was suffering enough without Zoe adding to her misery.

Catherine just hung her head. She knew Zoe was right, but it pained her to hear the words coming from her daughter. She was beginning to feel like the child in their relationship. Life was all mixed up and very little made sense to her any more. Only in her relationship with Christ did she feel like she was standing on solid ground.

Looking at her mother so humbled by her words, Zoe jumped up from her seat and threw her arms around Catherine. Both women wept in each others arms. It seemed as if Catherine and Zoe did a lot of that lately.

"Zoe, please forgive me for trying to run your life. You're right. I haven't done such a great job with mine, so what right do I have to give you advice."

"Mom, you need to forgive me. I shouldn't have said what I did. I do need your advice. It's just that I'm so confused and upset right now. My raw emotions seem to be the driving force in my life right now. And I sure could use some peace."

"You know, when I said an apartment would bring you peace, I was wrong. You need the Prince of Peace, Jesus, to have a lasting peace amid the storms of life."

"Here we go again." Zoe curled her lips up in a sneer.

"Zoe, I'm not going to preach to you. Jesus is trying to reach you, but He will not force you into a relationship. After all that's happened since you returned, I don't know what it's going to take for you to see the light."

"Mom, you act like I'm some criminal bound for hell."

"No, I'm not. The Bible says in Romans 3:23 that all have sinned and come short of the glory of God. Unless we have made Jesus our Savior, we will die in our sins."

"I learned all that in Sunday School when I was young. I don't need another lesson."

"The very fact that you display contempt for the things of the Bible shows your heart in not right with God."

Zoe didn't have an answer for that. She just wanted her mother to stop preaching to her. Maybe if she didn't respond to her mother, she'd give up and change the subject. Catherine must have had the same thought.

"Zoe, let's go to bed. I'm emotionally exhausted."

"Sounds good to me."

The following evening Austin parked outside the courtyard gate. This had become his evening ritual since he discovered that Catherine lived just beyond the little courtyard. These evenings gave him time to contemplate his tumultuous relationship with Catherine.

He couldn't believe that Catherine had rejected him so quickly after she had left her husband. She had even had the nerve to act angry with him at the museum. Certainly their one afternoon together had been brief, but they had forged a relationship when they would frequently meet at the library. This wasn't just a fling. They were meant to be together and he was going to make sure they were. Catherine must be confused to not recognize that they were in love. The thought that Catherine might have other ideas never crossed his mind. His self-centeredness would never allow it.

He didn't care how long it took. He would wait each and every evening until she came out to her car. Talking some sense into her was his only option. He realized that getting Catherine cornered at the museum might be a little dangerous for him. That security guard had scrutinized him when he had roamed aimlessly around the museum. A confrontation with security might result in being thrown in jail. He couldn't afford to violate his probation. He had to be very careful because he wasn't planning on going back to prison, ever. No, it was best to meet Catherine outside the museum. Certainly that wouldn't be part of the security guard's jurisdiction.

Austin was just about to fall asleep when he heard the gate rattle. He lowered himself in his seat in such a way where he couldn't be seen, but he could still survey the gate. Right away he saw that the figure closing the gate was not Catherine, but her daughter. He was about to get comfortable again and wait to see if Catherine emerged, when a plan began to form in his wicked mind. The more he thought about it, the more he concluded it would work. He couldn't help it if Catherine was forcing him to take drastic measures.

Zoe walked the short distance to her car, looking several times over her shoulder. Standing at the driver's door, she fumbled through her purse for the keys. *Why didn't I get the keys out while I was in the house and could see!* She was just about to walk next to a streetlight where the light was better, when her hand touched the car keys in the depths of her purse. Finally!

Before she could pull them out, a hand clamped forcefully over her mouth while an arm wrapped around her waist and lifted her ungracefully off the ground. Before she could react, duct tape was placed roughly across her mouth while her hands were painfully pulled behind her back and tied. Kicking with all her might, he dropped her on the ground then tied her ankles with course rope. Hitting the ground with a thud, she temporarily lost her breathe. Without being able to inhale with her mouth open, she panicked and felt her lungs begin to burn. Darkness clouded her brain as she fainted in the dust.

Steve decided to call Kate to see if she was available Friday night for a date. The phone rang several times before a sultry voice answered. She pretended not to know who had called, even though she had caller I.D.

"Kate, this is Steve."

"Oh, how are you?" She tried to sound surprised that he had called.

"I was wondering if you'd like to go out to eat Friday night? There's a great seafood restaurant I've been wanting to try."

"Sounds great!" Kate hated seafood, but they'd probably serve steak, too.

"Why don't I pick you up at 7:00?"

"That would be perfect. I should be home around 6:00." All she had was a hair appointment that afternoon, but she didn't want Steve to know she had nothing better to do on Friday than get her hair styled.

After hanging up, Kate smiled and considered things between her and Steve were so much better now that Zoe was out of the picture. *I just hope she never moves back.*

Having a date on Friday made Steve feel a little less depressed. While he technically wasn't divorced, he had felt like a single man for some time. After all, he reasoned, it was just dinner. No big deal. Right?

Catherine was enjoying a documentary on the television when she happened to see the time on the wall clock. Zoe had said she was going to run a few short errands, so she should have been home by now. Calling her cell-phone Catherine got no reply. *She must be in an area that has no reception. I'll wait a while then try again.*

After the documentary, Catherine decided to go get some fresh air in the courtyard. She still wondered where Zoe was, but she surmised that she might have only lost track of time. *I don't need to worry needlessly. But, I am going to have a little talk with Zoe when she gets home.*

Walking over to make sure the gate was locked, she saw Zoe's car in its usual parking space. *What is she doing sitting in her car?* Curiosity got the best of her and she walked over to the car. Not only was Zoe not in the car, but her purse was spilled out on the ground. Panic took over her brain as she ran around to the other side of the car to see if Zoe had fallen. No Zoe. A scream rose in her throat, but she stifled it quickly, knowing there was no one around to hear her.

Maybe Zoe dropped her purse accidentally and had gone into the museum. Catherine knew that was unlikely, seeing as she didn't come back into the apartment, but she was grasping at straws. She was determined not to become hysterical.

The security guard had not seen Zoe all that evening. *Maybe Steve picked her up and she forgot to call me.*

"Steve, this is Catherine. Is Zoe with you?" She tried to disguise the panic in her voice.

"No. I don't imagine she wants to see me right now. Is everything OK?"

"No. Maybe. I don't know." The harder she tried to sound calm, the more her voice betrayed her.

"Catherine, are you alright? You sound upset."

"Zoe left to run errands. When it got late, I walked outside and saw her car. She wasn't in it and her purse was on the ground with everything spilled out. Steve, I'm worried. Where could she be?"

"I'm coming over right now. Just stay put."

"Park in the back of the museum. I'll be waiting by the gate for you. Steve, you don't think something has happened to our little girl, do you?"

"Let's don't borrow trouble. I'll be there as fast as I can."

Catherine felt better just knowing Steve was coming over to help her figure this out. She felt she could hold her tears at bay until Steve arrived.

Meanwhile, Zoe woke up to engine noise and the whine of the tires on the road. Her cheek was pressed against a cold truck-bed, which caused her to shiver. The roughness of the rope binding her ankles irritated her skin, but it was her hands held behind her back that caused Zoe the most pain. She was forced to lie on her chest, which made breathing a little difficult. A tarp smelling of oil covered her body, but thankfully it did keep the wind off her back. Otherwise, the cold would have made things more unbearable than they already were.

Wherever she was, it was in a deserted area. No other vehicles could be heard. Not knowing where she was, who had her, and what she was going to face brought a desperate fear into her heart. Thinking of Catherine being worried sick made the tears run down her nose. Since she couldn't wipe her face, the tears caused her face to chill even more. Pulling her body into a twisted fetal position helped conserve a little heat.

When the vehicle turned onto a dirt road, sheer panic gripped her. It wasn't long before it sounded like they were going through some woods. Branches slapped at the truck and she could hear dry leaves fall into the bed. She had never been so terrorized in her life. *God help me!*

The truck stopped and the driver's side door slammed. When the tarp was viciously jerked from her body, cold, damp air permeated her thick clothes. As hard as she tried, Zoe couldn't stop shaking. There was no moon so the night was pitch black. Cruel hands dropped the tailgate and unceremoniously jerked her onto the ground. Cutting the rope around her ankles, he snatched her to her feet, grabbed her upper arm, and led her down a narrow path.

A dark structure loomed ahead. Fearing she was going to be held captive or worse, she kicked savagely at the man. A violent slap across her head caused Zoe to trip and almost fall. Not wanting to be struck again, she obediently staggered next to her captor.

Keys jingled and a lock sprang loose. The door hadn't been used in ages. He had to use brute force for it to open. Once inside, a damp, musty smell filled her nostrils. It was darker inside than out because all the windows were boarded up. After he pushed her onto a nasty mattress, she wondered if he was going to rape her. She had never been with a man and the thought of this monster getting intimate with her made her physically ill.

When he roped her ankles again, she breathed a sigh of relief that rape was not part of his plan, not yet anyway. He walked to the door, slammed it closed then locked it. She soon heard the engine start and the truck slowly drive away. Laying her head on the mattress, she cried herself to sleep.

It took Austin awhile to finally go to sleep. The adrenaline in his system had to abate before he could settle down. As sleep was slowly taking over his consciousness, he replayed the events of the evening in his mind.

He wondered how Zoe was doing in the old shack in the woods. He didn't want to hurt Catherine's daughter, or cause her any real harm, but he had to do whatever was necessary to keep her contained. Catherine's love for her daughter would force her to surrender to him. Austin was convinced that once they were together, Catherine would see his many charms and fall deeply in love with him. She had been through a lot with the divorce and moving. There hadn't been enough time for her to sit down and really contemplate how good her life could be with him. That had to change.

She had forced him to extreme measures to get her full attention. Once she was reunited with her daughter, her mind could settle on his love for her. Unfortunately, she would have to wait. Austin needed for Catherine to suffer a bit since he had suffered due to her rejection of him at his ranch months and months ago and more recently at the museum.

The next morning Austin packed a few snacks for Zoe and some bottled water. Never could Catherine say he hadn't kept her daughter fed. Once everything was in the backpack, he set off for the shack, eager to see how Zoe had fared during the night.

That morning a cold blast of wind whistled through the boards of the dilapidated structure. Zoe's eyes flew open and her teeth began to chatter. Besides the sound of the wind, she heard little rustling sounds in her room. Unable to turn over, she imagined it was mice scurrying around. She told herself they were mice because the thought of rats in such close proximity made her want to shriek.

Just as she was attempting to get a little warm by curling up her legs to her body, she heard the truck. She waited nervously for the sound of the key jiggling the lock. Did she want to close her eyes and pretend she was sleeping or look him square in the eye, giving him a look of defiance. Choosing the former, she tried to look like she was soundly sleeping.

When he opened the door, he mistook her sleeping act for death and ran over to feel her pulse. His hand at her throat, Zoe screamed loudly. His hand flew back against his chest he was so startled. Crying replaced her screams, while Austin stared at her with cold indifference. Pulling her to an upright position, he roughly brushed away the strands of her hair that had gotten caught in her mouth. He untied her hands only so she could eat. After dumping the contents of the backpack into her lap, he went to a corner where an old stump had been placed and watched her slowly nibble at the food, if you called beef jerky and chips food.

Knowing she had to eat to survive and keep her strength, she choked down the junk food and drank all the water. Not sure of his intentions, she placed the trash inside the backpack and leaned against the wall with her eyes almost closed. Zoe couldn't stand looking at him or trying to guess his next move, so she concentrated on an ant that had scrambled over to pick up the few crumbs that had fallen on the floor.

It was when Austin's boots scrapped the floor as he was getting up that Zoe looked him full in the face. It was the man in the museum. No wonder her mother was worried. He had a ruggedness about him that suggested he had lived outdoors. While he had some handsome features, his cruelty made him extremely undesirable. Zoe didn't want to look at him, but she stared in panic as he walked toward her. After kicking the backpack to the other side of the room, he pushed her face-first into the mattress and secured her hands with the rope again. The smell of the mattress was so intense that she knew she'd never forget that odor as long as she lived.

Without speaking a word to her, he retrieved the backpack and was gone again. After hearing the truck drive off, she successfully flipped herself over to get some fresh air. The pain of having her arms behind her caused Zoe to turn on her side. It wasn't comfortable, but it allowed her to breath in air not contaminated by the foul mattress. Tears flowed again as she contemplated her fate in the hands of this madman.

When darkness fell, Zoe knew it was another cold and lonely

night in the woods. There wasn't a body position that would comfortably allow her to maximize her own heat by curling up. It wasn't long before the damp chill of the night had her shivering and her teeth chattering.

Steve jumped into action after the call from Catherine. Not knowing what the night would bring, he packed a small overnight bag and headed to his car. Kate was just pulling into her driveway after an evening out with girlfriends when she saw Steve and the overnight bag.

"Running away or leaving for business?" she joked. The look on Steve's face told her he was not in the joking mood.

"Zoe is missing! I'm going to find her," he said in a panic.

Before she could stop herself, Kate said, "You are going to be back for our weekend date, right?"

Steve looked at Kate as if she was a three-headed dog. He had never looked at her with such disgust and anger. She would have done anything to take back the words, but it was too late. They seemed to just hang in the air.

"Kate, I have never known anyone as self-centered and callous as you. Zoe was right about you all along. You're worried about our date when my precious daughter may have been kidnapped. Don't count on seeing me this weekend or ever!"

Before she could retort, his car was backing out the driveway and flying down the road. Kate knew there would probably be no second chances with Steve. She had always suspected that Zoe would come between them one day. Zoe probably wasn't even missing, just hiding out somewhere to get some attention. What a pain in the neck!

After entering her house, she closed the door and went directly to bed. Loneliness soon wrapped around her like a fog. It was her turn to cry. *I had such great plans for me and Steve, but Zoe's ruined everything.*

When Steve pulled up in front of the Catherine's courtyard, she was waiting by the gate. He couldn't get out of the car fast enough.

"Have you heard anything from Zoe?" He was trying to put

on a brave face, but wasn't sure how long that would last. Seeing the distress in Catherine he knew he had to be the strong one, at least for now.

"No. I've checked everywhere I know. Even the security guard in the museum hasn't seen her. Steve, what are we going to do?"

"Calm down, Catherine. We will find her. I promise. The first thing we need to do is call the police."

"Oh, Steve. I just hate calling them after the trouble you were in with them. They're going to think we're some kind of crazy, dysfunctional family."

"Who cares? Getting Zoe back is all that matters!"

Steve dialed 911 and reported Zoe's disappearance. It was after he hung up that the full weight of Zoe's predicament fell upon him. He began to cry in a way that Catherine had never witnessed before. Wrapping her arms around him, they both cried and clung to each other.

It wasn't long before a patrol car arrived. Thankfully, the police officer was not the same one that had arrested Steve. After taking down all the information that Catherine and Steve could give him, he radioed in the apparent kidnapping and led them into Catherine's apartment. The officer saw that the couple had been crying and his heart was touched by their grief.

"Don't worry. We are going to do everything we can to get your daughter back. Your job right now is to pray. Are you Christians?"

"Yes, I am," Catherine answered, while Steve just lowered his head.

"You need to contact every friend and family member to start praying also. Prayer can make all the difference in the world."

Just knowing this officer was a Christian gave such hope to Catherine. God must have orchestrated it so that this particular officer would be on duty and take the call. Praise the Lord!

After he left, Steve and Catherine sat on the sofa and stared into space, lost in their own thoughts and grief. It wasn't until Steve grasped Catherine's hand that she was able to shake loose from the grip of doom she felt.

"Catherine, our little girl will come back. If it's OK with you, I would like to stay here until she returns."

"Oh, Steve, thank you. I don't think I could make it on my own right now without you."

They clung to each other while the tears spilled down their faces. After what seemed like an eternity, exhaustion from the trauma of the situation settled over both of them. Steve fell restlessly asleep while sitting on the sofa. Catherine retrieved a blanket from her closet and covered him. When she climbed onto her bed, she wondered if she should have invited Steve to sleep with her, after all, they were still married. Before she could make up her mind she fell asleep without undressing or getting under the covers.

It seemed like just minutes after she laid down that the phone rang. She glanced at the clock and saw it was 8:00 a.m. Thinking it was the police, she snatched up the phone before it rang again. Steve rushed into the bedroom with wrinkled clothes and his hair sticking up in every direction.

"Hello?"

"Good morning, Catherine." The voice made the hairs on the back of her neck rise.

"What do you want? I have an emergency going on right now and I need to get off the phone!"

"I know. That's why I called."

Steve was mouthing, "Who is it?" Catherine put her forefinger in front of her lips to signal that he needed to be quiet and wait.

"What are you talking about?" Catherine's voice was getting louder.

"I have Zoe." Catherine felt like cold water was running through her veins.

"You have Zoe? Where is she?" At that point, Steve grabbed the phone from Catherine's ear.

"Who is this? What's this about Zoe?" Steve was almost screaming into the phone.

"I will only talk with Catherine. Hand the phone back to her or I'll hang up." Austin sounded cool as a cucumber.

Steve reluctantly handed the phone back to Catherine. She stared at it for a moment like it was radio-active.

"He will only talk to you." Steve had to temper the rage in his heart so he could speak to Catherine without exploding. Steve had a good idea who this man was and the fact that Catherine had brought him into their lives made him want to pound the wall with his fists until it was full of holes.

"Austin, where is Zoe? She needs to come home." Tears filled her voice and she hated sounding so helpless.

"I need to see you alone and I mean alone. No cops, no husband, nobody. Do you understand me? If you do bring someone with you, you'll probably never see Zoe again."

"I promise. I won't. Please don't hurt her. Where can we meet?" she pleaded. Austin could hardly understand Catherine for the tears in her voice. He knew he had her just where he wanted her.

"I'll call you tonight. I have one of those disposable phones, so don't think you can have it traced to my whereabouts."

The phone went dead. Catherine held it in her hand like it was a lifeline. Steve took the phone, listened to see if anyone was on the line then hung it up.

"What did he say?"

"He'll call me tonight to arrange a meeting. He said if I bring anyone with me we'll never see Zoe again." Catherine covered her face with her hands and wailed. Steve placed his hand on her back.

"You will not go alone. I won't lose you and Zoe, do you hear me?" At this moment Steve couldn't decide which emotion filled him more-rage at this man and at Catherine's involvement with him, or the love he still had in his heart for this woman who had shared his life and given him their precious child.

Catherine dropped her hands and stared at Steve agape. Did she hear him right? He didn't want to lose her? Without a moment's hesitation, she grabbed Steve and hugged him until he had to pry her off.

"Steve, I thought you didn't love me anymore. Did you mean

what you said about not losing me?" Her eyes sparkled through the tears.

"I meant it, but we need to concentrate on Zoe right now, not us. We're going to call the police to update them about his demands."

Catherine grabbed the phone away from him. She believed that Austin was evil enough to hurt Zoe if she brought the police with her to meet him.

"No, Steve, no! He'll hurt Zoe! I think he's capable of anything."

Steve was dying to yell, "Then why did you get involved with him in the first place!" Not wanting to hurt her further, he kept this to himself. What good would it do to punish Catherine at this point? She was suffering enough.

"Catherine, when you meet that man, I'm going to go, too."

"But he said if I wasn't alone we'd never see Zoe again! I can't take that chance. I have to save Zoe." Catherine's emotions were so raw right then she felt she could have clawed her way to the ceiling.

"I have a plan. We will both save her. Can you trust me?"

"Yes, Steve, I trust you. It's Austin I don't trust. What is your plan?"

"We'll talk about it after he calls tonight."

Neither could eat a bite all day waiting for the phone to ring. Catherine had explained everything to Ms. Talbot that afternoon and she was more than understanding. She told Catherine that any resources she had were available to her. Whatever she needed to get through this nightmare and get Zoe home was hers for the taking. Again, Catherine sent a prayer of thanksgiving up to God for being blessed with such a good employer.

Exhausted from the strain of listening for the phone to ring and not eating, Steve and Catherine dozed sitting up in their chairs. The loud jangle of the phone in the quiet apartment caused both of them to jump abruptly to their feet. Catherine picked it up on the second ring.

"Catherine, are you ready to meet me?" His voice almost had

a seductive quality to it that made Catherine's skin crawl. This was all a little game to him, a mind game. How could he be so twisted?

"Where is Zoe? Am I going to see her when we meet?" Catherine tried to sound humble because she was afraid of angering Austin.

"Yes. We're going to go get her together."

"Where shall we meet?"

"Not at the museum. I assume everyone is aware of Zoe's disappearance there. No, we'll meet at the corner of Bartow and Fifth. I'll stand on the corner and get into your car when you come to the corner. Don't pull any stunts, Catherine. Zoe's life is at stake."

"What time are we meeting?"

"Let's meet at 9:00 sharp."

Before she could give her assent, he hung up. Steve was looking intently at her to see what the plan was. She relayed Austin's message then collapsed back into the chair she had just been dozing in.

"Since it won't take but 10 minutes to get to Bartow and Fifth we have time to discuss my plan. It will work. It just has to."

Catherine only nodded her head. She began to silently pray in earnest for this evening to end in victory, with Zoe safely home and Austin in jail.

Just before nine Catherine slowly drove down Bartow Drive looking for Austin. When she got to Fifth, there was no sign of him. Her heart dropped when she deduced he had set her up. Panic set in as she considered that Zoe may be lost to her forever. After going past the intersection, she turned around in a loading zone and headed back to Fifth Street. Perspiration was flowing down both sides of her face as consternation filled her heart and mind.

When she finally spotted him standing beside a parking meter, she felt a fleeting spark of joy. It quickly dissipated when she came to grips with the fact that she would be sharing the car with the most despicable man she knew.

When he jumped into the passenger seat, she could smell

alcohol and extremely unpleasant body odor. If he tried to touch her she was afraid she might faint or at the very least vomit. Thankfully he never made a move towards her.

"Keep driving until I tell you where to turn."

"Austin, where is Zoe? I'm not going to just keep driving if I don't know where we're going or if Zoe is waiting at our destination."

"Shut your mouth up! Do you hear me? If you don't drive you won't ever see Zoe. That's a promise." It was all she could do not to slap him.

Afraid she'd have a wreck if couldn't see, she willed her tears to dry up. This was no time for crying, even if she felt like she could flood the car with her drops of panic and pain.

"Turn right at the next street."

From her peripheral vision she saw a man who had not shaved in a number of days. From his smell he hadn't bathed either. How she could have ever fallen for this guy was beyond her comprehension. If only God would redeem this situation and give her a second chance at happiness and peace of mind. She promised herself and God she would never make this mistake again. That was probably why God had let this disaster happen in the first place. If she hadn't suffered the consequences of her actions, she might not have drawn so close to Him.

Austin had her turn down numerous lonely streets and dark avenues. She had never been to this part of town before.

"Where are we going? Are we lost?"

"No. I'm just making sure no one is following us."

"Austin, please. No one is following us. I want to get to Zoe as soon as possible." She could tell he liked for her to plead. She felt such revulsion towards him that she could have easily stabbed him repeatedly if she had had a knife.

Riding along for several miles, they turned onto a rural two-lane highway. Again, panic started to rise as she imagined he was taking her somewhere, not to Zoe, but to a place he could dispose of her. Her teeth began to gnaw on her bottom lip and she could taste the blood.

It was when they pulled onto a dirt road that Catherine began to sob. Austin was probably going to kill her right in the car in the woods somewhere. After getting to the point where she couldn't even see the road for her tears, she slammed on the brakes.

"Why are you stopping, you fool? Don't you want to see Zoe again?" Austin was literally yelling at the top of his voice.

"I'm not going to let you kill me in the woods. You'll have to do it right here if that's your plan." Catherine raised her chin in defiance. After all, what did she have to lose at this point?

"I'm not going to kill you. I'm going to keep you alive for myself. I plan to let your daughter go free once I see you're willing to stay with me. Once we're married, you'll see how much I love you and you love me." Even in the dark car she could see his psychopathic smile.

This man is insane. I'll just have to play along until Zoe is released from his clutches. Oh, Steve, you're plan has to work!

The car began to roll again down this lonely dirt road. Because it was dark, Catherine had no idea where they were. She wasn't sure if it had been light she would know. Her heart ached thinking about Zoe being alone in the woods with this madman. She couldn't wait to get her arms around her. Certainly he hadn't hurt her, or had he? She knew if her thoughts traveled down that road she'd fall to pieces. Staying alert and calm was her only option in order to rescue Zoe.

Branches slapped her car as they turned into a wooded path. She could hear them start to scrape the sides of her car the further they traveled. Finally a tree stump prevented them from going any further. She looked at Austin for instructions and trembled.

"Turn the car off. We're here."

As her eyes adjusted to the pitch dark, a structure seemed to appear a little ahead of them. Catherine swallowed hard as she pictured Zoe in that place. She wanted to run and rescue her, but she had to be patient and let Austin think he was running the show.

"Get out and follow me. Don't try any funny stuff, Catherine.

Give me the keys to your car. I don't want you to attempt any heroic rescues."

Handing him the keys made her feel even more vulnerable. Even if he just abandoned her here, she wasn't sure how she would find the way home. The thought of Steve's rescue plan was the only thing that kept her from running through the woods, screaming her head off.

Coming to the door of the dilapidated structure, Austin jiggled some keys and opened the door. Catherine saw a figure curled up on a mattress.

"Zoe, is that you?"

"Mom, you're here. Help me!"

She ran over to Zoe and threw her arms around her. It didn't matter that she smelled rank from the mattress she was on. Catherine could just squeeze the life out of her she was so elated to have her daughter in her arms again.

"Austin, please untie her."

"First things first. I need to tie you up, Catherine, then we can all have a nice, friendly chat."

"Please, Austin! I won't run. You don't think I'd leave my daughter here, do you? Please don't tie me up." *If I'm bound he might just kill both of us.*

Without replying Austin took a rope that was hanging on the wall and walked toward her. Catherine jumped up from the mattress and pushed him away.

"Catherine, I'm going to tie you up, one way or another. Do I have to hurt Zoe to get you to cooperate?"

He walked over to Zoe and grabbed her hair hard. She yelped from the sharp pain. Catherine ran over to get him to release Zoe, but he was stronger than her. Pushing her as hard as he could, Catherine went flying across the room and landed painfully on her bottom. Taking advantage of her being on the floor, Austin ran across the room and tied her ankles before she had time to react. After tying her wrists together, he lifted her up and ungracefully tossed her onto the mattress next to Zoe.

"Catherine, I don't want to have to man-handle you like that, but you left me no choice. If you don't stop fighting me and start cooperating with my plan for us to be together, it's going to be tough on you and Zoe."

Both women looked at each other as if to say, "What is he talking about? He's crazy as a loon."

Catherine and Zoe were able to twist their bodies in such a way so they could lean on each other. Catherine could feel Zoe's body shivering from either fear or the cold. She snuggled as close to her as her constraints would allow. If she could only wrap her arms around her and warm her up.

Catherine's body comforted Zoe, but she still couldn't stop shaking. She hadn't a clue how this nightmare would play out. Noticing that her mother didn't seem as upset as she, Zoe began to calm down a little.

"I'll come back in the morning and bring you both something to eat."

"Austin, what exactly is your plan for us?" Catherine asked boldly.

Before he could answer a sound like a branch snapping interrupted him. Running to the door he stepped out into the yard, leaving the door wide open with the wind rushing coldly into the room. A large cracking sound came next, like metal hitting a hard object. Catherine and Zoe waited, both women wondering what would come next.

When Steve's form filled the doorway, they cried for joy. He quickly crossed the room and began to untie them. Once untied, Catherine and Zoe hugged his neck fiercely. Neither woman wanted to let him go.

"Where is Austin?" Catherine whispered, as if he was standing outside the door.

"He's on the ground, tied up. I think he's unconscious, so he's not going anywhere." Steve's strong arms encircled them protectively.

"Daddy, how did you get here? Did you follow Mom's car?"

"Let's get into your mother's car, warm up, and call the

police. You don't need to be out in this cold anymore. I'll explain everything there."

Steve and Catherine had to almost carry Zoe to the car. Being bound for so long had caused her legs to go numb. One inside the car, Steve fired up the engine and the heat. Catherine and Zoe slumped against their seats and let the heat thaw out their bodies, while Steve called 911.

"I'm calling to report that I have recovered my kidnapped daughter. I'm not sure where we are, but my GPS tracking system should alert you to our whereabouts. Also, I have the man who kidnapped her bound in ropes."

After giving more details, he closed his phone and examined his wife and daughter. Zoe was still shaking from the cold and the whole ordeal.

Catherine just looked at Steve with such love that he thought his heart would bust. *Why did it take this disaster to bring us all back together?*

"Daddy, how did you find us?"

"Well, when that monster wanted to meet Catherine, I wasn't about to let her go alone. He had warned that he would hurt you if she let anybody know about his plan and follow her car. The car has an emergency latch inside the trunk which can release the trunk door in case a child gets trapped inside. I hid in the trunk and waited until I knew he and Catherine had gotten out of the car. After they entered the shack, I followed and waited.

I broke a branch deliberately so he would come out of that place to investigate. I was waiting for him by the door with the car's tire iron I found in the trunk. When he came out, I whacked him hard across the head and he fell to the ground unconscious."

"Mom, no wonder you weren't as nervous as I was when that man brought you into the shack. You knew Daddy would save us."

"I knew he would do everything in his power to rescue us, but Austin was so unpredictable, there were no guarantees. I should have known Steve couldn't be outsmarted by that lunatic."

The warm heat lulled them all into a somber mood. The effects of the trauma of the last few days began to settle into their bodies. Sheer exhaustion took over and the police found them almost asleep when they arrived. When an officer tapped on the window, both women screamed. Steve was so startled he yelled himself.

Rolling down the window, Steve said, "I'm so glad to see you guys!"

"We're here about the kidnapping of Zoe Russell and the arrest of Austin Winters."

Before he could say more, Zoe cried out, "I'm the one who was kidnapped. My father saved me!"

"Why don't you all step out of the vehicle."

All three slowly emerged from the warm car, exhausted and in various stages of dirtiness. The police shone their bright flashlights in their faces, so they had to quickly shut their eyes. Shivering, with their eyes shut, and their clothes all disheveled, they looked more like a group of captured refugees than a normal, American family.

"Have you got any identification?"

Steve and Catherine retrieved driver's licenses from their pockets, but Zoe had nothing to produce.

"My purse is back at my mother's home where I was kidnapped." Just thinking of how altered her life had been in the last few days and the relief of being rescued made Zoe suddenly start bawling. A policeman covered her with a blanket and offered one for Steve and Catherine to share.

"When you called in, you said Austin was here. Show me."

The women stood right by the car while Steve walked over to the body. The policeman checked for Austin's pulse then yelled back to another officer to call in an ambulance. Steve had wondered the whole time they were waiting for the police if Austin was dead or alive. Part of him hoped he was dead.

"Do any of you need medical help? Were you ladies harmed sexually by Mr. Winters?" The officer showed great concern for Catherine and Zoe.

All three shook their heads. There was nothing wrong with

them that a warm bath, a good night's sleep, and many hours of counseling couldn't cure.

"You three get back into your car. I'll follow you to the station to make a report. The other officers will wait for the ambulance. Do you have a GPS?"

"Yes, please just give me the address." Steve sounded a little curt, but he was tired and ready to get this whole catastrophe behind him. The officer just smiled discerningly at Steve and handed him a business card with the station's address printed on it. After turning the car around, Steve, Catherine, and Zoe headed back to town. Each deep in thought, the ride back to the station was long and quiet.

Things were hectic at the police station. Drunks, derelicts, and ladies of the night filled the station with their noise, smells, and behaviors, making it more like a madhouse than a police station. After taking Steve, Catherine, and Zoe's statements, the officers told them to go home and rest. They'd be in touch later. Of course, one day there would be a trial concerning Austin, but in the mean time he would be in jail until his court date. The family could rest assured he would not be a problem in their lives anymore.

Although they were weary to the bone, the three hurried out of the station, climbed into Catherine's car and sped toward her apartment in the wee hours of the morning. Once inside, they took turns taking showers. Afterwards Zoe fell across the sofa and slept so hard she was snoring. Catherine suspected she would fall asleep before her head hit one of the pillows on her bed. Steve, unsure if he should just go home, looked expectantly at Catherine. She motioned for him to follow her into the bedroom. They both were asleep before they could even pull the covers over their bodies. The apartment was quiet for the rest of the evening and into the day, except for the occasional snoring.

It was past eight p.m. when Steve woke up. He looked over at Catherine with her face pressed into her pillow. Stretching his aching body, he got up to check on Zoe. She, too, was fast asleep. Now that his family was safe, he was unsure what to do. Should he just go home and continue his lonely existence? He didn't really want to go. Besides the loneliness, he abhorred the idea of ever seeing Kate again. How could he have ever even entertained the idea of having a relationship with the likes of her? It was amazing how being lonely could drive one to such desperate measures. He couldn't help but shake his head at the absurdity of his actions. He could only imagine how Kate would have eventually made his life a living hell.

Just as he was contemplating slipping out the door, he heard Catherine stirring in the bedroom. He just couldn't leave without saying farewell.

"Steve, where are you?" Catherine had a touch of panic in her voice.

"I'm here in the living room, Catherine."

He walked into the bedroom and stood at the foot of the bed. Even though her hair had been tousled by her pillow, she looked so beautiful.

"You aren't leaving are you?" The look of panic on Catherine's face melted his heart.

"Well, to be honest, I wasn't sure what I should do. Catherine, right now we're all a bundle of nerves and emotions. I don't want to make the wrong move because I'm not thinking clearly today. Do you know what I mean?"

"Steve, I think I know what you mean, considering we've just been through one of the worst nights of our lives. I know it's going to be some time before we get our heads on straight again, but that doesn't mean we can't make decisions in the meantime."

"Catherine, are you just talking in general or are you talking about some specific decision?"

"Well, what were you talking about when you said you didn't want to make the wrong move?"

Steve hesitated and looked down at the floor. He wasn't really sure what he meant by that. He was feeling such a protective love for Catherine and Zoe, but he couldn't quite forget what caused them to be in this whole situation in the first place. He was ready to forgive, but what exactly were Catherine's feelings? It seemed to him that things had gotten in such a mess, like a tangled fishing line, that he wasn't sure what it would take to smooth things out. He wasn't sure if Catherine knew either.

Steve looked up and saw that Catherine was silently crying. He rushed to her side and held her tightly. How could he ever let her go again? She clung to him like a drowning man in the ocean. Finally, he looked into her eyes and took a deep breath. He needed to get a few things off his chest.

"Catherine, I love you, but what you did with that man hurt me more than you'll ever know. I don't blame you directly for what he did to Zoe, but if he hadn't been in your life at all, this would have never happened. I haven't a clue if Zoe's kidnapping has brought us back together or if we're clinging to a memory that feels too powerful to let go of because of the trauma we've been through. Like I said, I love you, but will that be enough to get us through this tragedy? I honestly don't know.

I do know that when I realized I might lose you and Zoe because of that lunatic, I about went crazy inside. Oh, I hid it well, but had this come to a tragic end, I'm not sure what I would have done. That's how strongly I feel about my family. Am I making any sense to you?"

The whole time Steve was speaking, tears flowed down Catherine's face. She used her nightshirt to wipe her tears until it was sopping wet. She wasn't sure where this conversation was going to take them and that scared her.

"Steve, I completely understand what you're saying. I guess my question is, 'What about us?'"

"I don't know, Catherine. I do know we're both feeling vulnerable right now because of what we've just been through. We were united in our fear for Zoe and our determination to rescue her, but does that mean we should get back together? I really would like to know. We don't need to jumpstart our relationship if we're not willing to give it our all. I don't think I could ever again go through what I experienced when you had that affair."

Catherine was so torn emotionally at this point. On one hand she wanted Steve to sweep her off her feet, comfort her, and love on her like he did when they were first married. On the other hand, his hesitancy made her feel that maybe his heart wasn't really into a reconciliation. She didn't want him to come back to her second guessing himself.

She got off the bed, smoothed her shirt, and walked over to Steve, who was standing again at the foot of the bed. She wasn't going to beg, even though she felt like it; she wasn't going to flirt, at this point, that would be a turn-off for both of them; she was going to be honest, then let the chips fall as they may.

"Steve, I love you. I've never stopped loving you. When you wouldn't take me back after the affair, I was devastated. There were so many times in the process of packing our belongings that I was sure you would change your mind and take me back. I remember one time you came over with flowers. My heart was sailing until you abruptly stormed out without an explanation. Do you remember that?"

"I do. I did bring flowers to romance you, but when I saw that all the family pictures had been taken down, I assumed you were moving on. It made me so upset to think our marriage could be so easily just packed away. That's why I said I just brought the flowers to make the house more attractive for perspective buyers. I didn't want to look like a fool."

"Oh, Steve. The reason I took the pictures down was because our agent, that irritating, little Kitty, told me houses sell better if you make them look less personal. Without family pictures the buyer can visualize their personal belongings in the house. I wish you had asked me about the pictures. It may have meant the end to the divorce proceedings and we could have gotten back together."

The knowledge that their misunderstanding of each other's actions had resulted in the life she lived now made Catherine's teardrops fall anew onto her damp shirt. What a waste! Steve was thinking the same thing. He gently wiped the tears off her cheeks with his handkerchief.

"Catherine, what do you want? I know you've started a new life here at the museum and I assume you like your job. We can never go back to the way it was before all this ever started. Emotionally, spiritually, and financially, we have been radically altered."

Catherine was shocked to hear Steve use the word *spiritually* because he had never been a religious man. Her concern for his salvation couldn't let this moment slip away.

"Steve, you said we have changed spiritually. I know what all that means concerning me, but what has changed with you?"

"This whole upheaval of our lives has caused me to reconsider what's important in life. I have been forced to my knees, crying out to God, on more than one occasion. I guess you'd call it a wake-up call. Never have I given God more than a passing glance in all my years, but now I know He is knocking on the door of my heart. I've seen the change in you and I have been in awe of that transformation, knowing it could only be the work of God. I just hate that it took my life being train-wrecked for God to get my attention."

"Oh, Steve. I've never heard you talk like this before. It just goes to show that God can take a tragedy and turn it into something beautiful."

"You call this beautiful?" Steve looked confused.

"The beauty is what God has done in our hearts. He has drawn us nearer to Him than we've ever been. He didn't cause the affair, but He used it to mold us. Had it never occurred, I wonder if we'd still be living the same old life, spiritually lost and headed for hell."

"You know, Catherine, I haven't been to church in a long time. It's about time I go because I can see there's a lot I need to learn."

"My Christian counselor, David, was the one you got me to see the light. I don't know what I would have done if it hadn't been for him. You know, he always said his prayer was for us to get back together."

Catherine stopped speaking because she realized that his prayer hadn't been answered yet. The ball was now in Steve's court. She had exposed her heart to him and now she could only wait and pray for Steve to act in kind.

"That's been my prayer, too, but under the circumstances I couldn't see how it would have ever worked out. Between the affair, our parting of ways, and Kate, I figured our marriage was as good as dead."

"But, Steve, you were the one that kept pushing about the divorce. I don't understand."

"Catherine, many times I was acting out of hurt and confusion. It was never that I really wanted things to end between us."

"Well, what about the divorce? Where do we stand now?" Catherine felt her body tense. At this point she couldn't decide if he just wanted to proceed with the divorce because things had gone too far, or if he wanted to start over. Whatever it was, she would honor it, no matter how much it hurt.

"I didn't finish the paperwork for the divorce. Something told me to just set the papers aside. My attorney has called at least once a week to ask me what the status was, but I ignored his calls. I don't know why I didn't pursue it."

"I do. The Lord was working to make sure the divorce didn't get finalized. He says in His word that He hates divorce. I hate it, too."

Catherine felt her heart soar because Steve hadn't completed the divorce papers. It's true that with God nothing is impossible.

"It looks like in spite of all we've done to tear this marriage apart God is going to have the last word."

"Yes, He's good at that." Catherine smiled as she reflected on God's goodness. Only God could have salvaged what was left of their marriage.

"Catherine, let's get back together. I'm willing to give it my all. What about you?"

"Steve, this is the second happiest day of my life. The first was when you asked me to marry you. Let's go give Zoe the good news."

"Before we do that, I just want to hold you in my arms. I've missed you so much. I think we ought to start going to your counselor as a couple. I want us to fix whatever it was that got us to this point. Our marriage is too important not to do all we can to make it last forever."

Wrapping her arms around his waist and laying her head against his chest, Catherine felt like she could stay like this for all eternity. In her heart she was praising God for what He had done to keep the marriage from being destroyed. She reluctantly disengaged herself from Steve.

"Zoe, come here. We have some good news," she yelled exuberantly.

Zoe stumbled into the bedroom. Her hair was sticking up in all directions and the pillow had put a crease in her cheek. To Steve and Catherine, she had never been more beautiful.

"What's up? I was dreaming so hard when you called that I'm surprised I woke up at all."

Steve said, "Zoe, your mother and I are getting back together. We haven't discussed the details, but it looks like we'll need to go find a new home for all three of us."

"Really? I can't believe it! This makes me so happy."

The smile on Zoe's face was the brightest they had seen since she had returned from Paris. She almost jumped into their arms. All three were hugging each other as hard as they could. It wasn't until there was a knock on the door that they pulled apart and stared at each other. Please don't let it be the police.

When Catherine opened the door, Mrs. Talbot stood there with a somber look on her face. It wasn't until she saw Zoe standing arm in arm with her father that she broke into tears of joy.

"I know it's late, but I came to see what was the status on Zoe. I see she's safe and being well cared for. Praise God!"

"Please come in, Mrs. Talbot. Steve, this is my boss. Mrs. Talbot, this is my husband, Steve. When we got home last night we were too exhausted to tell anyone the good news of Zoe's rescue and we've been sleeping all day. Steve was our hero and he rescued Zoe from that awful monster."

"No, I don't want to intrude. I can see you all just got up. We have all the time in the world for you to tell me all the details." Mrs. Talbot smiled and turned to go.

251

"Wait. There is more good news. Steve and I are getting back together and I've never been happier."

"It's written all over your face. I guess I'll be losing you, but I wouldn't stand in the way of your happiness for all the world."

"We haven't worked out all the details yet, but I'll let you know. It's going to take some time to set up housekeeping again for all three of us."

What a bittersweet moment! In her excitement, Catherine had forgotten all about her job. Giving up the apartment wouldn't be hard, but she liked the work with the children. Catherine turned when Zoe placed her hand on her shoulder.

"Mrs. Talbot, I would be thrilled if you'd offer me the same deal as you did Mom. By moving here I can spend more time in the museum, help you with the school groups, and live independently. I think Mom and Dad need to start their new life together without me around."

"No, Zoe. We want you to come live with us." Catherine didn't want Zoe to feel excluded especially after all she had been through.

"Zoe, I think that's a wonderful idea. I hope one day soon I can offer you a paid position, something besides the apartment. You'd be a real asset to the museum." Mrs. Talbot meant every word she said.

"Only God could take the mess I made and turn it into something so perfect," said Catherine with a heart full of gratitude. "He's taken the tangled threads of my life and woven a beautiful tapestry."

Mrs. Talbot, Steve, and Zoe all nodded their heads in agreement. After Mrs. Talbot left, the family held each other in a long, sweet embrace that would be repeated often down through the years.

CPSIA information can be obtained at www.ICGtesting.com
Printed in the USA
LVOW071250070812

293268LV00003B/1/P